THE SINGULAR EXPLOITS OF

WONDER MOM & PARTY GIRL

THE SINGULAR EXPLOITS OF
WONDER MOM & PARTY GIRL

MARC SCHUSTER

THE PERMANENT PRESS
Sag Harbor, NY 11963

For information, address:
   The Permanent Press
   4170 Noyac Road
   Sag Harbor, NY 11963
   www.thepermanentpress.com

Library of Congress Cataloging-in-Publication Data

Schuster, Marc–
   The singular exploits of wonder mom & party girl / Marc Schuster.
      p. cm.
   ISBN 978-1-57962-217-6 (alk. paper)
      1. Self-actualization (Psychology) in women—Fiction.
   2. Women—United States—Fiction. 3. Cocaine abuse—
   Fiction. I. Title.

   PS3619.C48327S56 2011
   813'.6—dc22   2010043994

Printed in the United States of America.

for Kerri

CHAPTER ONE

THE PACKAGE arrived while I was on the phone with Roger.

"Is it a date?" my ex-husband asked.

"Not that it's any of your business, but no."

Catherine and Lily were doing their homework at the kitchen table, so I was careful not to say the word *date* out loud. *Meeting*, yes. *Rescheduled*, certainly. *Friday night*, mostly harmless. But a word like *date*, with the questions it begged and the baggage it carried, was better left unspoken.

"Friday night? Dinner? His treat, I'm guessing? Sounds like a date to me."

"I didn't call to get your opinion," I said. "I called so you'd come for the girls on time."

"Are you kidding? I always come for the girls on time."

"You *frequently* come for the girls on time," I said as the mailman cut across my front lawn with a brown paper package in his hand. "And occasionally you make them wait for an hour."

"Okay," Roger said. "I'll send Chloe."

"Don't," I said.

"It isn't a problem. She doesn't mind at all."

"She's not the one I'm worried about."

There was a knock at the door, and Catherine looked up from her math homework. Her books were all open and stacked in front of her, the spine of each resting neatly in the crease of the one below. The glance that passed between us said she'd rather not be bothered by petty concerns like accepting deliveries from the mailman or the logistics of moving between one parent and the next, but Lily was more than eager to leap from the drudgery of her phonics workbook to whatever adventure lay between the kitchen and the front door. When her wide emerald eyes asked for permission to leave the table, I nodded.

"So what do you know about this guy?" Roger asked as Lily returned with the spoils of her short but triumphant journey. "Where does he live? What does he do? What kind of car does he drive?"

"I don't know," I said. "And it doesn't matter because this isn't what you think it is."

Lily showed me the package. It was addressed in my mother's letter-perfect script. Since the divorce, she'd been sending me self-help books like clockwork, so it wasn't a stretch for me to assume that this was one more in a long list of titles selected, above all, to remind me that my marriage had failed: *Surviving Divorce, Divorce and the Working Mother, The Spirituality of Divorce, Divorce for Beginners, Divorcing for Good,* and my personal favorite, *Divorced and Loving It: The New You Guide to Life without Him.* Sure, they were trite and completely unreadable, but who was I to deny my daughter the joy of opening a brown paper package sent with uncompromising love from her grandmother in Maryland?

"Can I?" Lily asked.

I gave her a nod. She tore at the package with greedy fingers. As the paper fell away to reveal yet another self-help volume, Lily cocked her head in a gesture of confusion and curiosity. Following her gaze to the lipstick-red letters that spelled out the book's title, I took in a sharp breath and told Roger that I had to go.

"What is it, Mom?" Lily asked as I reached out to revoke her prize.

"Nothing," I said. "Grandma made a mistake."

"Oh," Lily said. "What's master ... master?"

"God," Catherine groaned, looking up from her homework once again as Lily sounded out the one word I didn't want her to see.

"It's nothing," I said. "It's an adult topic."

"Does it have to do with divorce?" Lily asked as Catherine covered her ears.

"No," I said. "Yes. A little bit. It's a mistake is all. We'll talk about it later."

"Is it sex?"

"I'm leaving," Catherine said. "I'm gathering my books, and I'm walking out of the room."

"It's sex, isn't it?" Lily said as Catherine broke into a mortified run. "You can tell me if it is. I know all about sex."

"You're seven," I said.

"I'm very mature for my age."

I blamed television. I blamed the internet. I blamed the world we live in.

Most of all, I blamed myself.

The book in question was called *Singular Pleasures: The Womanly Art of Masturbation*, and when I called my mother to ask if she'd lost her mind, she explained in measured, even tones that masturbation was a perfectly legitimate option for a woman in my position to consider.

"My position?" I asked.

"Divorced," my mother said. In addition to plying me with self-help books, she had a habit of sending me newspaper clippings chronicling the accomplishments of boys I knew in grade school. Andy Gumble, who used to eat paste, was a gynecologist now. Chucky Friel, who once stole a case of beer from our neighbor's garage, was a district councilman. Danny Brooks, who was suspended for setting off firecrackers in the gym, was opening a pretzel franchise in Havre de Grace. *Single?* my mother asked on a three-by-five index card stapled to this last item, her query already pregnant with disappointment. "I assume you're still not seeing anyone."

"No, Mom, but I don't think I have to resort to *that*."

"Masturbation?" my mother said. "It's just a word, Audrey. You don't have to be afraid of it."

"I'm not," I said.

"Then say it with me. *Masturbation*."

"I'm not having this conversation."

"Women have certain needs," my mother insisted. "And believe me, we don't need men to fulfill them. Take your father and me, for instance."

"Mom, could you please stop talking?"

"Let's just say he's not the man he used to be."

"I'm hanging up now, Mom. Goodbye."

My mother started to elaborate upon my father's sexual dysfunctions, and I broke the connection between us. If I had time, I'd call back and apologize, but there was dinner to make, and Lily was still brooding over my refusal to discuss a certain singular topic with her.

"Are you ever going to get married again?" she asked later that night as I put a plate of mushy ravioli in front of her. "Because Dad says you're the kind of woman who doesn't need a man."

"He said that?" I asked.

"He was just kidding," Catherine assured me, refusing to make eye contact as she poked at her dinner. Magnets held last year's tests and report cards to the refrigerator. Before the divorce, she'd been a solid B student. Now all she did was study, and her grades were nearly perfect. I worried that she was trying too hard to please. I worried that she was trying to earn my love. "He says a lot of things he doesn't mean."

"But Chloe says *every*body needs *some*body," Lily said, picking up where she left off. "She says all *you* need is a little makeover, and guys'll go wild for you."

"Shut up," Catherine said through gritted teeth.

"Mom, what's liposuction?"

Catherine kicked Lily under the table, and Lily let out a yelp. When the telephone rang, I assumed it was my mother and let the machine deal with her. All I knew as her voice crackled over the line and my daughters started pecking at each other was that if something didn't change soon, the only pleasures I'd ever know again—sexual or otherwise—would likely be of the singular variety.

CHAPTER TWO

I WOULDN'T say I was naive, exactly.

I worked for a glorified coupon book called *Eating Out*, and ninety percent of the magazine's revenue came in the form of what people in the industry called trade dollars. I wasn't an expert on the subject, but from where I stood it wasn't unlike exchanging packs of cigarettes for favors in prison—the only difference being that our thriving little economy was restricted not by high concrete walls and barbed wire fences, but by the invisible edges of a seven-mile stretch of prefabricated restaurants, car dealerships, big-box department stores, and mini-malls known to the locals as the Golden Mile.

Though the masthead listed me as editor-in-chief, my job largely revolved around turning the chicken scratch of hung-over admen into magazine copy. Beyond that, all contact between me and everyone on the sales crew at *Eating Out* was restricted to discussing the specs of any ads that happened to trickle in: quarter-page, half-page, full-page; black-and-white or color; information on sales, specials, coupons, and seasonal menu items. More often than not, we avoided conversation altogether, and I received my instructions on tattered scraps of paper taped to the handset of my telephone in the dead of night. It wasn't that we had anything against each other. We just didn't have much in common. I was the prissy editor-in-chief of their glorified coupon book, and they were the rowdy, unwashed dregs who kept the money rolling in. We each lived in our own little worlds, and everyone was happy with the arrangement.

Except for the publisher.

"I want us to be a family," Vic Charles said on a Tuesday afternoon the week before my mother got it in her head to send me a book about masturbation.

"You and me, Vic? I appreciate the offer, but I don't think your wife would be up for it."

"No," Vic said with a sigh as he pulled a chair up to my desk. Sad-eyed, squat, and jowly, he bore a striking resemblance to a cocker spaniel. "Not you and me. I'm talking about everyone at *Eating Out*. Have you ever wondered why no one but Jerry and Melinda ever stays on board for more than a few months?"

"Low pay and a complete lack of benefits?"

"Bite me," Vic said. "They don't stick around because they don't see themselves as part of something that matters. They walk in here, and it's just another office. They look at me, and I'm just another boss. But it doesn't have to be like that. If we all got to know each other, we could turn this place into a home away from home and make *Eating Out* the family-centered enterprise I've always wanted it to be."

Vic and I had this conversation at least once a year, and the result was always the same. He'd rent a limousine and invite everyone involved with *Eating Out* to join him for a night on the Golden Mile, then they'd all get drunk and miss a good three or four days of work, leaving me to run the operation on my own. To get out of these events, I could usually cite an imaginary anniversary or birthday, and I'd be off the hook, no questions asked. A year after my divorce, though, the absence of a discernable husband combined with Vic's vague understanding of visitation rights made escape impossible.

"No excuses, Audrey," he said, placing a firm hand on my knee after laying out his plan. "You're coming with us."

"I'm busy that night," I said. "Whenever it is."

"Funny. We'll pick a weekend when Roger has the girls."

"You don't have to do that," I said. "Not on my account."

"You're not seeing the big picture, Audrey. Your old family's shot to shit. I want *Eating Out* to be more than a business. It's a win-win situation for everyone."

"When you put it that way, how can I resist?"

"So you'll make the arrangements?"

"Not in my job description."

"I'm thinking Friday night at Nick's."

"Why are you telling me this?"

"Silver Hummer. Stretch. We can get it on trade."

"You think I'll drop everything to set this up?"

"I know you will, Audrey. It's how you're wired."

"If I were one to curse, do you know what I'd say?"

"But you're not," Vic said. "That's the whole point. It's the mother in you. That's why you'll do this for me."

"Melinda's a mother," I said. "Get her to do it."

"Melinda's a woman who happens to have kids. There's a difference."

"I'm not doing this, Vic."

"It's a simple phone call."

"Then *you* do it."

"I can't do it," Vic said. "I'm a busy man."

"And I'm a busy woman."

"Then you better make this call and get it out of the way."

Vic reached for my telephone and held out the receiver. The dial tone buzzed. Vic's gaze met mine, and though I did my best to stare him down, we both knew I'd be the first to blink.

"Spouses and children?" I said, grabbing the receiver from his hand.

"God no," Vic said. "Have you met my wife?"

DESPITE VIC'S request for a silver Hummer, the best I could get on trade was an absurdly elongated Chrysler PT Cruiser—pink, with tinted windows. Meandering through the long, winding streets of my neighborhood, the limousine rolled over curbs and took out trashcans as it traded paint with every parked vehicle on its route. By the time it touched down in front of my house, all of my neighbors were standing on their lawns and staring at the monstrosity with an odd mix of curiosity and alarm, so I kept my head down and hurried to the curb.

"Shhh! Shhh!" Vic said, gesturing for everyone to simmer down when the driver climbed out from behind the wheel and opened the door for me. "Everyone be good. Mom's here!"

"Cute," I said, though I knew he wasn't joking.

Settling in across from Vic and his crew, I buckled my seatbelt and caught a smirk from Melinda Monroe, Vic's Vice President of Marketing and Sales. On most days, she wore spandex and sunglasses beneath her wild mane of dirty blonde hair, but tonight she'd opted for tight black jeans and a tee shirt that read *My Mommy's a Hottie!* By the time I joined the party, she'd already helped the guys on the sales team polish off the better part of a bottle of tequila, and the hard rock anthems thundering over the vehicle's sound system reminded me that this wasn't exactly a seatbelt kind of crowd.

"Planning to wear that thing all night?" Vic asked.

"Sorry," I said. "Force of habit."

"So there are good habits, too," Melinda said, pouring a shot of tequila and holding it out for me to take. "Live and learn."

"Maybe later," I said, declining the drink. "I hate to do shots on an empty stomach."

Shrugging, Melinda downed the tequila in a single gulp and passed the bottle to Jerry Adams. Tall, rumpled, and perpetually reeking of stale cigarette smoke, Jerry was the only member of the crew who'd been with Vic since the magazine's inception, and he once claimed to have given Vic the idea for *Eating Out*. It was a play on words, he explained, hovering over my desk with a list of restaurants he'd promised glowing reviews. Jerry's tongue flicked briefly past his lips to clear up any uncertainty about what he was getting at, and I spent the next month avoiding eye contact with him.

In addition to Jerry and Melinda, Vic's sales force consisted of an ever-changing crew of desperate hucksters who were either just getting their feet wet in the marketing business or trying to fool themselves into believing that they weren't washed up. This time around, Vic had managed to conscript a nineteen-year-old Indian boy named Raj and a scowling full-figured platinum blonde named Svetlana into the latest version of his family. The point of Raj, Vic announced, slurring his syllables and putting an arm around the quiet Indian's shoulder, was to infiltrate the ever-increasing, yet notoriously insular, community of South

Asian shopkeepers he embarrassingly referred to, both in public and in private, as the Patel Cartel. And the point of Svetlana, he added after giving the matter a full minute of thought, was to get Raj laid before the night was through.

Vic cackled at his own joke.

Jerry raised a shot glass to toast Raj's good fortune.

Melinda took the bottle back.

Raj grinned sheepishly.

Svetlana continued to scowl.

"To family," I muttered, turning to the window as our hot-pink limo trundled toward the hazy neon glow of the Golden Mile.

WITH THE exception of Fatso Ratso's Pizza Depot, no business on the Golden Mile owed more in trade to *Eating Out* than Nick's American Grill. Sandwiched between a dry cleaner and a nail salon in a strip mall valued for its proximity to a PetSmart, Nick's served greasy variations on something the menu referred to as the kind of meal your grandma used to make. Assuming your grandma's kitchen held a dozen deep-fryers, a fifty-gallon drum of lard, and an industrial freezer stocked entirely with Salisbury steak and chicken fingers, this claim was only slightly less misleading than the suggestion that anyone named Nick had anything to do with the establishment.

The real driving force behind Nick's was a man named Owen Little, who had already stood me up on two separate occasions. Both times I was scheduled to interview him for a profile in *Eating Out*, and both times I sat in a booth for close to an hour, sipping iced tea and checking the messages on my cell phone. When I finally met the man on the night of Vic's big family outing, he shook my hand and apologized profusely for leaving me in the lurch.

"Twice," I reminded him.

"Business," he said by way of explanation. "What can you do?"

Even in his own restaurant, Owen looked out of place. Slicked back, his longish black hair barely brushed the collar of his three-button suit, and his narrow horn-rim glasses gave him the air of a hipster who would have been more at home in a bar that boasted two hundred variations on the martini than in a glorified diner whose decor and clientele both looked as if they might have been transplanted directly from a yard sale.

"What do you think?" Melinda asked when she caught me looking.

"Please," I said. "The last thing I need is a relationship."

"Who said anything about a relationship?" Melinda asked. "I just want to know if you'd do the guy."

"I think no," Svetlana said, rescuing me in a thick Eastern European accent. "That man is girl. Too skinny. Will break like cheap toy."

"I'd do him," Vic said. "I mean, if I were a woman, I'd do him in a heartbeat. What about you, Raj? Would you do him?"

Raj snickered but said nothing.

"Not me," Jerry said, shaking his head as he perused the beer list. "I only do chicks."

"We're saying *if*," Vic said. "*If* you were a woman, would you do Owen?"

"If I were a woman, I'd still only do chicks," Jerry said.

"What if Owen were a woman?" Melinda asked. "Would you do him then?"

"Sure," Jerry said. "I'll do any woman."

"And we all thank you for it," Melinda said.

"You're one to talk," Jerry said. "How'd you get this account again?"

"Grow up, asshole."

"Okay, kids," Vic said. "Who's up for jalapeño poppers?"

To get through the night with any semblance of sanity, I ordered a glass of white wine and then another while Melinda, Vic, and Jerry pounded cheap beer and took turns absconding to the restroom. Though they did their best to ply us with increasingly lame alibis each time they returned to the table, I'd heard enough over the years about the chemical dalliances of the *Eating Out* sales crew to know what they were up to.

"I admire your bosoms," Raj confided to me after an hour of sipping from a mug of beer and stealing furtive glances in my direction. "They're full and round, like my mother's."

"Thanks," I said. "You really know how to make a girl feel special."

Out of the corner of my eye, I could see Melinda whispering something in Vic's ear. *God no,* Vic mouthed, shaking his head, but Melinda insisted on whatever she was saying with upturned palms and a sideways nod in my direction.

"Svetlana has good hips," Raj whispered. "But she's far too old to bear children. You, on the other hand, still have a good childbearing body. I'd marry you if you were Indian."

"Lucky me," I said.

"But you're not, and my parents would never approve."

"That's too bad."

"But we can still be lovers," Raj said as I reached for my drink. "My family is wealthy, and I'd always provide for you and our children."

"Thanks, but no," I said, and Melinda rolled her eyes in sympathy.

"You'd never go without," Raj said. "And you'd never have to work a day in your life."

"You know something, Raj?" I said. "I'm starting to get tired of this conversation."

He was about to say more when Jerry returned from his latest trip and pressed something into Melinda's hand. Giving me a wink, she asked if I felt like joining her in the women's room for some girl-talk. Personally, I never saw the attraction of cramming into tight spaces with small gangs of women I barely knew to primp and dish on members of the opposite sex, but when Raj placed a hand on my lap and whispered that we could be so good together, I leapt at Melinda's offer.

"I will come, too," Svetlana said, rising from her seat.

"I was asking Audrey," Melinda said through a forced smile.

"It's okay," I said, hoping that Svetlana's presence might keep Melinda from doing anything I didn't want to be a party to. "The more the merrier."

"But there was something I wanted to ask you," Melinda said. "In private."

"Can it wait?"

"No," Melinda said. "I don't think it can."

"You are doing coke, yeah?" Svetlana asked, loud enough to make Melinda cringe.

"Yeah," Melinda hissed, sneaking a quick glance over her shoulder. "We're doing coke, but you don't have to announce it to the whole world, okay?"

"Is not a problem," Svetlana said. "I'm cool."

Did Melinda just say *we*, I thought as she gave up on trying to dissuade our determined Serbian friend from following us to the women's room? As in *Audrey and I are doing coke*?

No, I told myself. *We* meant Melinda and the guys.

There was only one toilet in the bathroom, and a single, plastic rose sat in a vase atop the tank. Standing, the three of us barely had room to move, so Melinda pulled a tiny spoon from the pocket of her tight, black jeans and took a seat. Dipping the spoon into the packet that Jerry had given her, she brought a minuscule pile of white powder to her left nostril and snorted. After repeating the process with her right nostril, she rubbed her nose and held the packet out to me.

"Your turn," Melinda said.

"Oh," I said. "I don't. I mean, I never."

"Then is my turn," Svetlana said.

"You're sure?" Melinda asked as Svetlana snatched the packet from her hand. "It's good stuff."

"No thanks," I said. "I better not."

"Seriously, you'll love it."

"That's what I'm afraid of."

"What, getting hooked? Please. That's what they tell you in fifth grade to keep you from having fun. You're a big girl now. Besides, there's barely enough to give you a buzz."

I opened my mouth to say something, but Svetlana spoke first.

"So you have more, yeah?"

"More?" Melinda said. "What do you mean?"

"Coke." Svetlana held the empty packet between her thumb and forefinger. "What you had was nothing."

"Half of that was for Audrey."

"It's okay," I said. "I really wasn't up for it anyway."

Which was true, I told myself as Melinda launched into a mini-tirade about cocaine etiquette. I was absolutely, one-hundred-percent sure that I was about to say no.

Wasn't I?

Unlocking the door, Svetlana stomped out of the women's room in a huff as Melinda called after her that it was one hell of a bitchy move to invite oneself to a private party. Certain that everyone knew what she was talking about, I kept my eyes on the frayed carpet as I made my way back to our table. Muttering behind me, Melinda found her seat just in time for Owen to ask what we thought of the dining experience at Nick's American Grill.

"Food was crap," Svetlana said. "And women's room was hell-hole. But night was free, so who can complain?"

"Oddly enough, that was our original slogan," Owen said, and I allowed myself to smile at his wry sense of humor. "Can I interest anyone in coffee or dessert?"

"We'll take to go," Svetlana answered for all of us. "Is late, and I need beauty sleep."

"You'll need more than sleep to fix what you got," Jerry said and glanced around the table for laughs that never materialized. "You'll need a goddamn beauty coma."

"You want for us to step outside, pretty boy? I'll kick your bony ass."

"Just a check, I think," Vic said, pulling a thin sheaf of gift certificates from his wallet. "The kids are getting cranky."

We were halfway to the exit when Owen caught me by the arm and said he still owed me an interview. He was free most mornings before the lunch rush, he added as the rest of my party drifted out the door and into the parking lot.

"That's what you said the last time," I told him.

"And the time before that, I know. Let's say Wednesday at ten."

"Wednesday at ten," I said. "And if you're not there, Svetlana writes your next review."

"Ouch," Owen said. "Isn't that a little harsh?"

"A girl needs to watch out for herself," I said. "Especially when she's already been stung."

CHAPTER THREE

Fɪᴠᴇ ᴍɪɴᴜᴛᴇs turned to ten, and ten minutes turned to twenty. When the waitress brought my second glass of watery iced tea, I asked if she expected Owen to arrive any time soon. The girl had dark curly hair and angular features that reminded me of my ex's fiancée, so when she answered my question with a practiced look of sympathy most likely reserved for occasions when she had to explain to disappointed customers that Nick's American Grill served Coke and not Pepsi or that the kitchen was fresh out of beer-battered onion rings, I decided to hate her. Owen rarely showed up until late in the afternoon, she said. But if I wanted to fill out a job application, she would make sure he saw it.

"Tempting," I said. "But I think I'll pass. Tell Owen that Svetlana spent the weekend sharpening her hatchet."

A few minutes later, I was unlocking my car when I heard my name ring out across the parking lot. Looking up, I saw Owen hurrying toward me and waving his arms. Though I wanted more than anything to jump behind the wheel and leave the man in a cloud of exhaust fumes, good breeding got the better of me, and I waited.

"I know, I know," he said. "Three strikes, right?"

I looked at my watch and said nothing.

"At least let me make it up to you."

"Let me guess. Ten percent off my next meal at Nick's American Grill."

"Tax and tip not included," Owen added.

"You'll notice I'm not laughing."

"You're right," Owen said. "I'm sorry. How about dinner sometime?"

"Here?" I asked.

"God no," Owen said. In the cold light of day, the restaurant's sun-bleached cedar-shake façade gave it the appearance of a Jersey shore bait shop. "I'm trying to get back on your good side."

"Not hard enough," I said.

"Do you like jazz?"

"Not especially."

"Chinese?"

"Take it or leave it."

"Perfect. Let's say Friday at eight."

"Don't you have a restaurant to run?"

"This place?" Owen asked. "Practically runs itself. Besides, that's what managers are for. What do you say to dinner and a show? We'll do this profile thing right."

"Whatever," I said.

"You think I won't show."

"I know you won't show."

"I'll show," Owen said, and I gave him my particulars.

CHAPTER FOUR

ON THE Friday of my non-date with Owen, I came home from work to find Lily teetering on the spine of the sofa and the scent of something sweet wafting from the kitchen. Calling her name, I told Lily to get down before she broke her neck, but she told me not to worry. If she fell, she said, the sofa below would cushion her fall. Given that I was her mother, however, all I could see were the dozen or so sharp corners she might strike if she lost her footing: the coffee table, the end-tables, the ottoman, and, if she bounced far enough, the television.

"Hi, Mom," Catherine said, emerging from the kitchen in an apron that reached her toes. "I'm baking cookies for Chloe."

Caught off guard by her sister's sudden entry, Lily lost her footing. All at once, her eyebrows shot up, her jaw dropped, and she let out a soft cry as she fell to the faded blue sofa cushions beneath her. Bouncing once, she rolled off the couch and onto the floor only to spring back to her feet with an embarrassed grin.

"I don't need this," I said as my heart started beating again. "Especially not today."

"Sorry, Mom," Lily sang. "What's so special about today?"

"Nothing," I said. Because it was only an interview and nothing more. "Be more careful, okay? You're the only Lily I have."

A sheet of greenish paper adorned with a hundred variations on the letter Q lay on the coffee table. When I asked about it, Lily informed me that it wasn't just any Q but the Chrissy Qualtieri Q.

"Chrissy Qualtieri?"

"The designer," Lily said. "God, Mom. Don't you know anything? She's Chloe's favorite and mine, too."

Turning the paper over, I saw that she had been drawing on the reverse side of a flyer seeking members for the Good

Shepherd Teacher-and-Parent Organization, which no one ever thought twice about calling the GESTAPO. I'd been meaning to join the organization for years, but something always got in the way. Case in point: smoke wafting from the kitchen. Catching a whiff of burning sugar and dough, I ran after Catherine as she slipped an oven mitt over her hand and pulled a tray of slightly blackened Nestlé Toll House Break-and-Bake Cookies out of the oven.

"Don't worry, Mom," Catherine said, fanning the cookies with her oven mitt before I could admonish her. "It's no big deal. I do this all the time."

"It *is* a big deal," I said. "You know you're not allowed to use the oven without adult supervision."

"But I wanted to make these for Chloe. You did tell me to be nice to her, didn't you?"

"Fair enough," I said, grudgingly grinning on the inside at the thought of my ex's skinny fiancée forcing herself to down just one of my daughter's crisp, blackened tokens of high-calorie good will. "But make sure she eats them all. I don't want a single cookie going to waste."

I felt a minor seismic shift, and Lily reported that Chloe's Lincoln Navigator was touching down in the driveway. The report was confirmed seconds later when Chloe honked her horn, so I found a plastic bowl for Catherine's cookies, told my daughters to grab their overnight bags, and walked them across the lawn to the waiting behemoth.

"Roger told me about your date tonight," Chloe said, leaning out of her open window as the girls buckled themselves into the backseat. "Sounds like fun."

"It isn't a date," I said.

"You're going on a date?" Lily asked.

"Why didn't you tell us?" Catherine demanded.

"It isn't a date," I said again.

"Sorry," Chloe said. "I didn't realize it was a secret."

"It's not a secret," I said. "It's nothing."

"You're not supposed to keep secrets from us, Mom," Catherine said.

"I don't," I said. "I didn't. It's not a date."

Chloe gave me a sympathetic head tilt. It was meant, I supposed, not only to convey how sorry she was for throwing a monkey wrench into the delicate machinery of my relationship with Catherine and Lily, but also to hint that she couldn't wait all day for me to repair the damage.

"Whatever it is, have fun tonight," Chloe said.

"And be careful," Catherine added.

"Don't worry," I said as Chloe's window rose and the Navigator lumbered out of my driveway. "I'm always careful."

Fifteen minutes after he was supposed to arrive, Owen knocked on my front door with a limp rose in his hand and an excuse on his thin, pink lips. He'd left early, he said. And he'd given himself a good margin of error. A half-hour. Fifteen minutes, at least. But then he hit my neighborhood, and even the most basic principles of cartography went straight out the window. The streets weren't marked, or at least not clearly, and the ones that were, in fact, marked had an uncanny tendency to intersect with themselves. Then there were the houses, each an exact replica of a red motel on a Monopoly board. Add a little green Monopoly house out back, and you had everybody's garage. Street after street, all exactly the same.

"It's a wonder I'm standing here at all," Owen said with an air of mock hysteria. "Another wrong turn, and I'd have given up altogether—not only on finding your house, but on ever getting out of this neighborhood alive. Seriously, I was ready to park my car under the nearest oak tree and call it home."

"That's how most of us ended up here," I said. "So what's the deal with the rose? Were the Moonies having a sale?"

"The Exxon station, actually."

"Classy," I said as a petal fell away from the bud and fluttered to the ground. "Let's put that thing out of its misery before the neighbors get the wrong idea."

"The wrong idea?"

"There's a rumor going around that this is a date."

"You mean it isn't?"

"Please."

"What if I told you it was all a ruse? That I stood you up three times so we'd have an excuse to go out?"

"I'd say you were full of it."

"Full of what?"

"Guess. I'm a mother. Some words I don't say."

"Not ever?"

"Never. It's a question of habit."

"Habit," Owen said, handing me the sad rose. "I understand completely. Get used to certain words, and the tongue slips at the least opportune time. So what am I full of?"

"Excuses, for one thing."

"And?"

"You tell me."

"Charm?" Owen said. "Good looks? Personality?"

"I wouldn't go that far."

"So this isn't a date," Owen said as we walked to his car. "All opinions to the contrary be damned."

"The boy catches on quick."

"What about the rose? Isn't that a sign?"

"Haven't you heard? A rose is a rose is a rose."

"And if I open the door? That has to count for something, doesn't it?"

"It makes you a gentleman—no more, no less."

"So I'm a gentleman," Owen said, opening the door to his BMW and inviting me to sit with a courteous bow and a showy, majestic sweep of his hand. It was a dark blue two-seater with a tan leather interior. Head-on, the car looked like a grinning shark. "A step in the right direction, I think."

"Almost makes up for the fact that you were late." I sank into the soft leather seat and admired the burled oak trim of the dashboard. "But then there's that lame rose to consider, and you're two steps back again."

"So I guess there's no winning, huh?"

"Sorry," I said. "None."

Owen started the car, and a tune on his CD player picked up where it had left off. Mainly piano. Light drums. Maybe a stand-up bass. Beyond that, I had no idea.

"So," Owen said, dropping his car into second gear, then quickly into third. "Chinese?"

"Anywhere but Nick's."

"Why? You have something against botulism?"

"Cute," I said. "Can I quote you on that?"

"Oh, right. The profile. So is everything I say on the record?"

"Everything," I said. "Especially the bad stuff."

To my surprise, the restaurant Owen had in mind wasn't the cheap one I called for takeout whenever the girls and I were in the mood for Chinese, but the most expensive one on the Golden Mile. Its deep-red carpets were flecked with gold, and carp swam in a gurgling fountain in the center of the dining room. Roger took me there on our fifth anniversary but refused to return after seeing the bill. He also got annoyed with my insistence on using chopsticks. I mentioned these facts to Owen as a man in a loose-fitting tuxedo showed us to our table, but then I quickly apologized for bringing up my ex. The point of this dinner, after all, was not to force him into service as my analyst but to mine the minutia of his life so I could stitch together a reasonably interesting piece of pseudo-journalism in a thousand words or less.

"No problem," Owen said. "I've never been married myself, but I've come pretty close."

"Interesting," I said. "Any thoughts on why?"

"For the article?"

"What else?"

"I guess I'm waiting for the right girl."

"Maybe that's our angle. 'Local Restaurant Proprietor Waiting for Miss Right.'"

"Ooh," Owen said. "*Proprietor.* Do your readers know that word?"

"Good point," I conceded. "But I'm not allowed to write *asshole* in the headline."

"*Asshole*, hey?" Owen raised his eyebrows. "I thought you never cursed."

"In your case, I can make an exception. And besides, asshole isn't exactly a curse. It's a part of the body."

"Find me a dirty word that isn't a part of the body," Owen said.

"Shit," I told him.

"Doesn't count," he said. "It's a product of the body."

"What about the f-word?"

"Hmm," Owen said. "I'm not sure what you mean."

"Come on," I said.

"Nope. No idea. You'll have to be more specific."

"Fuck," I mouthed.

"What?" Owen said, cupping his hand behind his ear. "I didn't quite catch that."

"You know what I said," I told him.

"Say it again," Owen said. "For the record."

I rolled my eyes and said the word.

"You're blushing," Owen said. "That's so endearing. Unfortunately, fucking is as tied to the body as shitting, so no points for that one either."

"Now *I'm* the one who can't win."

"Looks that way," Owen said. "What do you say we call it a draw and admit that this is a date?"

A busboy in a maroon vest poured water from a metal pitcher, and the waiter came to take our order. Owen asked for spicy chicken. I ordered steamed vegetables. When our food arrived, Owen scraped some of his chicken onto my plate without asking and told me that his favorite thing about going out for Chinese was sharing.

"See?" he said. "I'm not a total asshole."

The fountain gurgled. Conversations murmured on all sides of us. Asian-sounding strings plinked in concealed speakers. After dinner, the waiter brought our check, and my fortune cookie informed me that I was an individual of many moods while Owen's noted that a rushing man can't walk with dignity.

"You mean like Vladimir Putin?" I said with a straight face.

"No, not Russian—" he started to say, then laughed. "Very funny."

This wasn't chemistry, I told myself. We were nothing more than a couple of clever wits trading barbs and one-liners in the dim light of a Chinese restaurant. Desi and Lucy. Burns and Allen. Tracy and Hepburn. Sure, we were speaking in the same ping-pong rhythms I'd shared with Roger back in the early days of our relationship, but how long before those rhythms turned into yet another rut?

"There's something you need to know before we go any further," I said as I settled back into the soft leather seat of Owen's BMW. "I really don't get jazz. I know it's supposed to be good, and I know it's what smart people listen to, but I'm sorry, I just can't figure it out."

"Not a problem," Owen said, sliding a disc into his CD player. "I prefer virgins, anyway. Close your eyes and tell me what you hear."

I closed my eyes and listened.

A stand-up bass crept along like a mouse peeking out of a hole in the wall. A trumpet sang softly, and I pictured a yellow sliver of moon. I heard soft drums and the tinkle of a piano, and I imagined the mouse stepping out into the moonlight. I told Owen what I was picturing and asked if I got it right. But it wasn't a right-or-wrong proposition, he said. Because there was no right or wrong in listening to jazz. There was only the music, and letting it into your heart.

"Deep," I said.

"You mock me."

"But of course. What do *you* hear in this one?"

"Ships at sea," Owen said. "Murky water. I imagine sea serpents rising to the surface and disappearing into the ocean like the Loch Ness monster. It's something mysterious. Something no one would ever believe even if they saw it with their own two eyes."

"I like that," I said. "Who are we listening to?"

"Miles Davis. On the trumpet, anyway."

"The sea serpent."

"Yeah, the serpent."

"The way his trumpet fades in like a sunrise. I can definitely hear it."

"See?" Owen said. "It's not hard at all."

GUNNING HIS engine, Owen piloted the small, nimble car down the highway, and the Golden Mile disappeared in the distance behind us. Jazz was a state of mind, he said, shifting gears as he wove in and out of traffic. You had to be willing to improvise. You had to be open to anything.

"Let's try one more," Owen said, reaching across my lap and popping open his glove compartment when the tune we'd been listening to reached its end. "Pick something at random and tell me what you hear."

I pulled a CD from the wallet in his glove compartment and slid it into the player. The track started with an odd drum beat followed by a trotting piano. I heard men in gray business suits, I said. Pulling big, gray cars into whitewashed garages, all in unison. All across America, men placing hats on hooks. Hugh Beaumont as Ward Cleaver, multiplied by thousands, multiplied by millions. I saw men smoking pipes behind newspapers. I smelled pot roast in the oven. I saw girls in poodle skirts, freckle-faced boys with crew cuts. There was the rotten-egg smoke of cap guns, and I felt a longing for toy trains, cowboy hats, and rubber dolls that cried and wetted themselves with a squeeze of the belly. I was walking through homes with ashtrays, homes with pianos, homes with radios built from solid oak and hi-fi record players cast in shiny, black plastic. I was crossing fresh-clipped lawns to the clink of ice cubes falling into glass tumblers. I saw bridge games silhouetted in dining room windows, men in v-neck sweaters, women in lipstick and pearls. The music had a wobbly feel to it, and Owen said it was because we were listening to Dave Brubeck, who always played with time signatures, so it was only natural for me to feel like I was riding on a horse with five legs.

"I like it," I said. "It takes me to a whole other world."

"Out of time," Owen said. "I know what you mean."

THE SPARE, spiky Philadelphia skyline glittered in the night and reminded me of the days when I used to dream of being a hip, young urbanite scraping by on the meager earnings of a freelance writer, and though we'd barely driven a half-hour, the sturdy old neighborhood where Owen touched down was light years away from the prefabricated neon sheen of the Golden Mile. Surrounded by redbrick row homes and meticulously restored brownstones, Owen's favorite jazz club stood in the imposing shadow of Eastern State Penitentiary, the abandoned prison in the heart of the city. Ordering our drinks as we sat down at a small, round table, he winked and said that whether I drank it or not, I should at least have a martini in front of me whenever I listened to live jazz.

"Not a fan?" Owen asked when I made a sour face at my first sip.

"Let's say it's an acquired taste."

"Like jazz," Owen said. "You'll get used to it."

The low, wooden riser at the front of the club was barely large enough to accommodate the drummer, but a guitarist and a stand-up bass player made do in its tight corners while a woman in a slinky red evening gown brought a slide trombone to her lips and sighed the first few notes of a song I knew I'd heard before.

"Summertime," Owen said when the title eluded me. "George Gershwin. Nine out of ten jazz musicians hate it, but it's the song everyone wants to hear. A friend of mine plays bass in a little trio in Brooklyn, and everywhere they go, his dumb-ass brother-in-law shows up and asks if he can sit in for a song or two. Then he shuffles onto the stage like the second coming of Sammy Davis, Jr., and says something ridiculous like, *Summertime, boys, and let's make it swing!* Everyone hates the guy, but they can't fire him because he's not technically a member of the group."

"Quite the conundrum," I said.

"It's getting to the point where they'll either have to kill him or break up the band."

I reached for my martini and took another sip. "So tell me, Mr. Little, what was the inspiration for opening Nick's American Grill?"

Owen laughed.

"What?" I said.

"I thought we were past this whole profile thing."

"I'm a professional," I said. "And besides, this whole profile thing is all there is."

"You're sure about that?" Owen said. "Because I could swear for a minute or two that this felt a like a date."

"Sorry to disappoint you," I said. "But if you want to go on a date with me, you're going to have to ask."

"Okay," Owen said. "Do you want to go on a date with me?"

"That depends," I said. "When?"

"How about right now?"

"Ooh," I winced. "I'm busy."

"Doing what?" he asked.

"Interviewing some guy who owns a restaurant."

"Sounds like a jerk," Owen said.

"Pretty much, but he has his finer points."

"Then how about next Friday?"

"I have the girls."

"Hire a sitter."

"I suppose it's a possibility."

"Can I take that as a yes?" Owen asked.

"Why not?" I said, reaching for my martini. "Assuming I can find a sitter, yes."

After the show, Owen drove me home, and we continued to play our game as traffic zipped by on all sides of us. Stan Getz was a warm summer breeze. Duke Ellington was the dogwood tree in front of my grandparents' house. Art Tatum was the grand lobby of an upscale luxury hotel in midtown Manhattan. Wishing the night could last a little longer as we passed beneath the phony rainbow of corporate logos and neon lights that lit the Golden Mile, I guided Owen off the main strip and through the confusing topography of my neighborhood. When he pulled up to the curb in front of my house, I asked him in for coffee.

"And by *coffee*, I mean *coffee*. Nothing more."

"That's too bad," Owen said, reaching for his glove compartment. "Because there's one more track I wanted you to hear. You do have a stereo, don't you?"

"Of course I have a stereo," I told him, though I failed to mention that its primary function was to play Lily's favorite numbers from the *Grease* soundtrack *ad infinitum*. "Who doesn't have a stereo?"

"Philistines mainly," Owen said. "You know, people who aren't into jazz."

"Very funny."

"I thought so."

Inside, I put the coffee on as Owen fiddled with my CD player. The track in question, he explained, was a free jazz composition by a saxophone player named Ornette Coleman.

"Free jazz?" I called from the kitchen.

"You'll see."

The coffeemaker gurgled. I poured each of us a mug and placed the mugs on a tray with a ceramic sugar bowl stuffed with white and yellow packets of sugar and Splenda. Pouring a thimbleful of milk into a tiny pitcher, I placed that on the tray, too, and checked my makeup in the slick surface of the door to my microwave.

"It's still not a date," I mouthed to the wide-eyed face looking back at me. "So don't get any ideas."

Laying the tray on the coffee table, I took a seat next to Owen on the sofa. The width of half a cushion said look but don't touch.

"Are you ready?" he asked, the remote in his hand.

"I don't know," I said. "Sounds ominous."

"It is," Owen said, pressing a button. "But I think you'll get it."

The horns screeched and squealed. The bass was all over the map. The drums rattled along, splashing and bubbling, seemingly heedless of the other instruments—in time, sure, but only grudgingly so. I couldn't even begin to guess how many instruments were playing, so when Owen asked me what it sounded like, I said the first thing that came to mind.

"I don't know. A cat falling into a washing machine?"

"Not exactly," Owen said.

"Not exactly? I thought there were no wrong answers."

"Usually, no. But for this one, I'm willing to bet we're hearing the same thing."

I listened to the rattling cacophony for a few seconds longer.

"Sorry," I said, reaching for my coffee. "I have no idea."

"Sure you do," Owen said. "I *know* you know this one."

I looked at him and turned up my palms in resignation.

"Hear how it's all screaming full-blast at once?" Owen asked. "Like the instruments can do whatever they want?"

"I guess so," I said. "Is that supposed to sound like something?"

"Yeah," Owen said. "I can't believe you're not getting it."

"Getting what? Tell me."

"It sounds like cocaine," Owen said. "Or at least getting high."

"Not you, too," I said, my heart sinking.

"You don't?" Owen said.

"God, no."

"But the other night. I saw you with Melinda and the Russian girl."

"Oh," I said. "That."

"It's such a small bathroom. I just assumed. I mean, what else could you have been doing? Especially with Melinda."

"It's a long story," I said. "Actually, it isn't. Melinda, yes. Svetlana, yes. Me, no."

"So you never?"

"Never," I said.

"Wow," Owen said. "Forget I mentioned it."

"No," I said. "I mean, don't worry about it. You're in the restaurant business, right? I should have known."

The music screamed away, and neither of us spoke for an awkward eternity. When it was finally time to break the silence, we both opened our mouths at once—Owen to apologize, and me to ask what cocaine was like.

"It's hard to say," Owen said. "Though I may have a little on hand if you want to try it."

"Me?" A picture of the girls hung over the fireplace, keeping an eye on me, reminding me to be good, reminding me to behave like a mother for Christ's sake. "I don't think so."

"No problem," Owen said. "Let's pretend I never brought it up."

I sipped my coffee. Would it really be so bad, I wondered? Just once? Just to see what it was like?

"I don't know," I said. "We're adults, right?"

"True," Owen said. "But I don't want to pressure you into anything."

"No," I said. "I mean, it's not like that. I'm curious is all, but I better not."

"Fair enough," Owen said, looking at his watch. "I should probably go."

"Yeah," I said. "It's getting late, isn't it?"

I walked Owen to the door, and we stood facing each other for a long, self-conscious moment. A hug, I wondered? A handshake? A peck on the cheek?

"You forgot your CD," I eventually said, gesturing toward the living room.

"It's okay," Owen said. "I'll get it next week."

"You're still up for that?"

"You think I'd miss our second date?"

"First date," I said. "Tonight didn't count."

"Right," Owen said, leaning in to give me a kiss on the cheek. "I almost forgot."

"Wait," I said before he could turn away.

Resting my hands on Owen's chest, I stood on my toes and kissed him on the lips. It was a soft kiss—tentative at first, but soon I felt his arms around me, and I fell into his embrace.

"That was nice," Owen said.

"Yeah," I said. "I thought so, too."

CHAPTER FIVE

CATHERINE AND Lily came home on Sunday afternoon, and I knew from experience that Roger hadn't allotted any time for homework. He was the fun parent, after all, so he had no choice but to fill every other weekend with trips to the mall and to the zoo, to ice cream parlors and toy stores, to video arcades and bowling alleys, to the movies and amusement parks, and, if Catherine insisted with enough vigor, to special exhibits at the Franklin Institute and the Academy of Natural Sciences. The girls could always do their homework, Roger explained on the one or two occasions when I tried to raise the subject, but the hours they had with their father were precious and few. Did I want to deprive them of face time with their dad, he asked? Did I want my daughters to remember him as the harsh taskmaster of their childhood? Did I want them to think of his apartment as nothing more than a place to do homework? It was an argument I couldn't win, so when the girls hit me with a flood of questions about my night out with Owen, I told them the answers would have to wait until they'd finished their homework.

"Did you kiss?" Lily asked in a vain attempt at postponing an inevitable rendezvous with a math worksheet.

"It's bad manners to tell," I said, sure my silly grin was giving me away.

"Were you careful?" Catherine asked.

"Of course I was careful."

"No, Mom," Catherine said, looking me in the eye. "I mean were you *careful?*"

"She wants to know if you used a condom," Lily said.

I looked to Catherine, who looked back at me, pleading.

Please tell me you were careful, her eyes seemed to say. *Don't mention condoms, and don't mention sex. Just tell me you were careful so I can sleep tonight.*

"Chloe hated my cookies," Catherine said quietly. "She took a bite and said they were great, but she was obviously lying or she would have had more."

"Catherine," I said, reaching for my daughter's hand. "You don't have to worry. I was careful, okay?"

"And even when she did take a bite, she was only pretending. She made dumb munching noises like I was a baby. How stupid does she think I am?"

"She's on a diet," Lily said. "So she shouldn't be eating cookies anyway."

Catherine rolled her eyes and looked at me again.

"I just don't want you getting hurt," Catherine said. "That's all."

"It's okay, Catherine. I'm a big girl, and I can watch out for myself."

"Promise?" Catherine said.

"Cross my heart."

As if the girls weren't bad enough, Melinda crept into my office on Monday morning and closed the door behind her.

"Did you do it?" she asked, palms pressed flat against the door behind her. "Did you get it on with Owen?"

"Don't say *get it on*. Roger always said *get it on*, and I hated it."

"You're not answering the question," Melinda whined. "Did you get it on or what?"

"That's between me and Owen."

"Please. You know he's at Nick's right now telling his entire wait staff that he kept you up all night and left you begging for more."

"I don't think he's like that."

"Honey, they're all like that."

"We talked," I said. "We got to know each other. It was nice."

"So was my grandmother's funeral. Tell me something good."

Part of me wanted to mention the cocaine and how Owen assumed that I'd been getting high with Melinda on the night of Vic's big family dinner. Should I be worried, I wanted to ask as I pecked away at my computer keyboard, pretending to have no interest in the conversation? Was he a big user, or was it strictly recreational the way it apparently was for her and the rest of the *Eating Out* sales crew?

And what about getting high? If we were truly friends and I could trust Melinda with the kinds of confidences she wanted from me, I'd have told her the thing I was afraid of admitting even to myself—that against every ounce of better judgment, I wanted to know what all the fuss was about.

"I drank a martini," I said, looking up from my work. "Well, half of one."

"And?"

I made a bitter face. "Not a huge fan."

Why not, I wondered as Melinda waited for more? A small amount under controlled circumstances. I'd probably hate snorting the stuff up my nose, but at least I'd know. And in a few years time, maybe I'd admit to doing it with a vague allusion over coffee and dessert to the time I tried cocaine. It wasn't a big deal, I'd insist with the air of someone who'd been around the block more times than she cared to admit. It didn't do anything for me. And really—I'd tell my daughters when they were old enough to know that their mother wasn't perfect, that she had a past, and that, despite all evidence to the contrary, she hadn't been a mom all her life—it was a stupid thing to do.

"So that's it?" Melinda asked. "That's all you're giving me? You talked all night and drank a martini?"

"Half a martini," I said, lest she get the wrong impression. "If that."

"Divorce is so wasted on you," Melinda said with a sigh. "Do me a favor next time and make something up, okay?"

"Who said anything about a next time?"

"Trust me," Melinda said. "With Owen, there's always a next time."

CHAPTER SIX

Catherine and Lily played shy when Owen arrived to pick me up on the night of our first official date. Watching from the kitchen with their babysitter as I answered the doorbell, they came when I called, but refused to look up from their shoes for more than a few seconds at a time. But Owen was a trooper, almost a natural at dealing with my daughters. He didn't condescend, didn't speak down to them, didn't try to be their buddy like Chloe did. Instead, he addressed them as if they were adults. Shaking their hands, Owen said it was a pleasure to meet them both and promised to have me back at a decent hour—a ploy that was bound to win Catherine over even if it was completely lost on Lily.

Kissing my girls on the way out the door, I told them not to wait up for me, and as we walked to Owen's BMW, he asked if he'd made a good first impression. I thought so, I whispered, but he still had to be careful because the girls and their babysitter were watching us from behind the living room curtains. Taking this as a cue, Owen opened the door to his car and stood like a chauffeur as I slid into the soft leather passenger seat, and it wasn't until he started the car that I brought up the subject I'd been mulling all week.

"About the cocaine," I said. "I need to ask you something."

"I'm really sorry about that."

"I'm not looking for an apology," I said. "I just want to know if it's a problem."

"You mean am I a cokehead?"

"Something like that," I said. "And I need you to be honest with me. How much and how often?"

"Rarely," Owen said. "Not much at all. I just had a little on hand the other night in case I needed to steady my nerves."

"Steady your nerves?" I said.

It was mid-September, and the sun was setting early. Owen was driving, and the radio was tuned to a sad trumpet accompanied by piano, bass, and drums. I knew the melody but couldn't place it. The DJ had a deep voice, and when the song faded, he said that we'd been listening to Miles Davis and his rendition of Someday My Prince Will Come.

"Of course," Owen said. "I always get nervous around beautiful women."

"Please," I said, turning to the window to hide my smile as a parade of strip malls, carpet outlets, and big-box department stores rolled by. During the day, this portion of the Golden Mile was nothing more than a shattered stretch of concrete and plastic, but as the sun sank and the neon lights came up, the stark, gray landscape gradually gave way to a host of glowing corporate logos floating, serene as angels, in the pink-orange haze on the edge of night. "You really think I'm beautiful?"

"I guess I have a thing for redheads."

"So you weren't high that night?"

"Absolutely not," Owen said.

"And tonight?"

"God no—though I was definitely nervous about meeting Catherine and Lily."

"Are you kidding? They loved you."

"I wouldn't go that far," Owen said. "We met for two seconds. I shook their hands and promised to have you back at a decent hour."

"Trust me," I said. "As far as Catherine's concerned, that's all that matters."

"And Lily?"

"I'm still trying to figure her out myself," I said.

Over dinner, I told Owen that Lily scared me sometimes, especially given the fact that she seemed to know more about sex than I ever would—or at least that she knew all the right things to say about it. What was behind the words was another matter altogether.

"The first time I ever heard anyone talk about rubbers, I thought they meant boots," I said. "My father always called out to my mother from deep inside the hallway closet to ask if she'd seen his rubbers whenever it rained. When I finally found out what the rest of the world meant when they talked about rubbers, I started to dread inclement weather and did anything I could to be out of earshot when my father went rummaging through the closet. If he ever asked me where his rubbers were, I swear I would have died."

"That's nothing," Owen said. "When I was six, a nine-year-old told me how babies were made, and I nearly threw up at the thought of it. I mean, here I am, six years old, and this pudgy kid with onion breath and sausage fingers tells me that in the middle of the night, my dad's parts go looking for my mom's parts so they can make a baby."

"Wow," I said. "Six years old."

"That isn't the half of it," Owen said. "My dad snored like a grizzly bear, so my mom made him sleep on the couch."

"What's wrong with that?" I asked.

"Well, when you're six years old and a nine-year-old tells you that your dad's thing goes looking for your mom's thing in the middle of the night, you take it literally. I figured it must have been about twenty yards long with a mind of its own if it was creeping from the living room to the bedroom in search of my mother every night. What if I woke up and tripped over it on the way to the bedroom? It would probably get mad and try to strangle me."

I started to laugh but caught myself.

"I'm serious," Owen said. "We're talking massive childhood trauma."

"I believe you," I said, and he laughed too.

We paused impatiently as our waitress hovered over the table to ask if we wanted fresh ground pepper on our salads or grated parmesan on our ravioli. Owen lost his virginity at fourteen to a girl with a driver's license and a banged-up Buick Century. I lost mine in college to a boy who wrote poetry and played raspy punk songs on an un-tuned acoustic guitar. Owen and I had both been through pregnancy scares, and we both got off easy—Owen with a girlfriend's first-term miscarriage, me with a faulty home pregnancy test. When he told me about the miscarriage, I reached across the table and touched his hand and told him I was sorry. It was the worst month of his life, he said, but he'd left the whole incident so far back in the past that he barely thought about it anymore.

After dinner, we went to a movie. Superheroes in anatomically correct body armor, a mad genius scheming to take over the universe, pyrotechnics to die for. Our hands touched in the wide mouth of the plastic cup-holder screwed into the armrest between us. Our fingers explored each other's boundaries. His hand eclipsed mine. Our forearms overlapped. He put an arm over my shoulders.

"I had fun tonight," I said later in the evening as Owen walked me to my front door. "I'm glad we talked about what we talked about."

"Me too," he said.

"So," I paused, swinging a nervous foot back and forth. "Maybe next time we can do more than talk."

"That would be nice," he said.

"Of course, we'll need protection."

"It's okay. I had an operation after the scare."

"Yeah, but there's still that other thing."

"Right," Owen said. "Goes without saying these days."

"So you'll take care of it?" I said.

"Yeah," Owen said. "I'll get some..."

"Rubbers?" I said, and we started to laugh like a couple of dumb kids.

If I wasn't careful, I might get used to it.

THE SITTER was asleep on the couch when I let myself into the house, but Catherine was wide awake, an open schoolbook resting in her lap.

"It's after midnight," she said.

"Sorry, Mom. I lost track of time."

The sitter stirred, then came awake with a start, black curls bouncing with the shock of my sudden appearance. After I paid the girl twenty dollars and watched her hurry across two lawns to get to her front door, Catherine asked why she needed a babysitter anyway. All the girl did was watch TV and talk on the phone with her friends.

"But that's what teenagers do," I told her.

"Not me," Catherine said. "When I'm a teenager, all I'll do is study so I can get into a good college."

"And when you get to college?"

"That's when the work begins."

I thought about my grandfather and for the first time seriously considered the possibility of reincarnation. He'd grown up during the Great Depression and served in the army during World War II. His father had been a coal miner, his mother the daughter of a dairy farmer. As a boy, he went down into the mines himself and kept an eye on the canary whose death would inform the miners that they'd struck a gas vein and that asphyxiation was imminent. The war, by comparison, was a piece of cake, and to hear him talk about it, you'd think that all he did was push a broom through Dresden to help tidy up after the bombing had stopped.

"Just promise me one thing," I said, squeezing Catherine's shoulder as we climbed the stairs. "Try to have a little fun once in a while, okay?"

It was the same piece of advice a little voice in my head had been whispering all week.

Loosen up. Try something new. Have a little fun.

I'd told myself for so long that being a mother was all I needed, that the daily rigors of waking up before the girls, of making their breakfast and getting them off to school, of going to work and coming home and making dinner and checking homework and making flashcards to help my daughters with their spelling and history and science and math were rewards in themselves, that driving Catherine and Lily to play dates and extracurricular activities strategically positioned at opposite ends of God's green Earth was a noble calling. I'd repeated these things to myself—not in words so much, but in the way that I lived—so often that it never once occurred to me that there might be more, that there might be life outside of my daughters, that—heaven forbid—there might be fun.

But now the girl I'd been before I was a mother—before Roger, even—was coming back to life. The girl who wore clunky black shoes and thrift-shop sweaters. The girl who read and wrote poetry and howled with laughter at Monty Python sketches. The girl who smoked cigarettes like she imagined a French intellectual might. Her heart was beating, her eyelids fluttering, her fingers twitching with new life.

As I spit out my toothpaste and gargled with mouthwash, I asked what she thought about the whole situation.

Seriously, the mother in me said. *What do you think?*

I think once would be okay, the girl said.

But this is cocaine we're talking about.

I know, the girl said.

Maybe if we don't ask. Maybe if we don't raise the subject. Maybe if we just let it go, and if he brings it, fine, and if he doesn't, we take it as a sign that it wasn't meant to be.

But if he does bring it? the girl said.

Then we have a little fun, the mother in me conceded. *And no one needs to know.*

CHAPTER SEVEN

THERE WAS a chill in the air on the night of our second official date, but the marquees on Broad Street in downtown Philadelphia gave the world a soft, warm glow. Old men in suits stood stiffly next to women in fur coats, their faces pale and wrinkled. The men were all skinny, the women a little plump, and they all had to shout at each other to make themselves heard. Before Roger left, I used to imagine the two of us fumbling through our golden years just like these couples, and as Owen guided me down a flight of concrete steps to his favorite jazz club, I wondered if I still had a shot at the old age I'd always dreamed of—reading glasses, hearing aids, and all.

The bar was dark and lit with purple neon. Owen and I sat at a small table and applauded whenever the music reached a climax. Two numbers into the show, I felt his hand brush up against mine, then close gently around my fingers. It was a soft grip, and my heart told me to trust him. Maybe this was the beginning of our life together, I allowed myself to think. Maybe this was my second chance at love. Maybe one day Owen and I would grow old together like the nearly deaf couples shuffling along on the sidewalk above, and maybe if I let my guard down, we could have a little fun while we were still young.

"So I was wondering," I said as Owen drove us back to my place after the show.

"Yes?"

Okay, so maybe I dropped a hint or two over the course of the week. Maybe I let it slip that a girl could always change her mind. Maybe I mentioned that even though no always meant no, there was always room for negotiation. Maybe I gave Owen the impression that I was open to trying coke just once, just out of curiosity, just to see if it would do anything for me.

"If maybe you brought a little something to top off the evening?"

"That depends," Owen said. "What did you have in mind?"

"Oh, I don't know. Maybe a little blow?"

The word was already out of my mouth when I realized how dumb it sounded.

"So it's *blow* now?"

"Not cool?"

"Too Hollywood," Owen said. "Are you sure you want to try it? I hear the stuff can be habit forming."

"I *am* an adult," I told him. "I think I know my limits."

Back at home, I poured myself a glass of wine and offered one to Owen. Before retiring to the bedroom, we sat on the couch and sipped our drinks until we were lost in conversation. Owen grew up in Hoboken before it went upscale. He'd been an altar boy in grammar school and once fell asleep on his bicycle while coasting to six o'clock mass. When he woke up, he found himself rolling across the hood of a parked car. He laughed when he told me this, and though I found the whole story highly suspicious, I laughed, too, and poured myself a second glass of wine. When I caught myself talking about Catherine and Lily, I changed the subject and invited Owen upstairs. Excusing myself for a moment, I slipped into a silky green kimono and returned to the bedroom to find him tapping a small amount of white powder onto a mirror.

"Hope you don't mind," he said.

A portrait of Catherine and Lily sat on my dresser, and I could feel them staring at me as I watched Owen chop at the powder with a razor blade. Any minute now, I guessed, I would come to my senses and tell him to stop, tell him that I didn't want to get high, tell him that if he ever wanted to see me again, he wouldn't get high anymore, either. But the words never came, and all I did was sit on the edge of the bed while Owen divided the powder into a pair of thin lines.

My breathing was shallow. My mouth was dry. A disc was spinning in the CD player on my dresser. Nina Simone, Owen said, concentrating on the task at hand as a tom-tom pulsed with a jump-rope rhythm and the singer sang of a woman in a black dress who, for a thousand dollars, could make a man love her and then fly away.

When he was satisfied with the lines in front of him, Owen rolled a twenty-dollar bill into a tight little tube and asked if I was sure I wanted to go through with it. Though I fully expected to hear myself say no as he handed me the rolled-up twenty, I just nodded and took the makeshift straw between my thumb and forefinger. It was no big deal, I told myself as Owen offered instruction. The stuff looked so innocuous—a line of white powder about half the length of my pinky—and I was only trying it once.

"Well?" Owen said when I came up for air.

"Ugh," I said, rubbing my nose as the voice of reason finally kicked in.

Cocaine? I thought. *What the hell am I doing? I'm safe. I'm reliable. I'm a responsible adult. I drive a fuel-efficient car and count my change. I make to-do lists and consult them religiously. I wear my seat belt. I buy generic groceries and save my receipts. I clip coupons and recycle and never charge more to my credit card than I have in the bank, and at the end of each day, I say a prayer for my daughters. I'm a mother, for the love of God, and experimenting with illegal and potentially deadly chemicals doesn't exactly fit the job description.*

At the same time, I couldn't help looking down at the rolled up twenty pinched between my thumb and forefinger and agreeing as a super-hip college chick in a black turtleneck looked up from her Kierkegaard, exhaled a plume of smoke, and whispered a single word in the dimmest, dustiest coffeehouse corner of my mind: *Cool.*

A minute passed, and then another. I closed my eyes and listened to my body—my breathing, my heartbeat, my poor, burning brain singing with joy. Aware of every atom, I could feel white light glowing in my veins as the acrid chemical taste of the coke dripped into the back of my throat. The feeling was like

Christmas. The feeling was like my wedding day. The feeling was like my first crush, my first kiss, my first valentine all at once. It was everything my life had always been missing, a feeling that made me complete.

"Earth to Audrey," Owen said. "It's working, isn't it?"

I nodded and smiled. Owen snorted a line. Soon we were pawing at each other, and his lips were on my neck, his hands on my breasts. For the first time in my life, I wasn't second-guessing myself, wasn't worrying about what the man in my bed was thinking or whether he was getting bored. Instead, I just went with my instincts and did what felt right, which was pretty much everything.

I knew for sure as Owen pinned my hands behind my back that this wasn't making love, but I also knew that it wasn't quite fucking. It was more like watching two strangers go at it, as if I were simply in the room with them or watching them on TV, and I kept thinking to myself how funny it was that this woman in bed with this man looked exactly like me, but sure as hell couldn't have been because, God, she looked like she'd been doing this her entire life—digging her nails into the man's back, talking dirty when he told her to, and screaming with wild abandon as if no nagging voice in her head had ever wondered if she was doing it right or worried that the neighbors might hear.

Between rounds, Owen tapped more coke onto the mirror, and I took little hits. A taste here and there. Part of a line. The dust that was left over. When Owen spread his legs, I sat between them with the rolled-up twenty in one hand and the mirror in the other.

"Don't take this the wrong way," I said as Owen reached forward and caressed my breasts from behind. "Because I like you—I like you a lot. But if I'd known about this stuff back when I was married, I guarantee Roger never would have left."

"His loss," Owen said.

"He called me wooden. Do you believe that?"

"You?" Owen said. "Never."

"Like a slab of oak, he said. Faithful. Strong. Reliable."

"Makes you sound like a pickup truck."

"My point exactly."

"Built Ford tough."

"Like a rock," I said. "That's totally me."

"I can tell," Owen said. "You're blowing through my coke like there's no tomorrow."

"Tomorrow?" I said. "Never heard of it."

"Even so, you better let up. You're still a bit of a lightweight."

"So sweet of you to worry," I said, rolling onto my belly and looking up at Owen with a smile. "But I think I know what I'm doing."

Even as I said it, something didn't feel right. My heart was still racing, and I could feel the blood coursing through every inch of my body, but it wasn't fun anymore, and soon my giddy euphoria dissolved into a nervous, jittery urge to get up and move.

"I really love my girls," I said, pacing the carpet at the foot of my bed. "You know that, right? Catherine and Lily. They mean the world to me. And I'm a good mother. At least, I want to be a good mother. But Catherine. She works so hard to please me. She's so smart, and I just want to tell her that I love her so much, but I can never find the words. And Lily. She's so funny. She thinks she's so grown-up, but I know she's not. She's my little baby. Do you understand what I'm saying? Do you know what I mean? My girls are my life. You see that, don't you? You understand what I'm saying?"

"Totally," Owen said. "I mean, yeah. I know exactly what you mean. Motherhood. It's what? The oldest profession? They should give medals. When I think back on what I put my own mother through? God. I mean, yeah. I mean, no. I mean, I can only imagine what it's like to give birth."

"You don't understand," I said. "This is more than giving birth. I'm talking about being a *mother*, Owen. *A mother*. It's who I am. It's what matters most. More than anything else in the world, I want my girls to be safe. I want them to be happy. I want them to know that I love them."

- 49 -

"Right. No. Exactly. I know exactly what you mean," Owen insisted, rubbing his nose.

He was still naked, and his penis lay limp and shriveled in his lap.

"No, you don't know what I mean. You don't know what I mean at all," I said, hugging myself against a shiver, certain that the neighbors could see us through the curtains. "God, I feel like I'm dying."

"It's okay," Owen said. "You're not dying."

He sat on the edge of the bed and beckoned for me to sit next to him.

"What about the girls?" I said, suppressing a sob. "They'll come home and find me dead, and they'll have to live with Roger."

"Honestly," Owen said. "You'll be okay."

"You don't understand. They'll move in with Roger, and they'll forget all about me."

"That isn't going to happen," Owen said. "You have my word on it."

"I'll be dead and in the ground, and they'll think she's their mother."

"It's okay, Audrey," Owen said. "You're just coming down a little hard."

"Never again, okay? If this is what it's like, then never again."

"It's not always like this."

"I don't care," I said. "I need you to swear to me. No more cocaine. Ever."

"Okay," Owen said. "I promise."

CHAPTER EIGHT

On Sunday afternoon, the hulking Navigator rolled into my driveway. Chloe was behind the wheel. The girls were buckled into the backseat. Roger, as usual, was absent from the scene. Standing at my front door in the threadbare bathrobe I'd been wearing for the past forty-eight hours, I watched Chloe descend from the vehicle and hold out a hand to guide Lily as she leapt to the ground. Though Catherine declined the same hand when it was offered, she didn't appear to have any qualms about joining her sister in a group hug with the woman who—please, let's be honest—destroyed my marriage.

What about the cookies? I wanted to scream as Chloe walked my daughters up the concrete path that led to my house. *What about the way she talks down to you? What about the way she treats you like a baby?*

Stifling my rage, I put on my best smile, but the expression on Chloe's face when I opened the door said it all: I looked like I'd been to hell and back.

"It's nothing," I said before she could state the obvious. "A cold, I think. I must be coming down with something."

"Do you want Roger to keep the girls?" Chloe asked, standing between me and my daughters. "I'm sure he wouldn't mind."

"I'm sure he wouldn't," I agreed. *Home-wrecker. Vulture. Baby-snatcher.* "But I'll be fine."

I turned my head and faked a cough, and Chloe said she hoped I'd feel better soon.

Bitch, I thought as she walked back to her Navigator.

"You're sure you're okay, Mom?" Catherine asked when Chloe was gone.

"I'm fine, honey. Don't worry."

"Can I make you some tea?"

"That would be nice," I said.

"Licorice or chamomile?"

"Whatever," I said, limping back to the couch where I'd spent most of the past two days. "Your choice."

In a few minutes, the water boiled, and I could hear Catherine setting the timer on the microwave oven. The instructions on the box called for allowing the tea to steep for three to four minutes, so three to four minutes it would be.

"You and Chloe looked pretty chummy out there," I said when Catherine emerged from the kitchen, carefully balancing a teacup on a saucer. "I'm glad to see you're getting along."

I patted a sofa cushion, and my daughter cuddled up next to me, nudging her way under my arm and resting her head on my breast. This was Catherine, I reminded myself. The one who always seemed so mature, so much older and wiser than her years, yet she was still my baby.

"She hugs like a robot," Catherine said, and it occurred to me that Lily wasn't anywhere to be seen.

"Where's your sister?" I asked.

"I think she had some homework to finish."

The door to my bedroom was open. The green kimono was lying in a silky puddle on the floor. A rolled-up twenty was resting on a mirror by the pillow. Would Lily guess what it all meant if she stumbled upon the scene, I wondered, frozen in a moment of panic? And more important, was there anything left on the mirror?

"Could you get her for me?" I asked.

It wouldn't be like getting high, I told myself. I just wanted to get back on an even keel. If I had a headache, I'd take an aspirin. If I needed a little kick to get me going in the morning, I'd drink some coffee. If I needed to unwind after a long week at work, I might pour myself a glass of wine. So what was wrong with doing a tiny bit of coke so I could focus on my daughters for the few hours left in the weekend?

No one would need to know, not even Owen.

Or *especially* not Owen, because I already told him that I was off the stuff for good, and I didn't want him thinking that I changed my mind.

Because I hadn't.

Because I only needed a taste.

Because I only needed the tiniest, tiniest bit.

"Lily!" Catherine shouted without getting up. "Mom wants to see you."

"Inside voices," I said, snapping back to reality.

"Sorry, Mom."

Lily came down from her bedroom with another call to arms from the GESTAPO. Every day offered a new opportunity to get involved in the life of a child, the handout said, and the Good Shepherd Teacher and Parent Organization had the resources I needed to do so. Sure, being an involved parent would take a lot of effort, but if I was willing to volunteer just a few hours a week with the GESTAPO, I'd be ensuring a brighter future not only for Catherine and Lily, but for every child in the school.

Because good schools didn't just happen.

They were created—by caring parents like me.

"I'll keep it in mind," I said to Lily.

"No, Mom," my younger daughter said impatiently. "The other side."

I turned the sheet over and realized that Lily was giving me her birthday list. She wanted clothing. She wanted jewelry. She wanted perfume, makeup, and high-heel shoes. Less than a year earlier, she was still content to play with dolls and imagine herself as the mother of a stuffed panda named Simon, but now the only names that held any interest for her were the kind I could never afford, even for myself. Armani, Prada, Gucci. And, of course, Chrissy Qualtieri and her art-deco Q.

"You're a little young for this kind of stuff," I told her. "And your birthday isn't until December."

"Chloe says you're never too young to think about how you look."

"I think she was talking to me," Catherine said. "She wants me to stand up straighter and not look at my feet so much."

"What's wrong with your feet?" I asked. "I think they're beautiful—as far as feet go, anyway."

Catherine looked up to see if I was kidding, and I looked back into her suspicious brown eyes with a perfectly serious expression before finally cracking a smile.

"I love you, Mom," Catherine said.

"I love you, too, baby."

I gave Catherine a squeeze, and Lily piled on top of us.

"I love both of you," I said. "You know that, right?"

My cup of tea sat cooling on the coffee table. Untangling myself from my daughters, I reached for it and asked how their weekend was.

"Oh my God!" Lily said. "I almost forgot! We're going to Hawaii!"

"You are?" I said.

It was news to me.

"Not just us," Lily said. "You, too. Dad says he wants an old-fashioned family vacation."

I started to tell her that she had to be mistaken, that her father probably had something else in mind when he used the word *family*—something that didn't include his ex-wife, for example—but Catherine confirmed Lily's story and said that Roger specifically mentioned my name in reference to the excursion.

They'd have to miss school, Lily gushed as I tried to wrap my mind around her father's definition of *old-fashioned*. But only for a week, Catherine added, promising to make up any work she missed while away.

"You *will* come with us, won't you?" Lily asked, commencing an enthusiastic if not entirely accurate impersonation of a hula dancer.

"I'll think about it," I told her. Meaning no. Meaning of course not. Meaning are you completely out of your mind? "Let me talk to your father before I commit to anything."

Knowing Roger like I did, I was sure he'd rationalized the whole scheme right down to the number of frequent flyer miles he'd accrue if I tagged along. In his mind, a vacation with me and Chloe probably represented nothing less than a great chance for all of us to set our differences aside and get to know each other better—and if my presence happened to provide a free babysitter while Roger and Chloe wandered off for long, romantic walks on the beach, then so much the better.

"I know what you want, Roger," I hissed into the phone after the girls went to bed. "You want the pretty fiancée and the perfect little girls and the faithful old ex to play the maid so you and your new family can go gallivanting across the island."

"Whoa," Roger said. "Who said anything about gallivanting?"

"I'm serious, Roger. I'm sick of you assuming that I'll do whatever you want just because I'm the mother of your children."

"Don't take this the wrong way, Audrey, but have you been drinking?"

"What's that supposed to mean?" I asked.

"Nothing," Roger said. "But you're not exactly being rational."

"Rational? What's rational, Roger? Inviting your ex-wife and fiancée on the same vacation and calling it old-fashioned? Pulling your daughters out of school so they can spend a week on the beach? Or how about this, Roger? How about sending your little chippie to your ex-wife's house to gather up your kids every week and then to drop them off again when you're done with them? Does that sound rational to you, Roger? Or does it sound like someone's trying to avoid something? Like—I don't know—having an adult conversation with the woman who gave him the best ten years of her life?"

"Look, I can tell you're upset about something," Roger said. "So how about if you just give this vacation a little more thought and get back to me on it?"

"Did you hear anything I just said, Roger?"

"Of course I did, and I really do sympathize. It's exactly why I think you should come along with us. We all need a chance to get to know each other better. Speaking of which, when do I get to meet this new guy in your life? We definitely need to double sometime."

"Yeah," I said. "Like that'll happen any time soon."

"I'm only trying to be civil," Roger said. "I wish you'd do the same, if only for our daughters. You're my best friend, Audrey. I've told you that a million times. I just wish you could see that. And I wish you'd give this vacation a little more thought."

"You don't get it, do you Roger? You made a choice when you asked for a divorce, and now you have to live with it. You wanted your freedom, and you got it. I'm not your wife anymore, and we're not a family. You can't have it both ways."

I said goodbye and hung up the phone.

I went to my bedroom and closed the door.

Traces of dust flecked my mirror.

If I really wanted to, I could probably scrape together a faint little ghost of a line and catch one last buzz, but the mother in me knew better. The last thing I needed was to mess with cocaine any more than I already had, and the last thing I wanted was another crash, so I put the mirror away and swore on my life that I'd never get high again—because who needs drugs when you can tell your ex-husband to go to hell?

CHAPTER NINE

THE NEXT morning, I dragged myself out of bed, got the girls off to school and trudged to work like a good soldier. My head was still fuzzy, and my arms and legs felt like borrowed property, but I knew I could manage—task by task, item by item, one cup of coffee at a time. If Vic and Jerry noticed anything odd, they didn't let on, but as soon as Melinda strolled into the office, she took one look at me, removed her sunglasses and placed them over my eyes. Big, round lenses, white plastic frames. I was still wearing them later in the day when I caught my reflection in the grimy mirror of the *Eating Out* bathroom and saw that they were decorated with Chrissie Qualtieri's art-deco Q.

"Those aren't a gift," Melinda said when she opened the door and caught me preening. "They cost *mucho dinero*, so I better get them back."

"Don't worry," I said. "You will."

"In the meantime, you can give me some details." Melinda lifted the glasses and examined my eyes with the practiced scrutiny of a physician. "Judging by these bags, the question obviously isn't *whether* you got it on with Owen but how many times."

"I don't know what you're talking about," I said.

"Nice try," Melinda said. "Give me a number."

"Would you believe I lost count?"

"Sweet," Melinda said. "We'll make a bad girl out of you yet."

"Don't count on it," I told her. "I'm really not like that."

"But you had fun, right?"

Biting my lip to conceal a grin, I decided to join the GESTAPO right then and there if only to prove Melinda wrong. I was still good, I told myself as I dialed the number on the back of

Lily's wish list. I was a responsible mother, and, yes, I was willing to do anything I could in order to ensure a brighter future for my daughters and their classmates.

The woman who took my call had a buttery voice and said she was glad to have me on board. The easiest thing for me to do, she said, was to start attending meetings, but if I was feeling especially generous, I could volunteer to host.

"Sure," I said, feeling more parental already. "I'll do anything."

The woman took my name and number, then asked some questions about Catherine and Lily—what grades they were in, who their teachers were, whether or not they participated in extracurricular activities. Like the good mother I knew I was, I rattled off the answers without thinking twice, and at the end of the call, the woman said she wished all parents could be a little more like me. It was exactly what I wanted to hear, and by the middle of the week, I was back to my old self. The coke, the crash, and the jitters were behind me, and I took it as a good sign when Owen suggested that it might be fun to invite Catherine and Lily along on our next date.

"You're sure you don't mind?" Catherine asked when I ran the idea by her.

"Of course I don't mind. You're my daughters."

Lily was walking the spine of the couch again, and I told her to get down before she cracked her head open.

"And Owen doesn't mind either?"

"It was his idea," I said. "He wants to get to know you guys."

"That means he's serious," Lily said, dropping onto the sofa cushions.

I hoped she was right but refused to say so. Though Owen and I had only begun to date, I was already starting to dream about my future with him, and when we took the girls out for burgers that Friday, it wasn't hard to imagine the four of us as a family. Sitting in a plywood booth next to a banged-up statue of Ronald McDonald, I poked at a soggy Filet-O-Fish while the girls loaded up on sugar, salt, and grease. Sure, the floor was sticky, and the restaurant smelled of ammonia, but I was loving every minute of it. For the longest time after Roger left, I'd felt as if people could smell my divorce on me, that they could tell by the way I walked or spoke that Catherine and Lily were all I had and that raising them was entirely my responsibility. But with Owen in the picture, I was beginning to feel normal again, less lopsided somehow—like we were finally the family I was always seeing on TV and wishing I could have.

I was feeling good, falling in love, and starting to come alive.

It wasn't cocaine, but it was definitely a rush.

CHAPTER TEN

BY THE end of October, my relationship with Owen was falling into a steady rhythm. I kept a toothbrush in his medicine cabinet. He left CDs in my carousel. When Roger took the girls, we'd hit the town and listen to jazz, and when the girls were mine, we'd go out for burgers and a movie and pretend to be a family. For all practical purposes, my wild night of drug-induced decadence might as well have been a dream. Even on nights when we were alone and I'd had a drink or two—nights when, okay, a tiny, tiny part of me was still curious, was still hungry for one more taste—Owen kept up his end of the bargain and never breathed a word of cocaine. But then came the party, and all bets were off.

A week before Halloween, Raj convinced an uncle of his to take out a quarter-page ad in *Eating Out*. Cash, Vic informed me, feet up on his desk and grinning broadly as if he'd landed the account himself. Up front, for a three-month run. Interpreting this turn of events as a sure sign that his campaign to win over the hearts and minds of every shopkeeper in what he still insisted on calling the Patel Cartel was finally turning a corner, he poured himself a drink from a bottle of Old Crow that he kept in his desk drawer and decreed that a celebration was in order.

"I'm thinking something Indian-themed," he said. "To welcome Uncle Punjab into the fold. Like maybe we all wear dots on our foreheads and call each other *sahib*."

"Could be construed as offensive," I said.

"You think?"

"Maybe a little."

"Hmm," Vic said, genuinely surprised. "Anyway, I'm sure you'll work something out."

"Me?" I said.

"Nothing big. Nothing fancy. No need to invite the world."

"Vic, I can't."

"Loyal customers only."

"In case you haven't noticed, I have a magazine to run."

"And don't forget to save your receipts for tax purposes."

"It's Halloween, Vic. I have two little girls at home, and I promised to make them costumes."

"Costumes," Vic said, snapping his fingers. "That's perfect. How does Saturday look?"

"That's two days from now, Vic."

"Then the following Saturday. We'll have it at your house."

"Seriously," I said. "I don't think so."

"Why? You have the girls that night?"

"No, Vic, but that's not the point."

"Are you kidding me, Audrey? It'll be fun."

"What'll be fun?" Jerry asked, breezing into the office.

"Costume party," Vic said. "Next Saturday at Audrey's house."

"Cool," Jerry said. "Can I bring a date?"

"Sure," Vic shrugged. "What's his name?"

Jerry cursed at Vic, and Vic cursed at Jerry. Soon Vic was up and out of his seat, and the two of them were taking playful shots at each other's biceps while reciting lines from *Raging Bull*. From what I could gather, this meant that my conversation with Vic was over, and since there was nothing I could do to stop a handful of strangers from showing up on my doorstep in a little over a week, I went back to my desk and started making a list.

ON THE night of the party, I filled an ice chest with cans of Miller Lite and, per Vic's instructions, bottles of Victory Festbier, neither of which, I feared, would be touched once my guests discovered the five-liter Heineken beer tap Roger left behind when he moved out. Since Vic was not forthcoming with the exact number of attendees he was expecting, I ordered two large trays of hot wings, each of which, the caterer assured me, could handle a hungry crowd of about thirty people. To play it safe, I also ordered a tray of finger sandwiches, filled a bowl with fun-sized Milky Way and Snickers bars, baked two pumpkin pies, purchased a third at the grocery store, and, in the event that anyone showed up out of costume, stacked a dozen translucent plastic masks in front of a neatly arranged row of wine bottles on the dining room table.

Despite all of my preparation, my mother's voice kept echoing in my head as I threw together a generic superhero costume of my own invention—a lemon-yellow dishtowel safety-pinned like a cape to the back of a kelly-green sweatshirt, a yellow skirt that almost matched the dishtowel, a pair of green stockings my mother had sent the previous March in honor of her questionable Irish heritage, a matching pair of boots and rubber gloves that fell somewhere on the color spectrum between the skirt and towel, and a yellow eye-mask I picked up for a dime the day after Halloween. There wasn't enough food, my mother's voice complained. My guests would go hungry. They'd finish off the hot wings in five minutes flat. They'd down the beers and swallow the candy and grudgingly polish off my pie, and in no time at all, the food would be gone, and my guests would start talking behind my back about how I was a terrible hostess, how I'd let them all down, how they could have done anything else with their evenings but decided, against their better judgment, to come to my lame and shamefully under-stocked Halloween party.

My guests were supposed to start arriving at eight o'clock, but my house was still empty at five-after. No big deal, I told myself. People always showed up late for parties. It was the fashionable thing to do. And so what if Owen promised to help me set up? Punctuality wasn't exactly his forte. In fact, I thought, idly stretching the fingers of my bright-yellow rubber gloves, he'd been showing up later and later for each successive date. Not by much, but enough to notice. Enough, in any case, for me to hint that he should probably break the habit.

When the doorbell rang at quarter-after eight, I wondered what the excuse would be this time. Traffic was always a good one, and so was the old standby that he'd lost track of time. Once in a while, he'd mix things up by telling me that something came up at the restaurant, but the something was never named, and I always let it slide.

"You're late …" I said as I opened the door, but stopped when I realized it wasn't Owen.

"For what?" Jerry said. "Who shows up for a party on time?"

He was wearing an old-time chain-gang uniform with broad, black-and-white stripes. Rubber manacles ran from his ankle to the hand of his date, who was wearing a black body-stocking that hugged her rotund figure. Her hair was tucked under a knit sailor's cap, and her face was concealed under a layer of black shoe polish so that the whites of her eyes glowed like a pair of porcelain saucers.

"Svetlana?" I said when I realized who it was.

"Don't say a word," Jerry hissed, and I held up my hands in mock surrender. "Where's the beer?"

I nodded in the direction of my dining room, where I had unscrewed half the light bulbs in the chandelier to give the party a moody glow.

"No beer for you, pretty boy," Svetlana said, tightening her grip on Jerry's chain. "Tonight you are designated driver."

"I drove last time," Jerry complained.

"And you drive again tonight."

"I get it," I said. "Old ball and chain. Cute."

Svetlana's face creased with confusion, and Jerry made a cutting motion across his neck.

"Ball and chain?" Svetlana said, casting a suspicious glare at Jerry. "You said I was dominatrix."

Why Svetlana thought a dominatrix might be wearing black-face was an issue I wasn't ready to deal with, so I decided to let it go as she dragged Jerry to the dining room and complained that there wasn't any vodka. In an effort to change the subject and also to ascertain that they wouldn't be my only guests for the evening, I asked Jerry if he knew who else was coming.

"The regular crowd, I guess," he said, piling hot wings onto a small plate. "Vic and Melinda, a couple of the kids from Fatso Ratso's Pizza Depot."

"Kids?" I said.

"Don't worry," Jerry assured me. "They're cool."

"But when you say kids, you mean?"

"I don't know. The kids who work there. Not all of them, of course. Just the day shift. I told them to keep it on the down-low, so, really, there's nothing to worry about."

Shit, I thought as the doorbell rang. *That better be Owen.*

But it wasn't. It was Polly, the pink octopus who played maracas and tambourine in Fatso Ratso's Rolling Thunder Review. Behind her stood Irving, the bespectacled mole who played keyboard, Leon, the bass-playing frog, and Stan, a creature who looked more like a pinkish cancer polyp than anything in the animal kingdom.

"Can I help you?" I asked as a giant rat joined the crew.

"We're here for the party?" the octopus said. "Jerry told us about it?"

"Hmm," I said, hoping they wouldn't notice my costume. "Are you sure you have the right address?"

"Hey, guys!" Jerry shouted from the dining room. "Grab a beer!"

"Or a soda," I said desperately as Polly brushed by, tentacles slapping me on her way through the door, her friends following closely behind in a single-file parade of multicolored fuzz. "The sandwiches are good, too."

Within a half-hour, my house was packed with people I didn't know, and the teenage logic of John Hughes films was starting to make an alarming degree of sense: if you throw a party, they will come. The only difference was that I wasn't Molly Ringwald, and there was very little likelihood that my parents would return early from a weekend getaway to break up the party and ground me for life.

Loud music I couldn't identify blared from the stereo as I followed my guests through the house with a trash bag to collect empty cups and beer cans. Once or twice, I turned the stereo down, but the volume always crept back up with a vengeance whenever I turned my back. Spills, I realized, were inevitable, especially when Polly the octopus entered the room, tentacles flailing wildly as she danced to a rhythm of her own invention. The only good news was that Svetlana had hoarded all of the red wine, indiscreetly taking it with her to a corner of my kitchen where she spent most of the night either making out with Jerry or simply smothering him. I was too busy emptying makeshift ashtrays to figure out the difference.

"Audrey!" Vic shouted over the music when he spotted me. "Great party, kid! Have you met my wife?"

"Several times," I said, smiling politely at the graying woman next to him. "You're not wearing a costume."

"Bah," Vic said. "Costumes. Who has time for that shit?"

"But it was your idea."

"I have lots of ideas," Vic said. "Where the hell's Jerry? I want to meet this new woman of his."

"You already have," I said.

"What do you mean?"

I tilted my head in the direction of Jerry and Svetlana.

"Oh, this is too good," Vic said. "I'll never let him live this one down."

Vic waddled off and left me with his wife. Her name was Ellie. Her front teeth stuck out like a pair of tombstones whenever she smiled, and if I didn't know better, I'd have guessed from her ugly sweater, fake pearls, and tortoise-shell cat glasses that she'd come to the party dressed as a librarian.

"I like your costume," she said.

"Thanks."

"Is Melinda here? I was hoping to score some weed."

"I wish," I said, scanning the crowd for a familiar face.

Judging by the earthy, skunky odor emanating from my living room, Ellie didn't need to wait for Melinda to get what she wanted. Based on the few times I'd met her, though, I guessed she wasn't exactly Fulbright material, and as she stood staring at me with her mouth slightly open as if I might pull Melinda out of thin air at any moment, I realized why Vic hardly ever allowed himself to be seen with his wife in public.

"So how did you guys meet?" I asked.

"Oh, you know," Ellie said. "The usual way."

She looked down at her feet, then up at the ceiling and said that my house was beautiful. Though the proclamation appeared to exhaust her entire store of small talk, the woman was determined to follow me from table to table saying nothing at all for the next sliver of eternity as I slid coasters under beer bottles and extinguished unattended cigarettes. The situation was so bad, in fact, that when Raj showed up at my door dressed as Abraham Lincoln, I was genuinely glad to see him. My relief, however, was cut short when he opened his mouth and I remembered why I always did my best to avoid him.

"Audrey," he said, locking onto me like a heat-seeking missile in a black beard and stovepipe hat. "First, you must know that I can't stop thinking of your bosoms. Second, my uncle sends his regrets."

"Hello, Raj," I said, all too aware that escape hinged entirely on timing. "Have you met Ellie? I'll bet you two have a lot in common."

Ellie exposed her gray front teeth, and as Raj took her hand, I bolted. Across the room, Melinda's husband, Alan, was dressed as a priest and chatting up Polly the octopus, whose head had come off to reveal the milky soft face of a girl who couldn't be any older than nineteen. Though I fully expected Melinda to be hovering within striking distance in the event that Alan forgot that he was not, in fact, a priest and therefore accountable to an exponentially more vengeful higher power, it took me a minute to find her sitting on the sofa across the room. Dressed as a slinky red devil with satin horns and a matching tail, she appeared to be engrossed in a conversation with none other than Fatso Ratso himself, whose giant fuzzy head, unlike that of his multi-armed colleague, was still planted firmly on his shoulders.

"Don't tell me," Melinda said, eyeing my costume as I approached. "You're Party Girl, and you're here to show the world how to have a good time."

"Close," I said. "I'm Wonder Mom, and I'm here to make sure no one burns my house down."

"Wonder Mom," Melinda said, disengaging herself from the giant rat with a promise to continue their conversation later. "I'll bet we can fix that if we try. Where's that man of yours?"

"I wish I knew," I said.

"Damn. There was something he was supposed to get for me."

"What was it?" I asked.

By way of response, Melinda touched the side of her nose with a long, perfectly manicured fingernail that matched her horns in color and sheen.

"Oh," I said with an air of disapproval. "That."

"Yes," Melinda said, shaking her head with a corresponding degree of ersatz horror. "That."

As far as I knew, only Owen was aware of my momentary lapse of judgment. To the rest of the world, I was still mild-mannered Audrey Corcoran—good mother, hard worker, solid citizen—and the thought of me experimenting with cocaine was about as plausible as my chances of winning a Pulitzer for my latest think piece on Fatso Ratso's stuffed-crust pizza.

"It's your life," I said, angling to perpetuate the myth of my unassailable moral fiber. "What you take into your body is your business. Just don't do it around here, okay? At least not in the open."

"Please," Melinda said. "You think I want to share with this crowd? The weed these kids are smoking is a cut above total shit."

"I wouldn't know," I told her.

"That's right," Melinda said. "Owen tells me you're more of a cocaine girl."

"What?"

"It's no big deal," Melinda said as I started to feel sick. "We had a little bet going on the side."

"About me?" I shouted before dropping my voice to a whisper. "Doing coke?"

"Don't take it so hard," Melinda said. Halfway up the stairs, I could see Ellie sharing a joint with Leon, the bass-playing frog. Standing alone by the fireplace with a beer bottle in his hand, Raj eyed me with what was, unfortunately, his best unblinking come-hither gaze. "Owen's wild about you. This bet, it was nothing. A little joke. Totally my idea."

"I don't believe it," I said.

"He told me about your first date, or whatever you want to call it—how you invited him in at the end of the night and he asked if you wanted to get high because he figured you and I were coke buddies."

"As if," I said.

"No kidding. He felt like a jackass."

"So, what? You came up with this sick little bet to make him feel better?"

"I told him he wasn't totally off base."

"Meaning?"

"Meaning you probably just needed a push in the right direction. Owen said he doubted it, and that's where the bet came in. He lost, by the way, though we were both sure you'd like it if you'd only give it a try."

"Well, I didn't," I said, keeping my voice down despite the noise of the party. "I seriously thought I was going to die."

"I heard."

"Is there anything you didn't hear?"

"Unfortunately, yes. He wouldn't tell me a word about the sex."

"Thank God for small favors."

"Really, Audrey. It was no big deal. You should give it another try."

"I don't think so," I said. "Once was enough."

"Let me guess," Melinda said. "He did the typical man thing and tried to impress you with a shitload of coke."

"That depends," I said. "How many lines in a shitload?"

Melinda rolled her eyes and said that Owen was an idiot. A girl needed to be careful with her first taste, she said. Which was why she only offered me a little bump on the night of our big family outing at Nick's American Grill. She was about to say more when Ellie squealed her name and bounded across the room.

"Melinda!" Ellie shouted. "Melinda! Melinda! Melinda!"

"Ellie," Melinda said without emotion.

"I'm so high!"

"I can see that."

"I was going to buy some weed from you, but then I found some *for free!*"

"It *is* a party," Melinda said.

"Yeah," Ellie said slowly. The thought seemed to come to her from a million miles away, and I wondered what she'd be like if she were smoking dope that wasn't, to borrow Melinda's phrase, a cut above total shit. "Can you really tell I'm high?"

"A little," Melinda said.

"But not too much, right? My mother's staying with us, and I'd die if she found out."

"I think you'll be okay," Melinda said, shooing Ellie away. "I think Vic was looking for you."

"Classy," I said as Ellie wandered away.

Still sick over Owen's indiscretion, all I wanted was for everyone to get out of my house and leave me to my misery. If I had to, I could probably make a scene or unplug the stereo or gradually start herding people to the door, but then what kind of hostess would I be? Even if the majority of my guests did happen to be a year or so shy of twenty-one, my unbending sense of etiquette refused to allow me to make them feel anything but completely welcome in my home.

"Hey," Melinda said, removing her red satin horns and placing them on my head. "You look a little down."

"Sorry," I said. "It happens when people place bets on my life."

"Let it go," Melinda said. "Have a little fun."

"I wish," I said.

"Do you want to get high?"

What the hell, I figured. My house was a wreck, my boyfriend couldn't keep a secret, and Raj was staring at me with hungry eyes. Given the circumstances, it seemed like a reasonable thing to do.

"Yeah," I said. "I think I do. But what about Owen? I thought he was your connection."

"Fuck him," Melinda said, nodding in the direction of the large fuzzy rat. "I'm working on a better one."

"Him?"

Melinda shrugged. "Is there somewhere we can go?"

"The bathroom, I guess."

"Too many intrusions."

"What about my bedroom?" I asked.

"Too early in the relationship. What's your basement like?"

"Messy," I said. "It's where the girls used to play house."

"Perfect," Melinda said. "Meet me in twenty minutes."

"No," I said when I spotted Raj laying an empty beer bottle on the wooden ledge above the fireplace and steeling himself for a second pass at my maternal bosoms. "Let's make it ten."

THOUGH ROGER and I had always planned on having our basement refinished, the media room we envisioned never quite materialized. Instead of the French drain, sump pump, and standard-issue putty-colored carpeting we envied in every finished basement on our end of the Golden Mile, we were still making due with a whitewashed stone wall, a concrete floor, and the occasional quarter-inch of groundwater at the time of the divorce. Instead of the flat-screen TV, the DVD player, and the surround-sound stereo system, we had a washer and dryer that shook violently and lurched like beasts whenever they ran. And instead of the sectional sofa, coffee table, and wet bar whose measurements Roger had gone so far as to outline in blue chalk on the concrete floor before the girls were born, we had Catherine and Lily's long-abandoned Fisher-Price kitchen set, complete with a white and lavender sink, a matching stove and microwave oven, and the tiny yellow kitchen table where Melinda was measuring out what she described as a sensible amount of cocaine for someone with my regrettable lack of experience.

"It's like I was saying," she said, using a credit card to form white lines on the mirror in front of her. "Guys are total assholes when it comes to cocaine. For them, it's all about power. They get a little coked up, and all they can talk about is who drives the fastest car and who can pound the most nails with his dick. But for us, it's different. For us, it's about connecting, about sharing."

Each of us sat on a small plastic chair on either side of the table. Unfurling a hundred-dollar bill, Melinda made sure I saw the denomination, then rolled it into a tight little straw. After she did her line, she handed me the straw and pushed the mirror across the table. Though the voice of reason told me to decline, I was already leaning over the mirror and liking what I saw. The mask gave me an air of playful mystery. The devil horns said I knew how to have fun. And to top the image off, the line of coke in front of me was a chance to let my worries go and pretend that everything in my world was just right—if only for a few hours.

"You know what I love about getting high?" Melinda said as I put the makeshift straw to my nose and snorted. "What we're doing right now. Opening up. Letting our defenses down. Really getting to know each other."

I slid the mirror back across the table, and the door creaked open at the top of the steps.

"It isn't that we *need* to get high," Melinda added. "As women, we're wired for nurturing. We're wired to care. All we want is to connect, and catching a little buzz every now and then helps us do it."

"Definitely," I said, already feeling the rush wash over me as a dark shadow clomped down the wooden stairway.

"You're doing coke again, yeah?" Svetlana said, pulling up another tiny chair and making its legs buckle as she sat. "I saw you go down, and when you didn't come up, I told Jerry I had to make pee."

"How romantic," I said.

"Romance is for little girls," Svetlana said. "I want sex, and I want money."

"Then what are you doing with Jerry?" Melinda asked.

Before Svetlana could answer, the door at the top of the steps opened a second time.

"Hello?" Ellie called from above. "Is anyone down there?"

"Shit," Melinda sighed.

"I hate this woman," Svetlana agreed. "All night, asking if I have weed. No, I told her. I don't have any fucking weed, so leave me alone. Five seconds later, a tap on the shoulder and it's the same damn thing. Do you have any weed? Do you have any weed? What the hell is her problem?"

"She's married to Vic," I said.

"Poor girl," Svetlana said. "But whose fault is that?"

Helping herself to Melinda's cocaine, Svetlana tapped a small amount onto the back of her hand, brought it to her nose, and snorted hard. Ellie, meanwhile, was doing her best to navigate the creaky wooden stairway.

"Hey!" she shouted upon reaching the bottom. "This must be where the cool kids hang out! Are you guys doing coke?"

"Christ," Melinda said. "Why don't you say it a little louder?"

"Sorry," Ellie said in a stage whisper. "I love cocaine."

"Too bad," Svetlana said. "Is private party."

"*Was* private party," Melinda said. "Until you showed up."

Ellie dragged a chair to our little yellow table, and Melinda reached for her purse.

"Mind if I smoke?" she asked.

"Not in the house," I said automatically.

"Don't worry," Melinda said, lighting a thin, hand-rolled cigarette. "I won't exhale."

"Is that weed?" Ellie asked.

"Yeah," Melinda said. "And no, you can't have any. You're dumb enough as it is."

"Tell me about it," Ellie said. "I'm pretty wrecked. But don't let me interrupt. What were you guys talking about?"

"We were saying how much we hate you," Svetlana said. "And what a mistake it was for you to marry Vic."

"Oh, that."

So much for nurturing, I figured as Melinda passed me her joint.

Taking a long drag, I started to hack violently, throat burning, eyes watering.

"Good stuff, isn't it?" Ellie asked. "Melinda always has the best weed. She grows it herself, you know."

"Really?" I asked.

"Heat lamps," Melinda said. "Down in the basement. No big deal, but it helps with the bills. Strictly friends and family, of course. It's more of a hobby than anything else. You should look into it if you want to make a few bucks."

"What, selling pot?"

"Don't think of it as selling pot," Melinda said. "Think of it as a part-time job in the fastest-growing industry in America."

"Pharmaceuticals," Svetlana said, in case I wasn't following.

"Drugs," Ellie volunteered, dumbing it down for the plush animals and rubber dolls in the room.

Ignoring her, I passed the joint back to Melinda, and she gave me a new one. For the morning-after, she said, taking another drag and grudgingly passing her joint to Ellie.

"You two are so pretty," Ellie said, exhaling her smoke without so much as a cough. "I wish I could be pretty like you."

"Pretty means nothing," Svetlana assured her. "In this world, only the strong survive."

"Yeah," Ellie said wistfully. "But I want to be pretty. Can you guys make me pretty?"

"I don't see it happening," Melinda said.

"But you know people," Ellie protested. "Hairdressers. Beauticians. Plastic surgeons. Vic always promises to get me a tummy-tuck on trade, but I know it'll never happen. He won't even let me see a real hairdresser. He says it's cheaper to cut my hair himself."

"Vic cuts your hair?" Melinda said. "That's pretty fucking disturbing."

"I know," Ellie said. "I'm a freak. Can't you do anything for me?"

"Sorry, darling," Melinda said. "No one has *that* much trade anywhere."

"I don't know," I said. The coke and the pot were coming together, and I was really starting to groove. Removing Ellie's glasses from her face, I gazed into her eyes and told her to smile for me. "I think she has potential."

"Really?" Ellie asked, her mood brightening.

"Sure," I said. "All we have to do is kick those ridiculous teeth down your throat and you'll be every man's dream."

Melinda let out a sharp cackle and Svetlana snorted like a hog as the smile disappeared from Ellie's face. For a second, I thought she was going to cry, and in that second, I hated myself. This wasn't me, I thought, glancing around the tiny table at the giggling overgrown children I'd fallen in with. But when I opened my mouth to apologize, Ellie just smiled and said that she needed to check in with Vic. It didn't happen very often, she explained, but once or twice he'd left her at a party because he forgot that she was with him.

"Kick her teeth in," Svetlana said as Ellie teetered away from the table. "That was funny."

"Yeah," Melinda said, tapping more coke onto her mirror. "I didn't know you could be such a bitch. I totally love it."

"A bitch?" I heard myself say demurely. "*Moi?*"

Melinda snorted a line and passed me the mirror.

What the hell, I figured. One more hit couldn't hurt.

It *was* a party, after all.

And I was one of the cool kids.

Around midnight, I decided to take my house back. Ellie and Vic were long gone by then, and though he was allegedly the guest of honor, Raj had given up, at least for the time being, on gaining access to my bosoms. Hitting Melinda up for one last tiny bump of coke, I made a beeline through a cluster of headless drunken cartoon characters from Fatso Ratso's Pizza Depot and searched in the vicinity of my stereo for the Ornette Coleman recording Owen had left at my house so many weekends earlier. When I finally spotted it under a half-empty bottle of beer stuffed with bloated cigarette butts, I wiped the CD on my sleeve and substituted it for the whiny homemade pop compilation some well-meaning but apparently tasteless partygoer had loaded onto my five-disc carousel.

Three seconds later, the cacophony began, and I cranked the volume.

Barely a second after that, the stampede was in full swing.

Grabbing their fluffy heads off the living room floor, the kids from the day shift at Fatso Ratso's were the first to leave, but it didn't take long for Svetlana and Jerry to follow suit, hands pressed to their ears as they fell in line behind their fellow party-goers, vying with each other to be the first out the door.

"I gotta hand it to you," Melinda said as her husband jerked a thumb over his shoulder to signal that it was time to go. "You really know how to kill a party."

"It's a skill no mother should be without," I said.

"I like you," Melinda said in a tone that implied that we'd never before had the pleasure of meeting. "You and I should do something sometime. Just the two of us."

"Sounds like fun."

"And give some thought to going into business with me."

"Business?" I said.

"You know. The fastest growing industry in America."

"Right," I said. "Pharmaceuticals."

"I'm serious. We could really make a killing."

Alan pointed at the spot on his wrist where a watch might be if he owned one and mouthed to his wife that she'd better hurry up. The man had long, mutton-chop sideburns that struggled to lend definition to his otherwise weak jawline, and the patch of black hair on his chin barely contributed to the illusion of a neck. Had Owen not appeared in the doorway at the exact moment Alan and Melinda were leaving, I would have been much less willing to forgive his egregious lack of punctuality and, more important, his violation of my trust. But as both men greeted each other with a bone-crushing handshake, I realized how fortunate I was to have a boyfriend with a square jaw and a real chin—especially at my age.

"You are so dead," Melinda whispered, pausing on her way out the door.

Gulping theatrically, Owen looked at me, and I nodded.

"Dead," I mouthed, drawing a finger across my neck.

Sure, I'd forgive him. But first he had to suffer.

"I, um," Owen said to Melinda, patting his breast pocket.

"Keep it," she said. "You're going to need it."

Telling me to be gentle with the poor guy, Melinda pulled the door shut and left us alone. My costume was still on, rubber gloves and all, as I adjusted the volume on my stereo and turned my attention to Owen. Other than a brown Stetson and a beat-up leather jacket, nothing about the way he was dressed stood out. In other words, it was the perfect non-costume. If he came to the party and everyone was dressed up, then, fine, he was Indiana Jones—*sans* whip, *sans* holster, *sans* pistol, and even *sans* sexy five-o'clock shadow, of course. And if nobody was dressed up, then, hey, all he had to do was ditch the hat, lose the jacket, and he'd blend in with everybody else. The only scenario he hadn't considered was the one where the party had already broken up before he arrived and he had to deal with a mildly perturbed woman dressed as an off-brand superhero.

"Sorry I'm late," Owen said.

"Don't want to hear it."

I crossed the floor, slipped a gloved finger between two of Owen's shirt buttons, and pulled him toward me so we were sharing the same breath. Reaching into his breast pocket with my free hand, I found the cocaine that Melinda had asked him to procure and, pinching the packet between the tips of two fingers, raised it to eye-level.

"It wasn't for me," Owen said in his own defense.

"No?"

"No, it was for Melinda, and it's why I was so late. My usual guy crapped out on me, and I had to drive all the way out to Bumblefuck, Egypt, to score from my number-two."

"All for Melinda?"

"We go way back, Audrey. You know that."

"Hmm," I said noncommittally.

"I swear I wasn't planning on getting high with her, if that's what you're thinking."

"Really?" I said. "That's too bad. But as long as you don't want any, I might as well have some fun."

I palmed the little packet and led Owen into the living room, one finger still hooked limply in his shirt. When we reached the sofa, I told him to sit. One word—*sit*—and he did, like a dog. Straddling his lap, I played a hunch and reached into the inner pocket of his beat-up leather jacket where I found a small flat spoon like the one Melinda had used all those nights ago when she invited me to join her in the restroom at Nick's American Grill.

"Interesting," I said. "I suppose this was for Melinda, too."

"A guy needs to be prepared," Owen said.

"I forgot. You're a gentleman. A handkerchief in one pocket, and a coke spoon in the other. In case you meet a damsel in distress, I suppose."

I dipped the spoon into the packet and brought a small amount of cocaine to my nose.

"It works better if you close one nostril," Owen suggested, pressing a knuckle to one side of his nose and lifting an imaginary spoon to the other. "I can show you how, if you want."

"I don't think so," I said. "You're still in the doghouse."

Heeding Owen's advice, I pressed a knuckle to my nose and snorted the coke. It wasn't much, but right away, I felt something. Not a high, exactly, but a nudge, a friendly reminder that my private little party was only getting started.

"I told you," Owen said. "I was late because of Melinda."

"You think you're in trouble for being late?"

"Seriously, the coke wasn't for me, but apparently that's not an issue anymore."

"You're getting warmer," I said, peeling off my gloves. "Melinda told me something about a bet."

"Ah," Owen said. "That."

"Yes, Owen," I said, unbuttoning his shirt. "*That*."

"It was her idea."

"But you played along."

"And lost," Owen said as I unbuckled his belt and undid his zipper. "Doesn't that mean anything?"

"It means you don't know me as well as you thought you did." Inching backward, I slid down to the floor and tugged at his pants. "It means you better watch out for me." He arched his back, and the pants came off. "It means I might be a little bit dangerous." I kicked off my boots and slithered out of my stockings. "It means, Owen, that I'm full of surprises."

CHAPTER ELEVEN

My BRAIN was still a little fried on Monday, so I didn't bother to tell Lily to get down from the sofa when I caught her in the middle of her tightrope act. Barely looking up from a thick textbook on the dining room table, Catherine informed me that there were three messages on the answering machine—one from her father, one from the GESTAPO, and one from Melinda, who didn't show up at the office that day and had never called me at home before.

"Cool," I said. "Did she leave a number?"

"Cool?" Catherine said suspiciously. "What does that mean?"

"She's an adult," I said, finding it difficult to look my daughter in the eye. "In case you didn't notice, I haven't had much contact with people my own age lately."

"What about the GESTAPO? *They're* adults."

"They're not exactly the kind of people I want to hang out with."

"You're a mother," Catherine said. "You're not supposed to hang out."

"It's okay," I told her. "She's only a friend."

"Like Dad?" Lily asked, still balancing herself on the spine of the sofa.

"Not exactly," I said.

"But you guys are still friends, right?"

"It's complicated."

"Dad says you're not just friends, but *best* friends."

"I'm sure he does," I said.

"I don't know about this woman," Catherine said, working, as always, to keep the conversation on point. "Her message said she was still pretty wrecked. Was there drinking at your party on Friday?"

"A little bit," I said. "But my friends are all adults."

"They weren't driving, were they?"

"Not if they were drinking."

"Are you sure?"

"Catherine," I said with a mild air of exasperation.

"Sorry," Catherine said. "But I worry sometimes."

"I worry, too," I told her. "But sometimes you need to let people make their own decisions."

"About drinking?" Catherine said.

"About everything."

"Well, you don't have to worry about me," Catherine said. "I'll *never* drink."

"But I will," Lily said. "I want to drink wine, champagne, and cosmopolitans when I grow up."

It was probably a good opportunity to sit down and have a chat with my daughters about responsible drinking, but I let the moment pass and checked the machine instead. The president of the GESTAPO was calling to remind me about a meeting later in the week, and Roger wanted to know when he'd get to meet the new man in my life. He was in the middle of saying something insipid (again) about being my best friend and having the right to meet all of my suitors when I skipped ahead to the message I really wanted to hear: *Hey, girl, it's Melinda. God, I'm still wrecked from your party. Give me a call when you get a chance.*

I played the message three times before getting her number, but didn't call back until after dinner.

"Hey," Melinda said as I took the cordless phone to my bedroom and locked the door behind me. "Did my little gift do the trick?"

"The joint?" I whispered. "Yeah, but I wouldn't have minded something a little stronger."

"What, like Valium? That stuff's bad news, darling. Stick with grass, and you'll never go wrong."

We talked like teenagers for the next two hours—gossiping, giggling, and whispering about sex. Back in college, Melinda said, she was in an all-girl punk band called the Sandbag Dykes. They used to get high before every show, then fondle each

- 80 -

other's breasts onstage. Once or twice they'd even get through an entire song, but the music wasn't the point, really. The point was to make money and meet boys.

"You wouldn't believe how hot they get when they think you dig chicks," Melinda said. "It's the ultimate turn-on. Just ask Owen."

"He's into that?"

"They're all into it, darling. If they deny it, they're lying."

"So you and Owen?"

"Strictly professional, I promise."

"But you do have a history," I said.

"Ancient. But I will say this—if I had any sense, I'd have kept him for myself."

Someone tried the doorknob, then knocked on the door.

"Mom?" Catherine said. "Are you in there?"

"I'm on the phone, honey."

"Why is the door locked?"

"It's a private conversation."

"I'm going to bed," Catherine said. "But Lily wants to stay up for the Late Show."

And fix herself a cosmopolitan during the evening news, I presumed.

"Hold on," I said to Catherine. "I'll be off in a second."

"Don't let me keep you," Melinda said. "Just remember what I said about Valium. Stay away from that stuff."

"Like I know where to get Valium," I said. "You and Owen are my only connections."

"Let's keep it that way," Melinda said. "If you ever need to score, you know where to find me."

"I don't see it happening," I said.

"I'm only saying *if*—should the need ever arise. And give some more thought to what I said about going into business. I have a good lead on some quality product."

"I thought you grew your own," I said.

"Mainly, yeah, but I'm thinking of diversifying."

"Good to know," I said as Catherine knocked on the door a second time. "Should the need ever arise."

CHAPTER TWELVE

On THE afternoon of my third GESTAPO meeting, I walked into a strange house and spied a deli tray wrapped in plastic. The same tray had been present at the last meeting and the one before that. Since it was only my third, I had no way of knowing exactly how many meetings this particular deli tray had attended, but given the fact that I'd never seen anyone so much as make a gesture toward breaking its airtight seal, there was a better than average chance that the tray had been around at least as long as the organization, and that the thinly sliced meats and cheeses inside had been silently—perhaps via mental telepathy—dictating the agenda of the organization since day one.

Next to the deli tray, a pitcher of iced tea stood untouched among a group of brand-name soft drinks in unopened two-liter bottles, a stack of disposable cups, and a bucket of ice. Though the host made a point of telling everybody to help themselves, no one dared break the seal on the deli tray or crack the cap on a single bottle of Pepsi, Sprite, or Canada Dry Ginger Ale. Instead, someone asked for a glass of ice water with a twist of lemon, someone else asked for the same thing, and soon it was a trend. When the eyes of the host landed on me, he insisted that there was plenty of iced tea, but I opted for the ice water like everyone else. Because water was good and pure, and the bare bones austerity of the drink—water with a twist of lemon—underscored the fact that this was no social event, no cocktail hour, no tea party. We were there to work. We were there to get things done. We were there for the good of the children, and even the twist of lemon was perhaps too much of a distraction from the serious business at hand.

The woman to my left was Catherine's teacher, Mrs. Woodring. She had a pear-shaped body and a round face and insisted that I call her Agnes, but whenever I opened my mouth, she was always Mrs. Woodring. Catherine was a wonderful student, she said. So serious. So studious. If only more parents were like me, Mrs. Woodring said, then maybe there would be more students like Catherine.

I thanked Mrs. Woodring for the compliment, and the GESTAPO president called the meeting to order. Like Mrs. Woodring, the president also had a pear-shaped body, and as I looked around the table, it hit me for the first time that prolonged membership in the GESTAPO could very well lead to excessive weight gain in the buttocks and thighs. In fact, the only longtime GESTAPO member who didn't have a pear-shaped body was the organization's secretary, Lyle Lesovitch, but that was only because he looked like a pasty bowling ball with a mustache.

Maybe there was something in the water, I reasoned, setting my glass aside. The twist of lemon, perhaps? The mere presence of the deli tray and soft drinks on the table in front of us? Maybe the calories passed through the plastic wrap via osmosis. Maybe the sugar molecules effervesced through the bottles before migrating through the air and attaching themselves to our hips and thighs like mold spores and other airborne allergens. Whatever the case, it occurred to me that I should probably ditch these people before the damage became irreversible. Another meeting or two, and I might balloon to twice my original size.

But how would it look if I left the GESTAPO after only three meetings? They'd think I was slacking off. They'd think I didn't care anymore. Mrs. Woodring would realize that I had nothing to do with Catherine's grace and poise, and she'd be sure to have Lyle Lesovitch record her doubts about my parenting skills in the minutes of the next meeting. Then Lyle would note that I'd been conspicuously silent whenever the president asked for a volunteer to help with the school's anti-drug program, and soon everyone would begin to suspect me of being on drugs—which I most definitely was *not*.

Sure, I'd been high once or twice, but I was a casual user—a far cry from being *on* drugs, or even *into* them, for that matter. For me, getting high was nothing more than a social gesture, like having a drink or laughing at a dirty joke. I did it to relax. I did it to unwind. And, okay, to the smallest of degrees, I did it to fit in, but it wasn't like I was the victim of peer pressure or anything. If I got high every now and then, it was only because I enjoyed doing it, because it made me more friendly, more gregarious, more outgoing, because it really *did* make me feel good, and most of all because it was fun.

The important thing was that I knew where to draw the line.

I'd only use on weekends, and never when I was lonely or depressed.

I'd never keep drugs around the house—not in significant quantities anyway.

And it went without saying that I'd never get high in front of my daughters.

In fact, I reasoned as the GESTAPO president asked for a volunteer to help with the school's anti-drug program, I was so clearly *not* into drugs that I was the obvious choice for the job.

"Audrey Corcoran," Lyle Lesovitch mumbled, scratching a note in his legal pad when I raised a finger to volunteer. "Drugs."

This was good, I thought, as Lyle slid a large manila folder marked *DRUGS* across the table and explained that my mission, since I'd already chosen to accept it, was to hire a speaker for the school's anti-drug assembly in March. All I had to do was get the date from the school secretary and set everything up with the police department or whichever act I decided to hire with my budget of two-hundred dollars.

"Personally, I recommend going with the cops," Lyle said. "You won't get all the bells and whistles you might get with some of these other jokers, but you *will* get a solid forty minutes of no-nonsense straight-talk on the dope scene."

"Sounds like fun," I said.

"It's all in the envelope," Lyle said. "Ask your kids for help if you get stuck. They know a lot more about this stuff than we do."

Wʜᴇɴ I got home, Catherine and Lily helped me sort through the materials Lyle had given me—all of which fell neatly into one of two categories. On one side of the kitchen table, we made a pile of monochrome pamphlets and press releases with titles like *MARIJUANA: What Every American Needs to Know* and *Winning the War on COCAINE*. On the other side, we compiled a short stack of slick, glossy, full-color artist bios and promotional packets from the tristate area's biggest anti-dope acts.

The No Squad boasted of being Philadelphia's top drug-awareness hip-hop trio, but Catherine said they were nothing more than a bunch of old men in baggy jeans. Even the teachers made fun of them, Lily added. The same went for the Drug-Free Party Posse and the No-Strings-Attached Controlled Substances Puppet Review. Everyone hated The Great Jussayno, too, despite the fact that his "hypnotic blend of music, magic, and true-life stories" proved that "messing with dope" could make even the hardest-working student's hopes of leading a happy and productive life "disappear without a trace," a phrase favored by each of the four magicians whose press materials were shuffled into the pile in front of me.

By the time we were through, the girls and I had worked our way through three folk acts, four fire-and-brimstone inspirational speakers, a dance troupe, two cheerleading squads, and a funk band whose members all dressed like visitors from another planet. And then there was Captain Panther.

According to his press release, Captain Panther was the brainchild of Chris Parker, a professional actor, musician, and dancer who started experimenting with alcohol and marijuana in high school to "escape the pain and isolation of feeling different from everyone else." Despite his escalating drug use, Parker's "mischievous good looks" landed him a ton of ad work in both print and television, and in no time he found himself making cameo appearances on such hot TV sitcoms as *The Ted Knight Show*, *Mr. Belvedere*, and *Charles in Charge*. Yet for all of his success, Parker's drug use was destroying his life, and after a near-death experience, he decided to make a change. Thus from the drug-ravaged ruins of an aspiring actor's career, America's favorite anti-drug superhero was born.

"Captain Panther!" I read dramatically. "Saving the world from the perils of drug abuse and underage drinking—one school at a time!"

Lily laughed, and Catherine shook her head in dismay.

"They all sound like they're on drugs," she complained.

"Maybe that's the point," I said. "You go to school, you see the Great Jussayno, and when you get home, you tell your mom all about this lame magician who kept going on and on about drugs. All of a sudden, your mom has an opening, and you're having the conversation she's been meaning to have with you for a long time."

"So we're trying to pick the worst one?" Catherine asked.

"In a word, yes."

"Then I'll have to go with Captain Panther."

"Me too," Lily said. "He sounds terrible."

"He is," Catherine said. "He came to give a talk when I was in second grade, and everyone hated him—even me."

"And she's a nerd," Lily added.

"Yeah," Catherine said. "And I'm a nerd."

"So someone named Captain Panther came to your school, and you never mentioned it?"

"I guess not," Catherine said. "Sorry."

"Does this mean we'll never talk about drugs?" Lily asked.

More than likely, my envelope contained a pamphlet called *Talking to Your Kids about DRUGS*, but I didn't have a chance to read it yet, so I wasn't exactly sure of what to say. Despite this fact, I was so engrossed in the business of being a mom that I'd almost forgotten that I was one of the bad guys now, and it wasn't until I told Lily that we could talk about drugs whenever she wanted to that I remembered that I'd done the unspeakable and tried cocaine.

"We really don't need to talk about this," Catherine said before Lily could ask any questions. "I'm not sure we want to know the answers."

"Don't worry," I said. "I'll try not to scandalize you."

"But you *do* promise to tell the truth, right?"

"Swear to God," I said, raising my right hand. "On Captain Panther's good name."

"Be serious, Mom," Lily insisted.

"I am. What do you want to know?"

"Did you ever use drugs when you were younger?"

"You mean in college?" I said, honing the question to suit my needs.

"Or high school," Catherine said, playing right into my hands. "Or even younger than that. But you don't have to answer if you don't want to."

"It's okay," I said. "Because I never did."

"Not even pot?" Lily said. "Katie Regan's stepsister's a senior in high school, and she said that everyone tries pot when they go to college."

"She's talking about marijuana," Catherine whispered. "Some kids call it pot. Other kids call it weed."

"Thanks," I said. "But I can honestly say I never used drugs when I was in college. Or high school, or anytime before that."

"Did you know anybody who did?" Lily asked.

"Sure," I said. "One or two people."

"Anybody we know?"

"Maybe," I said. "Actually, yeah. Definitely someone you know."

"Who?" Lily asked, hungry for gossip.

This was too easy. Even Catherine was practically jumping out of her seat to find out which of the adults in her life had committed the cardinal sin of smoking marijuana.

"I wasn't dating him at the time, of course, but your father experimented with marijuana when he was in college."

"Experimented?" Lily said.

"She means he got high," Catherine said.

"*Dad* was on *drugs*?"

"Not *on* drugs, exactly," I said. "He tried pot once or twice, but he always told me it was a dumb thing to do."

"Because pot is a gateway drug," Lily said. "We learned that in school. It leads to other drugs like heroin."

"So Dad could have turned into a heroin addict?" Catherine demanded. "I can't believe you're okay with this."

"It was a long time ago," I said. "It's ancient history."

"Is heroin the one with the needle?" Lily asked.

"Yes," Catherine sighed. "It's worse than cocaine. God, this is so embarrassing."

"And cocaine's the one you sniff, right?" Lily said.

"Right," Catherine said, hiding her face in her hands. "Don't even think of telling anyone about this, okay Lily? Not even Dad. I don't want him knowing that we know."

"Why not?" Lily said.

"Because we're supposed to think he's perfect. God, Mom, why did you have to tell us that?"

"You're the one who asked," I said. "And I *did* promise to tell the truth."

"It's okay, Mom," Lily said. "I'm glad you told us."

"That's because you're stupid," Catherine said, rising from her seat.

"I'm not stupid," Lily muttered.

"Yes you are," Catherine shouted, shaking a finger at her sister. "You're stupid, and Mom doesn't know when to keep her mouth shut."

"Catherine!"

"I mean it, Mom. Even Chloe would have known not to tell me that."

A little-known fact about Wonder Mom is that words can hurt her a lot worse than bullets. If you're looking to knock the wind out of her, all you need to do is remind her that she's not as pretty as her ex-husband's fiancée. Or as skinny, or kind, or smart, or funny. But if you really want to do some damage, if you want to bring Wonder Mom to her knees, just let her know that the one thing she's sure of—the one solid fact at the center of her existence—is a lie. Tell her that her ex's fiancée isn't just prettier, skinnier, smarter, and funnier. Tell her that this veritable stranger is also a better mother. If your goal is to kill Wonder Mom, this is how to do it.

"Don't worry, Mom," Lily said as Catherine stomped out of the kitchen. "I don't think she meant it. It's just that she doesn't adapt very well. She likes everything to stay the way it is."

"You noticed."

"I think that's why she likes books so much."

"They never let you down," I said.

"They never change."

I reached for Lily and pulled her close to me. I was still at the kitchen table, still sitting in my hard, wooden chair. Lily was on her feet, and as she rested her head on my shoulder, I could feel her little bones pressing into my body.

"To tell you the truth, I know how she feels."

"So do I," Lily said. "Sometimes."

"But if things never changed—" I said.

"Everything would be boring."

"I was about to say we wouldn't be alive, but I guess you're right. Everything *would* be pretty boring, wouldn't it?"

CHAPTER THIRTEEN

My smile was wide, white, and well rehearsed as Catherine picked sullenly at her pizza and Lily peppered Owen with questions about how much money he made and whether or not he had any intention of marrying me. The restaurant was filled with screaming kids and loud, thundering video games. A giant rat was waltzing from table to table and twirling his rubbery pink tail like a cane, and I wondered if he was the same rat who made an appearance at my costume party. When he arrived at our table and asked if everyone was having a good time, I looked him in the mouth and said that everything was peachy.

Sure, my older daughter hated me for besmirching her father's good name. And, okay, my younger daughter was turning eight in a few days but talked about sex, money, and fashion like she was closer to seventeen. And, yes, my boyfriend had gotten me to try cocaine once or twice. But we were still your average, run-of-the-mill, perfectly happy family—just like everyone else here at Fatso Ratso's Pizza Depot. The only real difference, in fact, was that we paid for our pizza with trade certificates.

"I almost forgot," Lily said, halfway through her third slice of pizza. "There was something I wanted to tell you about my dad."

Catherine shot her an angry glare from across the booth.

"Maybe this isn't the time, Lily," I said.

"Don't worry," Lily said. "It isn't about *that*."

"*That?*" Owen said.

"Don't ask," Catherine said. "I mean it."

Owen held up his hands in mock surrender.

"My dad really wants to meet you," Lily said. "He's been bugging my mom about it forever, but she keeps putting him off, so he asked me to say something while you were around."

"Really?" Owen said.

"Yeah," Lily said. "At first he thought maybe you didn't exist and Mom was just making you up so she wouldn't seem so lonely, but Chloe said no woman with any kind of self-respect would do something like that. Then Dad asked if there was something wrong with you, like you were short or fat or ugly or you had a hunchback or something, but I told him you were pretty normal."

"Thanks," Owen said.

"So do you want to meet him?"

"I guess that's your mother's decision, but I don't see why not."

"I think it would be fun," Lily said. "You and Mom and Dad and Chloe. Maybe we can all do something together sometime."

"I wouldn't exactly call that fun," Catherine muttered.

"Yeah, but you hate everything," Lily said.

"No I don't," Catherine said, and Owen stepped in to keep her from exploding.

"Hey, you know something?" he said, reaching for his back pocket. "I was thinking you girls could check out a few games and tell me which one's best." He fished a twenty-dollar bill from his wallet and handed it to Catherine. "Be sure to spend it all, and when you come back, I want a full report."

"Then what?" Lily asked.

"Then we all get to play."

"Mom, too?"

"Yeah, right," Catherine said. "Like that'll ever happen."

"Are you kidding me? Your mom's a total killer. All she ever does when we're not out with you guys is hang out at the video arcade."

"Nuh-uh," Lily said.

"Uh-huh," Owen insisted. "Just wait and see. When you guys come back, she'll blow us all away."

Shaking their heads in disbelief, the girls took off into the dark cacophony beneath a blinking neon sign that read *Fatso's Fun Zone*, and in seconds they were absorbed into the mass of screaming children who gave the place its charm.

"So what's up?" Owen said. "I've never seen Catherine so pissed."

"Oh, *that*," I said. "She found out that her father smoked pot in college."

Owen raised his eyebrows.

"Marijuana?" he said. "The demon weed?"

I nodded. "I kind of let it slip the other night when we decided to go with Captain Panther."

"Curiouser and curiouser."

"America's favorite just-say-no superhero," I said. "I agreed to coordinate the GESTAPO's drug program."

"Say no more."

"It's the teacher-parent organization at the girls' school."

"Classic."

"Anyway, I had to figure out which act to hire for drug day or whatever they call it, and I asked the girls to help out."

"And naturally it led to you volunteering that their father was a pothead in college."

"Not exactly," I said. "They asked if I knew anyone who ever used drugs, and I told them the truth. Isn't that what parents are supposed to do these days?"

"And now they know their dad was a reefer maniac."

"This is serious," I said. "Catherine won't talk to me."

"Of course not," Owen said. "You just knocked the only man she ever trusted off his pedestal. Doesn't Freud have a term for someone like you?"

"Yeah," I said. "Mother."

"There you go," Owen said, snapping his fingers. "The cruelest word in the English language. You didn't mention your own chemical dalliances, did you?"

"Are you kidding? Of course not. The literature only says you're supposed to come clean about past experimentation. It doesn't say anything about current use."

"Speaking of which," Owen said. "Are you in the mood?"

"You're holding?"

"Ooh, *holding*. Someone's picking up the lingo."

"Christ, Owen. You promised."

"That was before," Owen said.

"Before what?"

"Oh, I don't know," Owen said. "I seem to recall a little Halloween party."

"That was a one-shot deal."

"So was the first time."

"Owen."

"Just a taste?"

"No. And definitely not with the girls around."

"They're not around," Owen said. "They're lost in the Fun Zone."

"No," I said flatly. "And you better not, either. If I have to endure this nightmare without any help, then you do, too."

"Fair enough," Owen said.

Reaching across the table he pressed a small packet into my hand.

"In case you change your mind," he said with a wink as the girls returned to the booth, giddy from too much sugar, caffeine, and electronic stimulation.

"In case you change your mind about what?" Lily said.

"Your mom's just being a killjoy," Owen said. "We were talking about your little proposition—dinner with your dad and his girlfriend."

"Fiancée," Lily said.

"Right," Owen said as I slipped the packet into my purse. "We were talking about dinner with your dad and his fiancée, and your mom's dead set against it."

"I said I'd think about it."

"And we all know what that means." Owen rolled his eyes, and the girls laughed.

"Yeah, Mom," Lily said. "It always means no."

"Not necessarily."

"So you'll do it?" Lily asked.

"I'll think about it."

Owen rolled his eyes again and asked how the girls managed to spend his money so quickly. When he was their age, he said, adopting a creaky grandpa voice, he could play a game of Pac-Man for two hours on a single quarter. Of course, that was before Donkey Kong took over, back in the days when Ronald Reagan used to make surprise appearances at video arcades across the country, handing out free Rubik's Cubes to anyone who could beat him at air hockey or Pong.

"So did you find a few good games for us?" he asked when the girls made it clear that they weren't buying what he was selling.

"We found one," Catherine said. "But there's a line."

"There's a line everywhere," Lily added. "That's why we came back so soon."

"No problem," Owen said. "I love lines. And your mother does, too. Isn't that right, Audrey?"

"Yes, Owen," I said. "I love *standing in lines*. Doesn't everyone?"

"It's a motorcycle game," Lily said. "There's four of them, and we can race each other."

"Perfect," Owen said. "Lead the way."

THE GAME consisted of four plastic motorcycles, each connected to its own massive computer screen. Each motorcycle was armed with missiles, guns, and enough ammunition to take down a small nation.

"Extra points for hitting pedestrians," Owen said after bribing the kids at the front of the line to let us ahead of them. "And girls, this one's for all the marbles. If I win, your mother and I go to dinner with your dad. If your mother wins—"

"Don't worry," Catherine said, revving her engine. "She won't."

A green light flashed, and we took off down a virtual alley. Snipers popped out of trash cans and fired machine guns at us. Silly me, I started to tell the others to look out when Catherine veered to the left and forced me up against a brick wall.

"Power up, Mom!" Lily said as sirens screamed deep inside my plastic motorcycle and all of my gauges flashed red. "Shoot the next barrel of oil you see, and you'll get more power. Blow up a gas station, and you'll be fully recharged."

"I see you've played this game before," Owen said, racing ahead of us.

"No," Lily said. "It's just common sense."

We were out of the alley and onto an open highway when Catherine started to lag behind. Helicopters hovered over us, spraying the ground with bullets and dropping globs of napalm everywhere. I'd fired on two gas stations and destroyed one of them, so my fuel supply was healthy as Owen took out the tanks on the horizon with his sidewinder missiles.

"Be careful," Catherine warned him. "You want to save your missiles for important targets."

"Like what?" Owen asked.

"Like this one."

Catherine fired, and my screen came alive with warning lights.

"Serpentine, Mom!" Lily shouted, blasting a helicopter out of the sky.

I swerved to the left. I swerved to the right. Sparks showered the road on all sides of me, and Catherine's missile flew over my shoulder.

"I told you your mom was a killer," Owen said.

My fuel gauges were dropping to zero as a robotic voice calmly informed me that my shields were down. There was a tanker truck up ahead, Lily shouted. If I blew it up, I'd get half of my fuel back. All I had to do was avoid getting shot or driving over any landmines.

"And look out for napalm," she added.

"Goes without saying," I muttered as more lights started flashing on my screen again.

Another missile was coming at me, this one from ahead. My guess was that I wouldn't survive another set of evasive maneuvers, but just as the missile came within striking range, a metallic voice from deep within Catherine's motorcycle informed us that missile-to-missile firing had been engaged.

"Wow," I said as Catherine's missile took out the one bearing down on me. "Thanks."

The tanker truck was just ahead, but before I could refuel, my screen flashed red for the last time as Catherine riddled my motorcycle with bullets.

"No problem," she said.

"Ooh," Owen said, wincing. "Takin' mama down like a stone-cold gangsta."

My motorcycle informed me that I had thirty seconds to drop another dollar's worth of game tokens into its slot before my game officially ended.

"Hurry, Mom!" Lily said, blasting away at a school bus as she extended a handful of tokens in my general direction. "Or you'll lose all your points."

"It's okay," I said. "You guys keep playing. I have to use the ladies' room."

"God, Mom!" Catherine said. "You're so gross."

"Right, I forgot. Mothers aren't supposed to discuss their bodily functions in public."

"*Mom!*"

WHEN I returned from the ladies' room, a sweaty little runt in a football jersey had taken my place on the motorcycle next to Catherine's. Pressing a slightly curled, slightly crusty twenty-dollar bill into his hand, I told him to take a hike and leave the killing to the professionals. Then I hopped on my motorcycle, revved the engine, and took off like a shot after my daughters and my boyfriend.

My pulse quickened.

My eyes narrowed.

I could almost feel the wind whipping through my hair.

Focused as all hell, I blew away anything and everything that crossed my path. Police officers. Ambulances. Mothers pushing baby carriages. Stray cats and dogs. My gas tank was full, my shields were up, and I had a complete rack of missiles. There was no way my little girl was escaping this imaginary world alive.

As I approached Lily, her shields were flickering off and on, so I got her in my crosshairs and put her out of her misery. What the hell, I figured. It was only a matter of time before she started idolizing Chloe again and telling me how beautiful the bitch was. Besides, I could always make it up to her on her birthday.

"Quick, Owen, quick!" Lily shouted. "I need some more tokens!"

"Sorry, kid," Owen said, dropping his remaining tokens into the slot in front of him. "I'm tapped out."

"Sorry, baby," I said, zipping past the flaming wreckage of Lily's motorcycle. "But I'll make it up to you tomorrow."

"How?" Lily asked.

"We'll go to the mall, just you and me. Anything you want, it's yours."

"That's not fair," Catherine said, running over a crossing guard.

"Yes it is," Lily said. "My birthday's coming, and Mom just killed me."

"The girl has a point," Owen said.

A giant spider appeared on the horizon, and Lily shook her head. It was too bad that I killed her, she said. There was no way we were getting past the spider without her help.

"Something tells me it won't come to that," Owen said as I forced him off the road to get a better shot at a tanker truck. "I think your mother's on a mission."

Catherine was ahead of us, methodically firing on the spider's hairy legs like a smart little schoolgirl. Gobs of webbing and spider drool dropped onto the broken road all around us as tanks and helicopters fired missiles from afar. Catching her back wheel on a wad of spider goo, Catherine lost control of her motorcycle and skidded into a falafel stand.

"Oh, honey," I said. "Tough break."

From my perspective, I could see the propane tank with the skull and crossbones pressed up against Catherine's engine. It was hard to miss, of course, because the falafel vendor was gesturing at it wildly and shouting warnings in a language that sounded vaguely Middle Eastern. Meanwhile, various gauges on

Catherine's control panel were boiling over, and as the trapped falafel vendor alternately bit his knuckle, pulled at his hair and tried to free himself from the wreckage, I disarmed my missiles and told my daughter to relax.

"You're not going to shoot me?" she asked.

"Of course not. You're my daughter."

"What about me?" Lily said.

"That was an accident."

Owen was still in the game, but barely, and his motorcycle rolled onto the scene just in time to get caught in the mandibles of the giant spider.

"Gun your engine, baby, and we'll finish this race fair and square, okay?"

Catherine nodded grimly and revved her engine.

"Catherine, no!" Lily shouted, but it was too late.

Raising his eyebrows in terror, the falafel vendor shook his head and spit out a prayer as all of Catherine's gauges went red and the propane tank exploded, engulfing my field of vision in a ball of fire.

"You knew that would happen!" she screamed as the screen in front of her flashed GAME OVER! GAME OVER! GAME OVER! "You knew it!"

"Did I?"

I slid off my motorcycle, and the greasy kid in the football jersey hopped back on, revved the engine, and left the burning wreckage behind him. His shields were low, but the spider was dead, and there were plenty of gas stations to obliterate on the road ahead.

CATHERINE WAS sullen and silent as we walked back to the car, but I wasn't about to let her ruin my good time. Before we even pulled out of the parking lot, I started stomping my feet and clapping my hands to the beat of Queen's We Will Rock You. When Lily joined in and Owen started pounding the steering wheel, I turned to the backseat to shake my finger at Catherine and belt out the only line I was relatively sure of. To wit, my daughter had mud on her face and was a big disgrace because she'd let me kick her can all over the place. After a few more rounds of the chorus, which involved informing Catherine that we would, in fact, rock her, we passed beneath a streetlamp, and I saw that she was beginning to well up. Though she turned toward the window to hide her tears, Lily was too quick for her.

"Catherine's crying!" Lily said.

"That's because she doesn't know how to have fun," I told her.

I expected Lily to take this as her cue to start adding more insult to injury, but she didn't say a word. Instead, she sat silently as if trying to figure out what I was up to. Normally this is where I was supposed to keep the peace and tell Lily to leave her sister alone, but my behavior tonight brought us into uncharted territory. As we passed under another streetlight, the look on Lily's face said she wasn't sure if she liked where we were going.

"God," I said, winking at Lily in the shifting light. "Some people can't take a joke."

"Yeah," Lily said after a short pause. "Some people need to lighten up."

When we arrived at home, Catherine went straight to her room, and Lily told Owen and me that we probably needed some alone time.

"Especially after all *this*," she said, rolling her eyes in Catherine's direction. "To tell you the truth, I wouldn't be surprised if it's hormones. She's getting to that age, you know. The next five years are going to be H-E-double-hockey-sticks for everyone."

"Five?" I said. "Try ten."

Lily disappeared, and I put some music on the stereo. Clifford Brown playing Blue Moon—soft jazz with a string section. It was just loud enough to cover any indiscreet noises two adults might make in the night, and when Owen emerged from the kitchen with two glasses of wine, he whispered that I had to be the sexiest woman he'd ever met.

"Tell the truth," he said, handing me a glass. "You liked it, didn't you? Beating Catherine. Seeing her jaw drop when her motorcycle exploded."

"It was just a game."

"But you were out for blood." He raised his glass. "That's pretty hot."

"Owen, don't."

"Sorry," he said.

I opened my purse and took out the little bag. I dipped a fingernail into the coke and raised it, awkwardly, to my nose.

"So what about this double-date?" he asked. "You, me, Roger, and Chloe?"

"Yeah, I don't see that happening."

"We had a deal," Owen said, reaching for the coke. "You were the first to die, so, technically, you lost."

"I don't think so," I said. "First of all, I never agreed to anything, and second of all, *I* was the one who came back and mopped the floor with *your* sorry butt."

"On that sweaty kid's dime," Owen said. "So it hardly counts. If you don't agree, we can call the girls down and settle the matter once and for all."

I grabbed the coke back and told Owen to fuck himself. Roger's number was on the speed-dial, and the phone was in the kitchen. If he was so intent on taking my ex out to dinner, then he could make the arrangements himself.

"You think I won't?" Owen said. "Because I will."

"Then do it," I said. "I don't care."

Owen got up off the couch and headed for the kitchen. When I realized he wasn't bluffing, I stashed the coke in my purse and sprang up to stop him.

"Hello, is this Roger?" Owen said into the telephone. "This is Audrey's imaginary boyfriend."

"Give me the phone, Owen."

"Yeah, she's standing right here and trying to get the phone away from me."

"Owen."

"No kidding. Her belly button?" Owen extended a finger, and I jumped back instinctively. "Yeah, she jumped about ten feet. It's funny, you think you know a person. Anyway, I thought the four of us could get together this Friday. I know it might be a pain finding a babysitter so late in the game, but I figure we've put this off long enough, right?"

I took a step forward, and Owen wiggled his finger at me.

"That's great," Owen said. "I know Audrey's looking forward to it, too."

"Asshole," I whispered as Owen said goodbye.

"There, you see? That wasn't so hard."

"We can't see them next week," I said. "They're celebrating Lily's birthday."

"That's on Saturday," Owen said. "Lily told me all about it right after Catherine blew you away. Any other objections?"

"How about the fact that I don't want to do it?"

"Irrelevant."

"It'll be weird," I said. "Seeing Roger with Chloe is bad enough, but the four of us together? In the back of my mind, I'll keep thinking that I should go home with him, but then I'll see Chloe and remember that I'm not the woman he loves anymore. That I wasn't pretty enough for him. That I wasn't young enough. That I wasn't sexy enough."

"He's an idiot if he doesn't think you're sexy."

"You haven't seen Chloe yet."

"Are you kidding? Experience and attitude beat the hell out of a good figure any day."

"You're saying I don't have a good figure?"

"I'm saying you're sexy. Where's my coke?"

"It's mine now," I said. "I'll need it in the event of an emergency."

"Like?"

"Like when my boyfriend calls my ex-husband and invites him on a double-date. I think that qualifies as an emergency, don't you?"

"Okay," Owen said. "But if this keeps up, I'll have to start charging you. That stuff isn't cheap, you know."

"Please. You love it when I steal your coke. It's part of my bad-girl mystique."

"Yeah?" he said. "What else do I love?"

He took a step closer and brushed my breast with the back of his hand. Soon we were kissing, and I had to steady myself against the kitchen countertop to keep from stumbling backward.

"Owen," I said as he kissed my neck. "The girls."

"What about them?"

"They're upstairs."

"And?"

"They might hear."

"Then we better make it quick."

I thought about pushing Owen away and telling him to stop, but then I remembered why Roger left. How many times did I shy away from his advances before he started to lose interest? How many times did I tell him to behave himself because the girls had just gone to bed and maybe they'd hear? How many times, I wondered as Owen lifted me off the floor and my shoulder brushed the snub-nosed attachment hub of my KitchenAid stand mixer, could a woman throw cold water on a man before his eye started to wander?

So we made it quick and mostly quiet, and when we were done, I sprayed the countertop with Formula 409 grease and grime remover while Owen crept off to find the cocaine that I'd hidden in my purse. When he returned with his quarry, it didn't take much convincing for me to join him in a quick line, and seven minutes later, I was breaking out the 409 again to wipe down the kitchen table. Except in regard to location and my choice of cleanser, this pattern recurred several more times with no alteration over the course of the next hour-and-a-half, and by the time Owen left, my kitchen was immaculate.

CHAPTER FOURTEEN

THE FIRST thing that hit me as Lily and I walked through the steel and glass vestibule that opened onto the shopping plaza was the overpowering scent of pine, cinnamon, nutmeg, cloves, dried oranges, and what I could only imagine was either frankincense or the sweat of a multitude of unheavenly shoppers weighed down with children and packages, dragging their feet, pushing baby carriages, gorging on giant cookies, and slurping down buckets of Coca-Cola. Then came the music. Sugary sweet and, more often than not, delivered with a Texas twang, each tune promised a host of miracles ranging from rooty-toot-toots and rum-a-tum-tums to peace on Earth and good will to all. A giant pine tree stood at the center of the mall, and beneath the tree sat an ornate golden throne. Though there was no sign of Santa Claus yet, parents and children had already begun to line up for their free consultation with the jolly old elf, and a pair of teenagers were booting up the machinery that would stamp a commemorative photo of each unique and magical meeting with the big guy on a tee shirt, diaper bag, baseball cap, tree ornament, coffee mug, or all of the above for a modest fee.

The old Audrey would have done everything within her power to get in and out of the mall as quickly as possible—including, but not limited to, mapping out the most direct route from her car to the items she needed to purchase, sticking to the center of any and all footpaths so as not to fall prey to the charms of smarmy store managers, and, above all, avoiding eye contact with anyone conducting commerce in a cart or a kiosk. But on an automatic, intuitive, and instinctive level, the new and improved Audrey felt right at home amidst the garland, the gift wrap, and the chrome-plated pine trees.

These people were my people, I thought, as I handed over my credit card time and again, buying lacy lingerie at Victoria's Secret, a cast-iron panini press at Williams-Sonoma, and, for Lily, because I was feeling generous, a pair of sweats whose seat read *JUICY*. Everyone here spoke my language, and we were all on the same wavelength. The shoppers, the cashiers, the security guards. The mannequins in the showrooms. The models on the larger-than-life posters that hung, Chairman Mao-style, in every shop window. Here was our communion, our joy, our greater calling. Here was our peace on Earth and good will to all. We were part of something bigger here, living exclusively on the razor's edge of the present tense and burning with the certainty that we could be as happy as the models in the posters, as beautiful and shapely as the mannequins in the stores, as loved and adored as Hollywood royalty if only we'd spend just a little more money, if only we'd part with a few dollars more.

I bought a wire head-massager from an Iranian woman who told me I had beautiful eyes. I paid twenty-seven dollars for an eight-ounce bottle of apricot facial cleanser. I slumped face-down on a padded table and paid a man with a Jamaican accent to rub my shoulders, arms, and lower back for five minutes while Lily consulted a map of the mall. I could stay in this place forever, I thought as my body turned to putty in the man's strong hands and hordes of shoppers swirled around me like a relentless human riptide. But then I heard Lily asking the Jamaican man if he was almost done, and I knew the only way to stay in the moment was to give her my credit card and tell her to buy herself something nice while I absconded to the nearest toilet stall for a bit of privacy.

"Hey, baby doll," I said when I finally emerged from the restroom to find my daughter scowling at the kids in the tail end of the line to see Santa Claus. "Why so down?"

"I wanted to buy a pair of sunglasses at the Chrissy Qualtieri store, but they wouldn't let me use your credit card."

"That's ridiculous," I said. "It's Christmas."

"I know. I told them I had your permission, but they wouldn't even let me in the store."

I shook my head in disgust and told Lily to follow me. The world was full of small-minded assholes, I explained as we broke through the line of Santa's true believers and plunged into the dense mass of humanity that stood between us and the art-deco Q that glowed like a beacon over the entrance to the boutique. When we reached our destination, I dropped my bags in the doorway and cleared my throat, but none of the girls who worked in the store so much as looked in my direction.

"Officious little bitches," I muttered, more determined than ever to help Lily realize her dream of finally attaining something—anything—adorned with the art-deco Q. "Watch this, baby doll."

Breezing into the store, I tapped my credit card against the surface of a glass display case. Barely distinguishable from the mannequins in the window, the saleswomen all looked at each other and, via mental telepathy, elected one of their number to deal with me. Like the others, she wore a fuzzy red hat and appeared to be more interested in sucking on the long end of a candy cane than in dealing with anyone who might possibly spend money in her store.

"Is this the woman who chased you out?" I asked my daughter as the saleswoman approached.

"I don't know," Lily said. "They all look the same."

"You're right. They do." I turned to the saleswoman. "So you're in the business of chasing people out of your store? Refusing people the right to buy your product? Is that the business you're in? Someone doesn't fit the profile, and they're not allowed to wear your precious little Q? Is that it?"

"She's a kid," the woman said. "It's store policy."

"Store policy. Right. I guess it's also store policy to ignore people when they walk in. I mean, really, what's the point of acknowledging me? I must look like I'm too poor to be doing anything more than browsing, right? Drooling over shit I can't afford? How can someone like me possibly have enough money to even buy a pair of socks in this place, right?"

"They don't sell socks, Mom."

"Quiet, baby doll. I'm talking."

"I'm sorry, ma'am. We were busy."

"I can see that."

"Ma'am?" another woman said. "Is there something we can help you with?"

"Yeah," I said, still tapping my credit card on the display case. "My daughter wants a pair of sunglasses."

I nudged Lily with my elbow, and she pointed to a pair of glasses that reminded me of Jackie Onassis. Big and round, they were perfect for hiding the dark circles that were beginning to form under my eyes, so as the saleswoman turned a key in the back of the display case, I told her to make the order a double.

"And she'll need a purse as well," I added. "Baby doll, pick out a purse you like."

"Really?"

"Why not?" I said. "It's your birthday."

Lily didn't have to think. As if by instinct, she zeroed in on a lime-green purse adorned with a tangled web of lavender Qs and plopped it on the checkout counter. All told, the purchase totaled nearly a thousand dollars, but I was okay with it because, hell, that's what credit cards were for.

"That's a lot of money, Mom," Lily said as the cashier ran my card through her machine and generations of my fiscally responsible ancestors turned in their graves. "Are you sure we can afford it?"

I waved Lily's concerns away with a flick of my wrist.

"See?" I said, donning my new sunglasses as we strode out of the store. "That's how you deal with small-minded people."

"Vicious little bitches," Lily muttered, donning her sunglasses as well.

"Vicious?" I said. "Try *officious*. It means, well, like I was saying. Someone who can't think for herself. Someone who keeps checking the rules all the time and making life miserable for everyone else."

"You mean like Catherine?" Lily said.

"I'm not saying a word. But while we're on the subject, don't tell your sister how much we spent today. You know how she can be."

"Yeah. I'll tell her everything was on sale."

"No, tell her they're knockoffs. We got them from a van in the parking lot."

"But what if she tells my friends?" Lily asked. "The Q only counts if it's real."

"You're right," I said. "Let me think this through. Do you drink coffee?"

"Sure," Lily said. "All the time."

"Oh, yeah? How do you take it?"

Lily fumbled for the right answer before spitting out the name of the nearest coffee shop: "Oh, you know. Berkeley's."

"So you like your coffee Berkeley's," I said.

"Un-hunh," Lily said. "Berkeley's."

"That's funny. Because most people like their coffee black or with cream or sugar."

"Oh, right," Lily said. "I don't know what I was thinking. I like it black."

"Sure you do," I said.

The Berkeley's logo consisted of a bald monk reading what appeared to be runes from a pair of golden tablets while a wise old owl peered curiously over his shoulder. Though I didn't know what the monk, the owl, and the book signified, my guess was that they somehow justified charging six dollars for a small cup of coffee and the quadruple espresso I hoped would keep me going for at least another hour.

"What's an espresso?" Lily said when we sat down with our drinks.

"Super coffee," I said. "Usually you get it in a tiny cup, like the size of a thimble. That's how strong it is."

"So why'd you get a big cup?"

"Because I ordered a quadruple," I said. "That's four espressos in one."

"I know what quadruple means," Lily said. "Why did you order it?"

"Because they don't make a quintuple."

Our chairs were hard and uncomfortable, and our table was about the size of a half-dollar. Even after I bolted my drink, I could feel the ground crumbling beneath me, and watching my daughter's face turn sour with disgust at her first sip of coffee didn't bring half the guilty satisfaction I thought it would.

"What do you think?" I asked.

"I think it needs sugar," Lily said, trying not to let on that she was scraping her tongue against her front teeth. "And some milk, I guess."

"Okay, but that's not how adults drink it. Sugar's for babies. But you knew that, right?"

"Oh, yeah," Lily said. "I knew that."

Lily took another sip, and her entire face rippled. She didn't have to drink the whole thing, I said, but she told me she liked it, and by the time she was halfway through, her facial contortions had grown so subtle that she made a halfway believable coffee drinker.

"I think I know what to do about Catherine," Lily said when she reached the bottom of her cup. "We hide my sunglasses and purse in the trunk and tell her all I wanted was a pair of Juicy sweats."

"No," I said. "She'd never believe it. If I'm taking you to the mall, we're definitely coming home with more than sweatpants."

"But they *are* more than sweatpants," Lily pointed out. "They're *Juicy* sweats."

"True," I said. "But she still won't believe that's all you wanted for your birthday."

"So what if I got something else?"

"That could work," I said. "Will fifty dollars do?"

"I guess," Lily said. "What should I buy?"

"Whatever," I said, handing her a few bills. "Just spend the money."

To KILL some time and at least make a gesture toward competing with Chloe and the skinny salesgirls at the Chrissy Qualtieri boutique, I dragged my pudgy ass across the mall to Dr. Treadwell's Home Fitness Emporium, where a cardboard cutout of a tiger listening to its own heartbeat through a stethoscope while walking on a treadmill enticed customers to drop loads of cash on fitness equipment they'd never use. The tall, broad-shouldered man who greeted me at the door was named Chris, and his bleach-white smile shined brighter than the three gold stars adorning the nametag over his heart. Looking my body up and down, he nodded studiously and told me that before starting at Dr. Treadwell's he'd been as flabby as a jellyfish. As soon as the employee discount kicked in, however, he bought himself an Ultimax 3000 cross-country skiing simulator, and now he had the muscle tone of a professional dancer.

"Touch my butt," he said, casting a glance over his shoulder to make sure his manager wasn't looking. "I mean it. Give it a good squeeze."

I reached for his bottom but paused before touching it. Something about the man struck me as familiar. His build, maybe. Or the heart-shaped pucker of his lips.

"Don't be shy," he said. "It doesn't bite."

I palmed his bottom quickly and said it felt nice.

"Nice and hard, right? That's the Ultimax advantage." He climbed onto a nearby machine and scissored his legs back and forth. "When you buy the Ultimax, you don't just get a machine. You get a twenty-four-hour health-support system. Charts and graphs. Daily tips on exercise and nutrition. Chat rooms. Blogs. Bulletin boards. Discussion groups. Everything you need to discover the new you."

He slowed to a stop and, once again, looked over his shoulder. "Touch my abs," he said.

I reached out and did as he told me.

"You know what that is?" he asked.

"The Ultimax Advantage?"

"Bingo."

"I know you," I said. "I've seen you somewhere."

"I get a lot of that," Chris said.

"I mean it. You're not a member of the GESTAPO, are you?"

"Not that I'm aware of."

Then it hit me. The smile, the build. All he needed was a satin cape and a pair of pointy ears, and the transformation would be complete.

"Captain Panther," I said. "America's favorite just-say-no superhero."

"You're a teacher?"

"No," I said. "But I did see your press kit. I just volunteered to run the drug program at Good Shepherd."

"Good Shepherd," Chris said with a nod. "I remember that show."

"My daughter does, too," I said, failing to mention that she hated it. "We're thinking of bringing you back."

"I wish I could help," Chris said. "But that line of work didn't exactly pay the rent."

"I'm sorry to hear that."

"No big deal. I'm still doing what I love."

"Shilling exercise equipment?" I asked.

"Keeping America fit."

"Right," I said. "That."

"Listen, I shouldn't be doing this, but since you're a Captain Panther fan, I can fix it so you get zero down, free delivery, and no interest on your purchase until January."

"It's December," I said.

"Fair enough. But the bottom line is that you're not in the market for an exercise machine. You're in the market for a whole new you, and that's exactly what I'm selling. With the Ultimax 3000 Home Fitness System, you'll see results in days. I'm talking belly. I'm talking thighs. I'm talking abs. I'm talking buttocks. All it takes is a signature."

What the hell, I figured. It was only money.

"Okay," I said. "But I want you to think about bringing Captain Panther out of retirement. My daughter tells me you're the best in the business."

"She said that?"

"Not in so many words, but more or less."

"I'll think about it," Chris said. "But no promises."

Keeping quiet about the exact nature of Catherine's commentary on the Captain Panther show, I signed everything that Chris put in front of me. When I was through, he offered me a firm handshake and congratulated me on accepting the Ultimax Challenge. I wouldn't regret it, he said, and in a few months, I'd barely recognize myself when I looked in the mirror.

After I left Dr. Treadwell's Home Fitness Emporium, I found a bench outside of a commercial learning center called the Math Lab and sat down with my packages and a sheaf of brochures and paperwork that the once and possibly future Captain Panther had given me. Shuffling back and forth in front of the Math Lab, a man dressed as what, at first glance, appeared to be a giant cross but which, upon closer inspection, turned out to be a giant plus sign handed out candy canes and white tee shirts that read *High on Math!* to anybody who wanted one. Though I thought about picking up a shirt for Catherine, any minor rush I'd gotten from accepting the Ultimax Challenge had already evaporated, and the five paces that separated me from the walking, talking plus-sign might as well have been a hundred miles.

By the time Lily found me, I was planted firmly in the realm of the living dead. Forcing myself off the bench and onto my feet, I knew that my daughter was talking to me, but her voice was barely registering. I nodded vaguely as she showed me the plastic wristwatch she had purchased, and I snapped at her when she started tugging at my Ultimax brochures and asking if she could read them.

"God, Lily," I said. "Why do you have to be such a pain sometimes?"

Lily looked up at me, and her eyes went wide.

"Mom?" she said.

"What?"

"Your nose is bleeding."

"Christ."

I pulled some tissues from my purse and wiped away the blood. There wasn't much, but the sight of it was enough to launch Lily into a fit of a million questions I didn't feel like answering: Was I okay? Did I hurt myself? Had someone punched me? Had I been mugged? Did I still have all my money? Could I remember my name? How many fingers was she holding up? Could I stand? Could I walk? Did I want her to call mall security?

"I'm fine, baby doll," I said. "It's the air conditioning in this place."

"The air conditioning?"

"I think it dried out my sinuses," I said.

If my daughter thought I was lying, she didn't let on. In fact, she was more than willing to change the topic if it meant that we could talk about my brochures for the Ultimax 3000. Had I accepted the Ultimax Challenge, she wanted to know, perfectly aping the candor and urgency of a late-night infomercial as we made our way to the parking lot? Did the salesman tell me about the aromatherapy option? Did the model I chose come with a biometric monitoring system? Had I signed up for the weekly newsletter? And when, just out of curiosity, would our Ultimax 3000 be delivered?

"Listen," I said by way of an answer. "Don't mention the nosebleed, okay? Because you know how Catherine is. She'll only worry."

"I know," Lily said.

"And it really wasn't anything. Just the air conditioning at the mall is all. And probably the cold medicine I've been taking. The combination must have dried out my sinuses—but Catherine doesn't need to know about any of this. You know how she is."

"I know, Mom."

"Good, because it's really not a big deal."

"*Okay*, Mom. I *know*."

"And don't tell her about the sunglasses either."

"God, Mom. How many times do you have to tell me?"

"Or the coffee. I don't think she'd stand for that."

"That's not fair," Lily said. "I *have* to tell her about the coffee."

"Come on, baby doll. I'll never hear the end of it from Catherine. She'll act like I took you to a bar and got you drunk on margaritas."

"You're the mother, Mom. Send her to her room."

"Please," I said. "Just do as I say, okay? Don't tell your sister about the coffee, and don't tell her about the Ultimax."

"But they're delivering it to the house," Lily said, looking over the paperwork I signed. "In three to five business days."

"Shit. Maybe she won't notice."

"It's an all-in-one workout machine," Lily said. "I think she'll notice."

"Shit," I said again. "Shit, shit, shit."

The only thing to do, I realized as I pulled into my driveway, was to come clean and tell Catherine what I'd done. Trudging heavily through the front door, I found my older daughter in her bedroom and told her about my big purchase. I knew she wouldn't approve, I said, interrupting Catherine's reading, but I'd bought us an Ultimax 3000 Home Fitness System. Yes, it cost me a lot of money, but—call me crazy—I thought our family's continued health was worth every penny, and as the only person in the house with a job, I had every right to draw on my paycheck as I saw fit.

"Okay," Catherine said.

"Okay?"

"If you think we need it, sure."

"You don't think it's a waste?"

Catherine looked up from her book and shrugged.

"But it's totally useless," I said. "You and I both know I'll never go near it."

"Then why did you buy it?"

"See?" I said. "This is what I was talking about. All you ever do lately is try to cut me down."

"I didn't mean—"

"It's because of your father, isn't it? He's turned you against me."

"No," Catherine said.

"Don't lie to me, darling. I'm your mother, and I can see right through you. You're still mad at me for saying that your father smoked pot back in college. Well, it's the truth, okay? I'm sorry if it changes the way you look at him, but your dad was a total pothead before I met him—a complete stoner."

"Stop," Catherine said. "You're scaring me."

"Please," I said. "Don't even *think* of starting with that routine. You're not the victim here. I am."

Catherine swallowed and wiped a tear from her eye.

"Don't you see, Catherine? I'm just trying to be a good mother, and you keep pushing me further and further away. Can you even begin to imagine how much that hurts, or are you too bound up in your own little world to care?"

"I'm sorry, Mom."

"Then be a little happy for me when I tell you that I've made an investment in the mental, physical, and spiritual well-being of our entire household."

"I am, Mom. I'm happy for you."

"Then try acting like it sometime," I said, before marching out of her room to find Lily building a shrine to her new purse and sunglasses high atop the tall dresser in her bedroom.

"*You* love me, don't you?" I said loud enough for Catherine to hear.

"Of course I love you," Lily said. "You're my mother."

Satisfied with her answer, I went to my bedroom to crawl under the covers and steel myself against the long, hard crash to come.

CHAPTER FIFTEEN

ON THE night of Lily's birthday, I picked at a box of cold Chinese food and chatted on the phone with Melinda while a pair of delivery men argued across the divide of two completely incompatible languages about how best to assemble my new Ultimax 3000 Home Fitness System. When Melinda asked what all the commotion was about, I told her that I hired a Romanian striptease act to celebrate my younger daughter's coming of age. Catherine rolled her eyes when I said this, so I stuck out my tongue and handed her the box of salty noodles with a gesture that said she should make herself useful.

"I love you," I said in mock sing-song as Catherine took away my trash.

"How sweet," Melinda said. "I wish I had a daughter."

"Do you want one?"

"Only if you take one of my boys."

"No thanks." I said. "Catherine isn't *that* bad."

"Catherine?" Melinda said. "I thought she was the good one."

"That's the problem. I wish she'd loosen up."

"Get her stoned," Melinda said.

"She's ten."

"I was twelve. Tell me about the strippers."

"They're not really strippers," I said.

"Oh," Melinda said, a trace of genuine disappointment in her voice. "That's too bad."

Cradling the cordless handset between my ear and my shoulder, I ducked into the bathroom and closed the door behind me. The reason I was calling, I said, was that I needed some coke for Friday night. Normally I had a rule against buying my own, but this was a special occasion. After all, it wasn't every day that a woman introduced her boyfriend to her ex-husband and his skin-and-bones fiancée.

"No problem," Melinda said. "Drop by on Friday."

"Your house?"

"Yeah," Melinda said. "There's something I wanted to talk to you about, but it isn't exactly for public consumption."

"Can I have a hint?"

"Do you really need one? Tell me about these strange men you let into your house."

"They're delivery men," I said. "I ordered an Ultimax 3000."

"I totally want one of those. Did you go for the aromatherapy option?"

"To tell you the truth, I don't think it matters at this point."

I poked my head out of the bathroom to check on the progress of my visitors. Lily was reading from an instruction manual in broken Spanish while the delivery men used rubber mallets to pound screws into metal brackets. When they got tired of pounding, they spit foreign epithets at each other between bites of the sheet cake I'd gotten on trade to celebrate Lily's birthday. When the sheet cake was gone, they resumed their hammering. Within seconds, my Ultimax 3000 fell apart with a crash, and I said goodbye to Melinda.

"We cannot," one of the delivery men said, approaching me with his hands turned out in a gesture of defeat.

"I don't understand," I said. "You cannot *what*?"

He tilted his head toward the pile of metal and plastic on my floor.

"You can't put it together? But that's your *job*. It's what you *do* for a living."

The delivery man pulled a business card from his front pocket. If I needed further help with my Ultimax 3000 Home Fitness System, he intimated, I could call the number on the card.

"So that's it?" I said. "You're giving up?"

The other delivery man stood over the wreckage and made what appeared to be some kind of blessing—perhaps an exotic form of last rites or extreme unction.

"But I paid two thousand dollars for that thing," I whispered so Catherine wouldn't hear. "The least you can do is put it together."

By way of a reminder that I could call Dr. Treadwell's toll-free helpline any time, night or day, in the event that I wasn't satisfied with my purchase, the first delivery man pointed at the card he'd given me while his partner packed their tools into a plastic toolbox. Satisfied that they'd put in an honest day's work, they both stood silently at my bedroom door until Lily whispered that they probably wanted a tip.

"For what?" I said.

Carrying the box, the first delivery man explained. The *heavy* box, his partner added by adopting a series of awkward poses and pained facial expressions. Up a fairly steep flight of stairs, no less, the first delivery man concluded with a combination of pantomime and broken English.

"Get out," I said. "Before I call the police."

Muttering some of the same curses I'd heard earlier in the evening, the delivery men headed for the stairway, out the front door, and into the damp, chilly night. When I dialed the number on the card they'd given me, I found myself trapped in a labyrinth of automated push-button menus, each equipped with a set of options more detailed and complicated than the last. If I wanted to speak directly with a customer service representative, the voice of a computer-generated British woman informed me after twenty minutes of wading through options that didn't quite meet my particular needs, my best bet was to call the licensed retailer who sold me my unit.

Exasperated, I hung up the phone and realized that Lily was still on my bedroom floor with the instruction manual and my unassembled exercise machine. She was hoping to squeeze in a workout, she said, checking the various pieces of metal and rubber laid out before her against the parts list in the manual.

Assuming, of course, she could piece the machine together before bedtime.

"I wouldn't count on it," I said, wondering where I left the business card of the former superhero who sold me the pile of junk on my bedroom floor. "Not tonight, anyway."

"Yeah, I guess you're right," Lily said. "Not without Dad's help."

It was starting already, I thought. Lily's pendulum-swing back to Roger. If I didn't start making inroads to Catherine's sympathies soon, I'd be out in the cold without any allies, so I knocked on her door and asked if we could talk.

Looking up from her book, my daughter shrugged.

Her never-ending book, I mused. Her perpetual shrug.

When I asked what she was reading, Catherine raised her book high enough for me to catch a glimpse of the cover. Her desk faced the door, and she sat behind it like a secretary guarding the inner sanctum of some highly placed government official or an equally powerful Hollywood mover and shaker.

"You know I'm proud of you, right?" I said. "And I'd never do anything to hurt you."

"I guess so," Catherine said.

"I know I said some things about your father that you didn't want to know." I sat down on the edge of her bed and motioned for her to sit next to me. "And I didn't realize until I said them that you'd take it all so hard."

"You said that Dad was a pothead before you met him," Catherine said, still at her desk. "You said he was a complete stoner."

"I'm sorry, Catherine. I never should have said that."

"Was he?"

"Probably not," I told her. "The truth is I was feeling sick all day, and the mall was crowded, and I took all my frustration out on you. I know it was unfair, but you have to believe me. I wasn't myself."

"Then who were you?"

"I don't know. I guess what I'm trying to say is that I'm sorry for killing you the other night."

"I'm sorry, too," Catherine said. "For killing you, and for getting angry when you told me about Dad. I don't know why I made such a big deal out of it."

"He's your father," I said. "You want him to be perfect."

"No one's perfect, Mom. I know *that* much."

"Don't be so sure," I told her. "I know a girl who's pretty close."

CHAPTER SIXTEEN

This wasn't going to be a regular thing, I told myself. A gram, maybe less. A small outlay of cash. A quick line before my big double-date. A bump or two to keep me going through the night. After that, I might have enough left over for the occasional emergency pick-me-up, but even if I didn't, I honestly couldn't see myself ever needing to score my own coke beyond this one time.

When I pulled into Melinda's driveway, her youngest son was running across the front yard in his underwear. There was no snow on the ground, but it had been a cold and wet December, and Melinda's lawn was stiff with frost. The boy froze when he saw me, then laughed and started running again to keep his circulation going. He was in his underwear, he informed me, and I asked if maybe he should go inside where it was warm.

"I'm not allowed," the boy said. "Donnie won't let me."

"But you'll freeze to death if you stay out here too long."

The boy looked to be about four years old, and he stopped for a moment to stare back at me as if the connection between the cold weather and his own mortality were nothing more than a paranoid delusion on my part.

"Does your mother know you're out here?" I asked.

Again, the look that said I couldn't be serious.

"Well, I'm a friend of hers, and I don't think she'd like it if I let you freeze to death."

The boy let out a shriek and started running laps around an oak tree in the center of the yard. He was pudgy and had a round face. His cheeks were red, his lips gradually turning blue. Steam billowed from his mouth in the cold winter air as he spread his arms and started to growl like a World War II fighter plane. Unsure of what to do, I knocked on the front door, and a blue periscope met me at eye-level.

"What's the password?" a child shouted.

"I don't know," I said. "Are you Donnie?"

"I'm Richie," the boy said. "Donnie's my brother, and you're not allowed in unless you know the password."

"My name's Audrey," I said. "I'm a friend of your mother's."

"She's in the basement," the boy said.

"Would you mind getting her for me? We have an appointment."

"No one's allowed down there." The boy lowered his periscope. Unlike his younger brother, he had a square head and looked as if he'd be more at home fleeing gunfire or mortar attacks on the evening news. "You can ring the bell, though. She'll probably hear it."

I rang the doorbell and waited. Out on the lawn, the first boy was still running and growling and breathing steam. When Melinda showed up, she let me in and called for the child to come inside.

"Do you believe this?" she asked, whacking her youngest son on the bottom as he rumbled through the door. "This is my life. Every day. And you think girls are tough."

"Could be worse," I said, though I couldn't imagine how.

Inside, Melinda led me to her basement steps through a battle zone of broken toys and abandoned sporting goods: action figures with missing arms and legs, a pair of unstrung tennis rackets, a deflated football, and a fleet of flattened cars and trucks that looked like trampled bits of scenery left over from a Japanese monster movie. As we reached the bottom of the steps, the boys began to stomp around on the floor above us, but if Melinda thought their antics were anything less than normal, she didn't let on.

"They sure have a lot of energy," I said.

"ADD," Melinda said. "There's nothing I can do."

I don't know what I was expecting, but her marijuana crop was less than impressive—six plants in ten-gallon flowerpots, a few heat lamps and a huge bag of Miracle-Gro. Turning the spigot in the large washtub at the back of her basement, Melinda filled a green plastic watering can and hefted it over to her garden.

"So," she said, tipping her watering can into one of the flower pots. "What do you think?"

"Nice," I said, wondering how the transaction was supposed to proceed and whether or not Emily Post ever mentioned anything about the etiquette of buying cocaine from a coworker. "But I was in the market for something with a little more punch."

"But of course," Melinda said. Lowering her watering can, she dipped two fingers into the pocket of her tight, black jeans and came out with a packet of cocaine. "The pause that refreshes."

"Cute," I said. "How much?"

"Forget about it," Melinda said. "Consider it a gesture."

"A gesture?" I looked down at the packet. It wasn't that I needed the stuff, exactly. It would just make the night go down a little more smoothly, make me more friendly and outgoing, make Chloe seem like less of a threat. "Let me guess. You're about to make me an offer I can't refuse."

"Refuse it if you want," Melinda said. "But I think we could both make a nice bit of cash if we went into business together."

"I don't know," I said. "I don't exactly see myself as a coke dealer."

"Dealer? Please. You'd be a connection. We're talking small quantities, completely under the radar."

"Sorry," I said. "It's just not me."

"I understand completely. You're worried about the legal angle, but believe me—it's not an issue. As long as you're not some kind of kingpin, the cops aren't interested."

"And you know this how?"

"My brother's on the force. He told me so. Out here in the suburbs, it's mostly kids on skateboards and drunk college students they're worried about. Soccer moms are practically invisible."

"So it's only natural to get into cocaine."

"It's easy, darling. You make a joke about getting high. You ask your friends what they do to unwind. You talk about acquaintances who smoke weed or do the occasional line, and—not that you're into the scene yourself—you ask your friends if *they've* ever been high. Maybe in college? Maybe more recently? From there, it's easy. Mention that you might know where you can get your hands on some topnotch pharmaceuticals. You know somebody who knows somebody. It's not the sale that matters, but planting the seed. Everyone says no at first, but they always come back. *You know that conversation we had? You said you had a friend? It's not that I'm into this kind of thing, but ...* Try it sometime. You might be surprised."

"Then what? They show up at my house? I don't think so."

"You're still thinking movies and cop shows," Melinda said. "Weirdo pimps and prostitutes. I'm not asking you to open a crack house. I'm saying work from home. Make your own hours. Build a client base. Doctors, lawyers, schoolteachers, accountants. Casual users. People like us. It's like champagne or fine wine. Pricey, but you keep a bottle around the house in case of emergency. Trust me, you'll make a small fortune."

"How much are we talking?"

"That's the beauty of it," Melinda said. "Ten, fifteen years ago, I saw coke going for ninety bucks a gram in some cases—street value, I mean. Now it's down to, I don't know, thirty-five, forty? Again, this is street value, and I've heard some people say they can get it for as low as fifteen. Probably shit, but it's a lot cheaper than it used to be. The kind of people we're selling to, though, it's not exactly like they know what they're doing. I mean, they buy the occasional gram, but not with any regularity, so it's, you know, whatever the market will bear. The last thing any of these people want is to drive down to some sketchy neighborhood with a wallet full of cash. They want to go somewhere safe. They want to buy from someone they can trust. And it's not like your customers are in a position to shop around. They find a connection, and they pay the asking price. Supply and demand. It's totally a seller's market."

There was another loud crash above us, and Melinda's boys stopped beating the hell out of each other just long enough to ascertain that no one had been killed.

"It's our whole culture," Melinda continued. "Everywhere you look, someone's telling you to get high. TV, movies, radio, magazines. You see an ad for brownies, and some overwrought mother is drifting off to la-la land after the first bite. Anything chocolate—I'm serious. Watch carefully next time. It's always the same woman, and by the end of the commercial, she always looks stoned, ecstatic, or otherwise lost in the throes of orgasm. Meanwhile the kids are off kicking the shit out of each other, but as long as Mom gets her brownies, everything's cool. And don't get me started on coffee commercials. Drugs in a cup. Prescription medicine? Please. Soap that wakes you up in the morning? Shaving cream that helps you face the day? Bath crystals that take you to another world? It's all about getting high. That's the forbidden fruit that all of these commercials are holding out to you, the promise they never quite keep. And that's where we come in. Everyone else promises to make you feel good, but ours is the only product that delivers."

"And this product," I said. "How much does it cost?"

"That's what I like about you," Melinda said. "You're all about the bottom line."

"Strictly out of curiosity," I said. "Nothing more."

"This guy I met can hook us up for twenty bucks a gram, twenty-five tops, and it's good stuff. We get an ounce and cut it with baby laxative, and all of a sudden we have two ounces, follow? Real fishes and loaves stuff, because the people we're selling to, they don't know quality product from confectioner's sugar. Then we take that and sell it for forty bucks a gram, and still it looks like a good deal because these people, they're used to paying like fifty or sixty, or probably more if the last time they scored was more than a few years ago. And if they've never scored, which a lot of them probably haven't, then they're nothing to worry about."

"How much is a gram, exactly?"

"Like the little bag I gave you. We buy an ounce, and it's twenty-eight grams."

"And that costs us, what? Five hundred bucks or so?"

"About that, yeah, but you never pay up front, so the cash isn't an issue. They front you the coke, and you pay them back later."

"So we get an ounce, and we cut it."

"Which gives us fifty-six grams altogether."

"We're making, what, thirty bucks a gram?"

"Times fifty-six, and we make over fifteen-hundred bucks. Split down the middle, of course, and it's almost eight-hundred for each of us, probably in a single week. Then we go for two ounces, three ounces, four. We're looking at two grand a week in walking-around money."

"That's a lot of people stopping by my house."

"On your own terms, I promise."

"And if we get caught?"

"We won't," Melinda said. "You're on the drug squad or whatever it's called. Who would suspect?"

I thought about my new Ultimax 3000 and the additional grand I blew at the mall.

"It's tempting," I said. "But I can't."

"No problem. Like I said, it's entirely up to you, so give it a little more thought and get back to me."

Commingling discreetly with my wallet, my checkbook, my tissues, and my keys, the little white packet barely looked out of place. Taking a quick hit in the grimy little restroom of Nick's American Grill, I thought about the first time Melinda offered me cocaine and how I turned her down—or would have, if Svetlana hadn't hoovered up her stash. Was I all that different now that I'd been high a few times? A little more open-minded, I told myself, checking the mirror for telltale signs of what I was up to. A little more relaxed. A little more daring. A little more willing to let the little things slide. But in the final analysis, I had to insist that I was the same woman I'd always been. Smart, self-assured, responsible Audrey.

Back in our cozy little booth, Roger and Chloe were snuggled together like a pair of lovebirds, but Owen had yet to arrive.

Not that I was worried—he probably had a perfectly reasonable excuse for being a half-hour late to dinner at his own restaurant. Sure, I looked like a jackass, and sure, with each passing minute, Roger and Chloe were becoming increasingly convinced that I'd hooked up with some kind of deadbeat, but I honestly didn't care. I had my coke, and I was feeling good. Beyond that, nothing mattered.

"You guys are so cute together," I said. "I mean that sincerely. I'm sitting here looking at you, and all I can think is, wow, these two are *so damn cute.*"

"Thanks," Roger said. "I think."

He made a fist in front of his mouth when he spoke, but Chloe pulled gently at his wrist and told her fiancé to show us his smile.

"Maybe later," Roger said.

"It's the gap in his teeth," Chloe whispered theatrically. "We're thinking about braces."

"Oh, are we?" I said, looking Roger in the eye.

"No," Roger said. "I mean, yeah, eventually, but not right now. After the wedding, maybe. When things have settled down."

"Does this mean you've set a date?"

"Almost," Roger said. "We're very close."

"Almost?" I asked.

"He means no," Chloe said.

"I mean we still have some variables in play," Roger said.

"Right," Chloe said. "Variables. Like the fact that Mr. Indecisive here is afraid to commit to anything."

Roger grimaced at the remark, but before he could respond to Chloe's allegation, Owen arrived and apologized for being late.

"Don't tell me," I said. "You had trouble finding the place."

"Something like that," Owen said with an embarrassed grin.

Sizing up the new man in my life, Roger rose from his seat, and the pair shook hands the way men always do—forearms tensing as they tried to squeeze each other's fingers into oblivion. No sign of pain, no sign of weakness on either side—just two Neanderthals bearing their teeth and saying how great it was to finally meet each other as their faces turned red and their bones slowly shattered. When the competition ended in a stalemate, both men settled into their seats, and Owen offered me a quick hello-kiss on the lips before asking if we'd had a chance to order dinner.

"Not yet," I said. "We were waiting for you."

"Uh-oh," Roger said. "I remember that tone. Someone's in trouble."

Owen hooked a finger inside his shirt collar and tugged at it, gulping comically.

"Cute," I said. "Now refresh my memory. We were saying something about Roger and commitment. What was it again, Chloe?"

"Actually, I think that conversation was pretty much over," Roger said before his fiancée could respond.

"Was it?" I asked. "Because I really don't think it was."

"Wow," Chloe said, defusing the situation before it could escalate any further. "Look at this menu. It's your restaurant, Owen. What do you recommend?"

"Honestly?" Owen said. "Sending out for pizza."

I punctuated his joke with a vaudeville rimshot that, in addition to letting Roger and Chloe know that Owen was only kidding, had the added benefit of getting the attention of our waitress, who read the specials from a ragged spiral-bound notepad and asked if we had any questions. If she knew that Owen was the owner of Nick's American Grill, she didn't let on, and the way she stumbled over words like *risotto, mesclun, Bolognese,* and *steak-frites* suggested that the girl wasn't just new to Nick's but to the foodservice industry in general. But she was young and skinny and cute and bubbly, so I had no doubt whatsoever that the customers here would treat her well—assuming, of course, she didn't mind the occasional drunken marriage proposal or the slightly more frequent pat on the ass from a dirty old man.

The girl repeated our order back to us three times before getting it right, a minor source of amusement that gave us something to talk about for a good three or four minutes after her departure. It wasn't long, however, before the topic got old and we found ourselves talking like couples do when they really have nothing in common. Chloe asked how Owen and I met, and though I did my best to make the story sound romantic, the bottom line was that the only reason we ended up together was that he owed me dinner after standing me up so many times. Owen asked Roger what he did for a living, and the answer, as always, came in fits and starts and left everyone, including Roger, wondering exactly what his job entailed. Something with numbers. Something with finance. Something to do with his accounting degree, but not quite accounting itself.

When I returned from my second trip to the women's room, Chloe was nestled against Roger's body, and it struck me that this wasn't how I ever used to sit with him when we'd go out to eat or to see a movie or even when we were watching TV at home. This was how Catherine used to fall asleep against his chest when she was younger. This was how, on very rare occasions, Lily still cuddled up with me. Was this what he'd wanted all along, I wondered? Was this why I lost him? Because I wasn't little, because I wasn't manageable, because I didn't fit comfortably and conveniently in the crook of his arm?

"Owen was just telling us about Dave Brubaker," Chloe said as I slid back into the booth. "He's—what did you say, Owen? In his nineties or something and still on the road?"

"Brubeck," Owen said with a shrug. "But, yeah, the guy's been touring forever."

"Jazz," Roger said, shaking his head. "I'm sorry, but I just don't get it. Junkies, alcoholics—what's the attraction?"

"You don't keep touring into your nineties if you're a junkie," Chloe said. "*Or* an alcoholic."

"True," Owen said. "But Roger does have a point. Pretty much everyone I love was into the dope scene. Getz, Parker, Chet Baker. Billie Holiday, of course. Miles Davis was a bit of a coke fiend in his own right, but look at everything he accomplished."

"Coke's obviously a different story," Roger said as if he knew anything about it. "But you can see my point, right? On the whole, we're talking about a population of degenerates."

"Absolutely," I said. "A bunch of goddamn dope fiends. As long as we're on the subject, though, Catherine might not be speaking to you this weekend."

"Pardon me?"

"I may have let it slip that you were a bit of a pothead in college."

"You're kidding," Chloe said. "*My* Roger? A *pothead*?"

"He's not *my* Roger anymore, kid."

"I wasn't a pothead," Roger said. "And why would you say something like that to our daughter?"

"She asked," I said.

"Is it true?" Chloe asked, disentangling herself from Roger.

"I was young," Roger said. "And stupid. Can we talk about something else?"

"Catherine's very disappointed in you," I said.

"Not me," Chloe said. "I'm intrigued. I want to know more. How much and how often?"

"I'll talk to her," Roger said, ignoring his fiancée.

"Do you want some pamphlets?" I said. "I might have some in the car."

"I don't need pamphlets," Roger said. "I'll just tell her the truth. I was young and stupid. She's a big girl. She'll understand."

"Just so I can pinpoint where you're coming from," I said, working my way under my ex-husband's skin. "You were, what, twenty years old at the time of your indiscretion? Which means that when you were a full ten years older than Catherine is now, *you* were young and stupid, but *she*, at the tender age of ten, is a big girl, and therefore capable of excusing the folly of a so-called youth who was, at the time in question, twice her age. Unless I'm missing something here, Roger, your logic doesn't exactly track."

"I'll work on it," Roger said.

This was more like it, I thought. Real chemistry. Not the lame-ass puppy-dog glances that passed for a relationship between

Roger and Chloe. That wasn't love. That wasn't commitment. That was infatuation at best, and I gave the marriage three years—tops—because if you want a real marriage, a good marriage, a meaningful marriage, you need to mix it up once in a while. You need to be willing to have it out. You need to be ready to lay all your cards on the table and go for broke in an all-out, no-holds-barred, knockdown, drag-out, full-blown argument.

Somewhere between the entrée and coffee, the conversation started to lag, so I excused myself to spoon a little more coke into my nose. By the time I returned, Owen was talking about a surfing class he'd taken years earlier in Hawaii. The waves on the north shore, he said, could reach twenty, thirty, forty feet tall. As tall as a house, he added. Not that he'd ever surfed the north shore himself, but he'd heard about plenty of guys who had. Some had drowned over the years, and some were paralyzed. The lucky ones only broke bones or tore ligaments as the massive waves smashed them up against the shore, but everyone who'd ever survived the challenge agreed that the thrill was worth the risk.

"We were just talking about our big trip to the islands," Chloe said, eyes wide at Owen's secondhand tales of derring-do as I slid back into my seat.

"Yeah, Audrey," Roger said. "You should really give some more thought to coming with us. We'll have a lot of fun, and God knows you need a vacation. Help me out here, Owen. Doesn't our girl here deserve a little getaway? Doesn't she owe it to herself to cut loose and enjoy herself once in a while?"

"Couldn't agree more," Owen said. "I love it when Audrey cuts loose."

"See? Even Owen thinks it's a good idea."

"Owen can go fuck himself," I said, riding the line between buzzed and edgy. "I told you before, Roger, tagging along after you and your little girlfriend isn't exactly my definition of a good time, and we both know the only reason you want me there is to take care of the girls while you two get all cutesy together. No offense, Chloe, but I don't feel like playing the old maid while you're in the next room going down on my husband."

"Oh," Chloe said. "I—oh."

"Jesus, Audrey, what the hell?" Roger asked.

"Please. You know I'm only kidding, Chloe. If Roger had his way, we'd *both* be going down on him while we palmed the girls off on the concierge."

"Okay," Owen said, raising a hand to flag down our waitress. "Wasn't this fun? We should definitely do it again sometime."

"What?" I asked. "You're saying it isn't every guy's fantasy? Two girls at once? Come on, Chloe, you have to admit that the whole situation's a little weird. Why else would Roger have invited me along?"

"I was trying to be nice," Roger said. "I thought you'd enjoy it."

"It *is* a little weird, honey," Chloe said. "I didn't want to mention it before, but Audrey's kind of right. Not about us going down on you, necessarily, but about the whole situation in general."

"Then why didn't you say anything?"

"I don't know. I thought you knew what you were doing."

"I *do* know what I'm doing. I'm trying to keep my family together."

"That explains the divorce," I said.

The waitress approached us carefully, and Owen told her that our meal was on the house. Her brow creased when he said this, and the crease threatened to become permanent as Owen explained who he was and how his position as proprietor of Nick's American Grill related to her own role as an employee.

"Poor, sad, balding, gap-toothed Roger," I said as the waitress went off to consult with the night manager. "The old wife's too old, and the new wife's too young. Another time, another place, and you could have been a king. You could have had wives and concubines and everything you ever dreamed of, but here we are in the land of the free, and all you can do is agonize. The young one or the old one? The skinny one or the faithful one? The sexy one or the mother of your children? You told yourself I was wooden, Roger, because that made the decision easier for you, but tonight you found out that I wasn't. Tonight you found out that I'm alive and smart and sexier than you remembered, and now you want me back."

Chloe checked her watch and said the hour was getting late.

The babysitter charged time-and-a-half on Fridays, Roger added.

The manager peeked out from his office, and Owen gave him a wave.

Out in the parking lot, the night air was cold. Once again, Roger and Owen shook hands, forearms bursting with the effort of crushing each other's bones. Leaning forward with out-stretched arms, Chloe offered me a bony, awkward girl-hug, meant, I supposed, to convey that all was not only forgiven but completely forgotten. When she decided that our embrace had lasted long enough, Chloe turned to Owen and offered him a dainty hand, which left only me and Roger.

"We should do this again sometime," my ex said as he leaned in to plant a friendly, sexless kiss on my right cheek. "Don't you think?"

"Oh, yeah," I said, returning the favor. "Absolutely."

"So we're good?" Roger said.

"As gold," I said.

"Still best friends?"

"Sure, Roger," I said. "Best in the world."

CHAPTER SEVENTEEN

Per Roger's instructions, I had the girls packed and ready to go at noon sharp on Christmas day. When he and Chloe rolled into our driveway at twenty-after, I was hoping my ex would simply lean on the horn, but the spirit of the season moved them both to make the twenty-foot trek to my front door. With our daughters standing at attention and sweltering away under their heavy winter coats, their wool caps, their puffy gloves, and the scarves my mother knitted for them the previous winter, Roger gave me a hug and wished me a merry Christmas. There'd been a slight change of plans, he explained. Instead of going back to his place, they were going to visit Chloe's parents in upstate New York.

"But that's a four-hour drive," I said. "The girls don't want to spend Christmas in the car."

"It's not *that* far," Roger said. "Besides, this is family we're talking about. Sometimes you need to make little sacrifices to be with the people you love. We'll just pretend like today's Christmas Eve, and tomorrow morning we'll have Christmas all over again. How does that sound, girls? Two Christmases!"

Chloe let out a half-hearted hurrah, but the girls remained silent, staring sullenly at Roger through the narrow slits between their caps and scarves.

"You'll love it," Chloe said. "My parents have stables and a tennis court and an in-ground pool."

"It's winter," Catherine observed.

Sensing the futility of putting up a fight, Lily shrugged her shoulders and extended the drag-handle on her suitcase. Though it wasn't officially licensed merchandise, she'd fashioned her own art-deco Q out of felt and attached it to the suitcase with a safety pin. It wasn't a knockoff, she insisted to anyone who asked, because the ersatz Q wasn't there to fool anyone. Its sole purpose was to help her visualize the luggage she aspired to.

"Well, time's a-wasting," Roger said, looking at a gold watch I'd never seen before. "We better hit the road if we want to get there before sundown."

Glancing conspicuously at the mess in my living room, Roger put an arm around Chloe, and I hugged the girls goodbye. Though their eyes begged me to do something, to put up a fight, to put my foot down and tell Roger that the plan was the plan and he couldn't simply whisk my girls away to upstate New York on a whim, I didn't say anything other than that I loved them and that I was sure they'd have a good time.

In all honesty, all I really wanted was for Roger and the girls to get out of the house so I could spend some time with a gift labeled *From Owen To Audrey—DO NOT OPEN UNTIL YOU'RE ALONE ON CHRISTMAS*. It wasn't that Owen *wanted* to be away from me over the holidays, I'd all but convinced myself as I slid a fingernail under the strip of tape that held the green and red gift wrap together. And so what if his excuse went without so much as an attempt at an explanation from having plans with his family in Hoboken to spending the week with some buddies in Vegas? Plans change, right? And, seriously, I didn't mind being alone, because being alone meant that I didn't have to share.

As the paper came away from the package, my heart raced with the hope that Owen—the old romantic—had seen fit to celebrate the holiest day of the year by giving the woman in his life a gram of cocaine. Not that I needed it, of course. I just wanted to catch a tiny buzz. I just wanted to spend the day a little coked up so I didn't have to think about my daughters and how they were off meeting their future step-grandparents with their stables and their tennis court and their in-ground swimming pool. I just wanted to do a quick line so I wouldn't mind as much when my mother called to wish me a merry Christmas and ask why I gave in so easily to Roger, why I let my boyfriend go gallivanting off to Las Vegas on Christmas day, and why I deemed the woman who raised me such a horrible person that I couldn't drive three hours to visit her in Maryland when my ex-husband could drive all the way to upstate New York to be with Chloe's family.

Given the circumstances, snorting a little coke was the most rational thing to do—except for the fact that the bastard hadn't given me any. All I found when I opened the package was a pair of fishnet stockings and a note that read *Let's put the X back in Xmas!*

Dropping the card, I let out a sigh and headed to the dining room to see what kind of booze I had in the liquor cabinet. Though I never had much of a stomach for hard liquor, I could easily picture myself sipping Irish whiskey and watching old movies until my mother called. *Miracle on 34th Street, It's a Wonderful Life, The Bells of Saint Mary's*—I had them all on video, and I had them all on DVD. Old-timey black-and-white morality plays that made people believe in happy endings, the sanctity of life, and the American dream. Not that I was drinking to get drunk, I told myself. I was drinking to unwind—and if, perchance, my mother started pestering me to make a last-minute trip to Maryland for a long round of passive-aggressive queries, comments, and suggestions masquerading as a holiday dinner, being too tipsy to drive would give me the perfect excuse to just say no.

GEORGE BAILEY was about to jump off a bridge in *It's a Wonderful Life* when the telephone rang. Assuming it was my mother, I answered the phone with a hearty *Merry Christmas!* only to hear a man's voice on the other end of the line—Chris Parker from Dr. Treadwell's Home Fitness Emporium. According to his records, I'd placed a call in reference to my recent purchase of an Ultimax 3000 Home Fitness System.

"Yeah," I said. "Three weeks ago."

"Sorry for the delay," Chris said. "I've been pretty busy lately."

"Let me guess. A pair of international terrorists masquerading as delivery men has been dumping piles of useless scrap metal in households up and down the Golden Mile, and no one but Captain Panther can stop them."

"Something like that. I forgot you were a fan."

"Your biggest," I said. "Have you given any more thought to coming out of retirement?"

Chris made a noncommittal noise—part sigh, part groan, part desperate cry of existential angst. Beyond the fact that I didn't want to revisit my envelope full of press kits and anti-drug propaganda, there was no real reason for me to pursue the issue of the Captain's return to showbiz any further, but I couldn't help myself. It wasn't that he looked good in tights, exactly, but the fact that the man had worn them at all, that at some point in his life he believed he could change the world by putting on a mask and cape and telling kids to stay away from drugs, was oddly endearing to me.

"Anything can happen," he said. "But I wouldn't hold my breath."

"We'll see about that," I told him, stealing a page from Melinda's playbook. "I can be very persuasive."

"I'm sure you can, but that's not why I called."

"Oh, right. The pile of junk in my bedroom."

"If you don't mind the intrusion, I can stop by today and have you up and exercising in no time."

"But it's Christmas," I said.

"Believe me, I know."

What the hell, I figured. It wasn't like I had anything better to do.

"Okay," I said. "But you'll have to sit through my sales pitch."

"For what?"

"The Captain Panther Comeback Special."

"You can't be serious."

"Those are my terms."

"But it's *your* exercise machine."

"And *you* are under contract to fix it," I said. "Do I need to show you the paperwork, Captain?"

Yielding to my undeniable persistence, Chris said goodbye, and less than an hour later, I found myself caught in the opening scenes of what was either a bad romance novel or an even worse adult-entertainment video: The swarthy repairman shows up on the lonely woman's doorstep wearing a pair of baggy gray overalls and carrying a metal toolbox. Placing a hand on a rock-solid bicep, she ushers him past the living room and up to her boudoir for a postmortem on her stillborn exercise machine. Gently laying his toolbox on the floor, the repairman stoops to inspect the damage. It could have been worse, he tells the woman, flexing his muscles before settling down to work. A lot worse.

"Tell me one thing," Chris said, opening his toolbox. "Did they use a hammer?"

"Mallets, I think. With rubber heads."

"Typical."

He went to work quickly, shaking his head in mild disbelief as he disassembled mismatched lengths of metal and repositioned them so that, in the space of minutes, the arrangement started to take on the general size and shape of the Ultimax 3000 Home Fitness System I'd seen on the showroom floor at Dr. Treadwell's Home Fitness Emporium.

"So," he said, tightening a bolt with his socket wrench. "What about that pitch you promised?"

"Right," I said. "The pitch."

"What did you call it? The Captain Panther Comeback Special?"

"The world needs a hero," I said.

"Is that the best you can do?"

"Give me a break. I'm new at this."

"At what, exactly?"

"Marketing superheroes. Or anything, really. I'm a magazine editor, not a salesman."

"Salesperson," Chris said.

The telephone rang before I could respond with something clever, and I knew right away that it was my mother. Since there was a strong likelihood that she wouldn't take kindly to the fact that I was giving her the brush-off to spend time with a strange man who showed up at my door on Christmas day, I let the phone ring until the machine picked up.

"Merry Christmas," my mother said. "It's only me. I guess you found something to do on your own today, unless you're out with Owen. Hope you're having fun wherever you are. Dad says Merry Christmas. Bye."

Translation?

I know you're there, Audrey, and you couldn't be bothered to pick up the phone. It kills me that you won't answer a call from your own mother on Christmas day, but I guess that's the kind of relationship we have. Keep on twisting that knife in my heart, Audrey, and don't stop until I die.

"Mothers," Chris said.

"Tell me about it."

"Thank God for small favors. If not for Dr. Treadwell's delivery goons mangling your Ultimax 3000, I'd be sitting down to dinner with my family right now."

"Sorry," I said.

"No, it's a good thing. I was strung out on heroin for years, and every time I visit, my mother puts a glass of wine in front of me and tells me I should at least have a drink to be social."

"You were on heroin?"

"Heroin, coke, speed," he said, counting the drugs off on his fingers. "You name it, I did it—and my mom pours me a glass of wine. I know why, of course. She wants to pretend it never happened. In her mind, I went out to Hollywood, had a few auditions, made some TV shows, and decided to come back east to sell exercise equipment. One glass of wine, she always says. What will it hurt?"

"Are you ever tempted?"

"Not really. Most times I wouldn't even dream of it."

"And other times?"

"It starts with an itch—this little voice in my head that says maybe my mother's right. Maybe *one little drink* wouldn't hurt. Or a little bit of grass. Or a taste of coke. That's when I know it's time to start running. That's when I know it's time to hit the weights. Endorphins, you know? That's what I used to focus on with the Captain Panther bit, anyway. If you want to feel good, I'd say, get out there and exercise."

"So why did you give up?"

"I told you before. It didn't pay the rent."

"Please. You're saying you were in it for the money?"

"Money would have been nice. A little recognition."

"This coming from America's favorite just-say-no superhero."

"Pure hype and nothing more."

"Okay," I said, sensing a dead end. "What made you realize you had a problem? With drugs, I mean. Though if you want to talk about your Captain Panther habit, feel free to do that, too."

"It's a tough call," the Captain said, making adjustments to my exercise machine as if by instinct. "I was living in L.A. with my girlfriend, and she got it in her head that she wanted to have a baby. We were both using at the time, and I told her that junkies really didn't have any business having kids. In my mind, I was only talking about her, but it was enough to get the word out in the open."

"And that's when you realized?"

"That's when I started to rationalize. I wasn't a junkie because I rarely mainlined the stuff. I wasn't a junkie because I was still getting work. I wasn't a junkie because I could quit any time. I had it all under control. But still the word was there—*junkie*. Haunting me like a ghost. Circling like a buzzard. Passing over the lips of everyone I met. Casting directors. Agents. The only place to hide was in the gaze of other junkies. I stopped getting work. I stopped paying my bills. I ended up on the street. If this sounds rehearsed, that's only because it is. I've told this story a million times. It's part of my act."

"Captain Panther?"

"No, Chris Parker. My skin was crawling all the time, and I hated who I was. All I wanted was to die, to shoot up in some toilet stall and nod off forever. Then one day I got my wish. I shot some dope and knew right away that it wasn't any good. I turned a dozen shades of green. Next thing I knew, I was in an ambulance, and I heard someone say I was flat-lining. When I woke up in the hospital, the doctors said my heart had stopped. They told me that I'd died. And to this day, my mother insists that one drink won't kill me."

If only I had a gram in the house, I thought as Chris told me to get on my Ultimax 3000 for a test-run. Then maybe I could channel Melinda and convince Captain Panther to get back in the superhero game. Failing that, I could at least work up the guts to ask him to stay for dinner and save me from spending Christmas alone. And maybe if he stayed long enough, I'd confess to being a little high. And maybe he'd tell me that it was okay, that for some people, cocaine wasn't a big deal. Then we'd talk a little more, and I'd have a little wine, and over candlelight and leftovers, the Captain or Chris or whoever he was at the time might just relent and have that holiday drink his mother had been bugging him about ever since he cleaned up his act.

"Okay," I said. "Cards on the table. Give me one show. We'll invite the local press. I'll do a profile in *Eating Out*, and we'll talk to Dr. Treadwell about sponsoring your act."

"There's no Dr. Treadwell," Chris said. "He's an imaginary character someone invented to sell exercise equipment."

"Then who better to join forces with America's favorite just-say-no superhero?"

"I told you—that was all hype."

"Yeah," I said. "And we're going to hype your comeback even more."

"I don't know. I got out of the business for a reason."

"Bottom line," I said. "The gig pays two-hundred dollars. Do you want it or not?"

"Two-hundred?"

"Cash," I said. "Not bad for an hour's work, right?"

I could see the wheels turning in his head as he worked through all the angles. A single show. A little bit of press. Who could tell what would happen next? If the right people heard about the Captain—a TV news director here, an influential blogger there—there was no end to the possibilities. Corporate sponsorships, a record deal, his own cartoon series.

"Okay," he said, carefully laying his tools back in his toolbox. "I'll do it."

CHAPTER EIGHTEEN

Two days after my Christmas with Captain Panther, I called Melinda to tell her that I'd given her proposition some more thought. I'd consider a new and exciting career in the fastest-growing industry in America, I said, but only on a temporary basis—long enough to pay off Christmas and my Ultimax 3000, but no longer. Accepting my terms, Melinda said that she had to make a phone call or two to set things up and that I could meet her at Fatso Ratso's for lunch. It was the perfect place to plan our next move, she said—dark and loud with the constant buzz of screaming children and thundering video games. It also didn't hurt that she could bring her boys along and let them wreak havoc on someone else's property for an hour or so.

"Bring the girls," she added. "We'll make it a play date."

Reluctant to get into all of the reasons I couldn't bring my daughters—especially Catherine—back to the house of the giant rat any time soon, I thanked Melinda for the suggestion and told her that the girls were with their father in upstate New York. What I failed to add, however, was that I wasn't completely sure that bringing children along to discuss a potential drug deal was necessarily the best of all possible parenting strategies. But as they say, to each her own.

"I need you to be honest with me," I said when we met up and her boys tumbled off into the neon darkness of the arcade. "You don't think there's a chance I'll get in over my head, do you?"

"Uh-oh," Melinda said. "Is Owen on one of his kicks again?"

"Kicks?"

"His whole clean and sober act. Nothing to worry about, really. Usually passes in a month or so—six weeks, tops."

"Actually, it wasn't Owen," I said. "America's favorite just-say-no superhero dropped by to fix my Ultimax 3000."

"Captain Panther?" Melinda said.

"You've heard of him?"

"Absolutely," Melinda said, signaling a passing rat for a helium balloon. "Donnie told me all about him when he came to Good Shepherd a few years ago. Said the guy was a complete loser, but he looked great in tights."

"Donnie said this?"

"About being a loser," Melinda said, undoing the knot in her balloon and taking a hit of helium so that when she spoke again, she sounded like a card-carrying member of the Lollipop Guild. "I said the thing about the tights. Donnie won an autographed picture of the guy because he knew the most about drugs. Hung on our fridge for weeks."

Our waitress brought a basket of breadsticks, and Melinda asked if someone named Michael was around. He was her nephew twice removed, Melinda explained, and she wanted to wish him a happy birthday.

"You're not the only one," the waitress said, nodding in the direction of the rat with the balloons. "That's him over there."

"I thought he looked familiar," Melinda said, holding her balloon out and asking if I wanted a hit.

"Never before lunch," I said, and Melinda ordered a large pizza with everything on it.

The giant rat gave away the last of his balloons and returned to our table so Melinda could wish him a happy birthday. There was an inflatable banjo slung over his shoulder, and he told us he couldn't talk for too long because he needed to get his tail onstage for Rockin' Ratso's Rolling Thunder Review.

"Not a problem," Melinda said. "I want to slip out of here while my boys are still flush with game tokens, so I'll just take our pizza to go if you don't mind."

"I understand completely," the rat said.

"You're really leaving them?" I asked as the rat scurried off.

"They know the way home," Melinda said. "Now tell me what Captain Panther said to spook you."

"Nothing really," I said. "I just worry sometimes."

"Look, these clean-living types all have their weird little hang-ups about getting high and their grand, sweeping theories about why everyone in the world is an addict waiting to happen, but the bottom line is that you like to do a little coke once in a while, and it isn't a big deal. As far as having a problem is concerned, it's a no-brainer. I wouldn't go into business with you if you did. The last thing I want is a partner who's going to hoover-up our entire inventory, right?"

The giant rat returned with our pizza, then took to a tiny stage at the front of the restaurant with the band of anthropomorphized animals who'd wrecked my house nearly two months earlier—the pink octopus on tambourine and maracas, the blind mole on keyboards, the frog on bass, and the squishy red cancer cell on drums. It certainly wasn't jazz, I thought as the opening riffs of their prerecorded set rumbled over the sound system and Melinda hurried for the door. But it sure kept the kids distracted.

"Your car or mine?" I asked when we reached the parking lot.

"For what?" Melinda said.

"To meet our connection."

"Are you kidding? That was him."

"The rat?"

"He's not really my nephew, in case you were wondering."

A police car glided by, and Melinda beckoned for me to take a look inside her pizza box.

"That's it?" I asked, peering down at what appeared to be a condom packed with baking soda.

"You were expecting something else?"

"I don't know. Guns and speedboats. A seedy motel room. I assumed it would be a little more dangerous."

"Exciting, you mean. If it makes you feel any better, Michael has a Glock taped inside his costume."

"Good to know," I said, guessing as I got into my car that a Glock was a gun of some kind and wondering if Michael was the same rat who visited my home on Halloween.

Down in her basement, Melinda had all the gear we needed to get our venture off the ground: scales, tiny plastic bags, an ounce of powdered baby laxative, and a small food processor. It had been a wedding gift, she said, but since she saw the kitchen less as a place to prepare food than to order takeout, it was still clean and ideal for the job she had in mind. Untying the knot in one end of the condom, she emptied its contents into the food processor, then emptied an equal amount of baby laxative into it.

"What if the product's already been cut?" I asked.

"Of course it's been cut," Melinda said. "It's always cut, and we're cutting it a little more."

"A little?"

"Okay, a lot. But do you know who our customer base is? People who don't know any better. Cocaine for dummies—that's what we're selling."

She put the lid on the food processor and turned it on. The blades chopped away at the powder, blending the two quantities together to make two ounces of what we hoped our customers would be willing to call cocaine. After a few minutes, Melinda turned off the food processor and asked if I wanted the first taste. Just a little, I told her. The girls were due home at the end of the day, and I didn't want to be too wired when they walked through the door with their Norman Rockwell tales of Christmas in upstate New York with their father, his fiancée, and her billionaire parents.

"Speaking of which, do you think Chloe gets high?" Melinda asked.

"Don't even joke about it."

"I'm serious. With all that money, she could be a real gold mine."

"Do you know how much time she spends with the girls?"

"Not nearly as much as you do," Melinda said.

"That's different. I know what I'm doing. Besides, what am I supposed to say to her? *Hey, Chloe, want to buy some coke? Strictly between you and me, okay? Not a word to Roger.*"

"Fine," Melinda said. "Forget I mentioned it."

The good news according to Melinda was that almost everyone in suburbia was looking for a reliable source for controlled substances. Or maybe not *everyone*, she added on second thought, but enough of our neighbors to put some decent money in our pockets. Because, sure, there was always going into the city and trying to cop from some stranger, but that was dangerous. The police were always watching, and the dope could be tainted. You asked for cocaine, and you got drain cleaner. You asked for marijuana, and you got oregano soaked in bug spray. Of course, there was asking your kids to score, but then they knew you were using and you lost all credibility when you told them to say no. In addition to that, kids were another middleman, another pinch, another drop in quality. You sent them to school to procure an ounce of pot, and by the time you rolled your first joint, half of it had been replaced with clippings from the neighbor's lawn.

No, you couldn't trust your kids to score dope for you, Melinda said, and you couldn't bring yourself to risk a ride into the seedier parts of town, so you convinced yourself that you weren't interested in getting high and that anyone who could, in fact, get their hands on some halfway decent dope was a moral degenerate and deserved to go to jail.

Until, of course, you found a new connection in the suburbs.

When people learned that Melinda grew her own marijuana, the first thing they asked—always in jest, always in a whisper—was whether or not she ever sold any. When she said yes, they always insisted that they were only kidding—no offense to Melinda, of course. If she enjoyed getting high once in a while, who were they to judge? But while they were on the subject, how much did, say, an ounce of pot go for these days? From there, the sale was almost guaranteed, and the first question that more than a few of her clients asked when they made their first purchase was whether she knew where to get her hands on anything else.

Again, not that anyone was ever really interested.

Just out of curiosity.

The tray on Melinda's scale was fitted with a tiny chute, and each time she weighed out a gram, she tapped it into a tiny bag and handed it over so I could seal it. By the time we were finished, we had fifty-six packets, and Melinda reminded me that we were holding firm at forty dollars a gram. No matter how much anyone complained, she said, forty dollars was the going price, the price the market dictated. Since none of our clients knew what the market looked like, how it worked, or, for that matter, where to find it, they couldn't argue.

"Keep track of everything," Melinda added, snatching up a gram for herself. "Our primary concern is to pay for the first ounce so we can get another one, but let's not forget the big picture. This is our retirement fund, right? Our healthcare. If we do this right, we'll be able to afford getting old."

And to pay off our creditors in the here and now, I failed to add.

"Have you given any thought to where you're going to hide the product once you get it home?"

"In a lock box, I guess."

"No good. That's the first place they'll look."

"They?"

"The cops."

"Whatever happened to under the radar?"

"Of course we're under the radar, darling, but you can never be too safe. What you want to do is pick a few different places. Take an empty jelly jar and hide some of the product in your freezer."

"Talk about the first place they'll look."

"In the toilet tank, then. With the good silverware. Under your bed, taped to your box spring. Keep a few grams handy for when our clients stop by, and the rest you scatter throughout the house—places your kids won't go, unless you're one of those cool moms."

"Trust me," I said. "I'm anything but cool."

"I know," Melinda said. "That's why I love you."

Upstairs, the boys had found their way home and were beginning to tear the place apart. First came the tentative footsteps as they opened the front door, but once they ascertained that Melinda wasn't within immediate striking distance, the full-tilt mayhem began with a string of crunches and crashes and the sound of a lamp crashing up against a window fixture. When one of the boys let out a bloodcurdling shriek, I took it as my cue to leave.

"Take me with you," Melinda said as I zipped fifty-five packets of our house-blend into my purse. "Please, Audrey. I'm not wired for this. Living with boys, it's not what I was designed for."

"Who is, darling?" I said, feigning an air of sophistication. "At least when we're millionaire drug lords, you can hire a maid. Or better yet, send the little bastards off to military school."

"Promise?" Melinda said.

"I promise," I said as I headed home to find a suitable place to hide two ounces of cocaine from my daughters and the police.

HALFWAY HOME, I stopped at a light only to spot a state trooper rolling to a halt in the next lane over. The trick, of course, was to adopt a look that said I didn't have fifty-five packets of cocaine in my purse, but for the life of me, I couldn't remember what that look looked like, so I smiled at the trooper and gave him a nod.

Just be cool, I told myself as the light turned green.

Edging my mom-mobile up to just under the speed limit, I proceeded with caution, and the cop car fell in behind me. The trouble, I realized, was that I was driving too slow. If I really wanted to look like I had nothing to hide, I'd be speeding at least a little bit, so I laid a heavy foot on the gas, and the trooper followed suit.

Five, six, seven miles per hour over the speed limit.

Eight, nine, and pushing ten.

When I hit eleven, I knew I was probably going a little *too* fast, but slowing down would be conspicuous, so I sped up a little more, and as the needle verged on fifteen miles per hour over the speed limit, the lights on the police cruiser started flashing and the siren started to wail.

My stomach turned, my heart leapt into my throat, and my foot hovered over the gas pedal as I calculated the odds of successfully outrunning a state trooper in a no-holds-barred chase through the streets of suburbia. Realistically, the only thing I could do was pull over, so I hit my turn signal and started to slow down. The coke was in my purse, and my purse was sealed. He could write me a ticket, and he could take away my license—if it even came to that—but if my knowledge of the law—which came entirely from watching cop shows—was correct, then he had no right to look in my purse without just cause—whatever that was.

All I had to do was remember to breathe.

Rumbling to a stop on the side of the road, I was still rehearsing my lines when the cruiser zipped past me and sped toward a car fire or a bus wreck or some other highway-related emergency. My heart was still pounding as I nosed my car back into traffic, but by the time I pulled off the Golden Mile and started the final approach to my house, I was able to pull myself back together. All I had to do, I thought, passing the red-brick homes of my neighbors, all still decked out for the holiday season—lawns decorated with inflatable reindeer and snowmen and Santa Clauses, windows blazing with electric candles and flashing Christmas trees in the late-afternoon sunset—was find a few places to hide my coke, then sit back and wait for the money to start rolling in.

That was the plan, anyway, until I pulled up to my house to find Chloe's massive green Lincoln Navigator parked in my driveway, a withering wreath of evergreen branches tied to the center of its massive grille. Parking on the street, I peered through the front window of my house and saw Roger sitting in his old easy chair, sipping coffee from a steaming mug while Chloe cleaned up the wrapping paper that had been lying on my floor since her last visit. Still lost in the joy of the season, the girls had returned to adoring the gifts they'd abandoned two days earlier, and except for the lateness of the hour, I felt like a voyeur peeking in on someone else's Christmas morning.

"Take your coat off, Audrey," Roger said without rising from his seat as I opened the front door. "Make yourself at home."

"Thanks," I said, clutching my purse.

"Merry Christmas," Chloe said cheerfully. "Or Boxing Day, or whatever two days after Christmas is. Hope you don't mind that I decided to straighten up a little. All this paper—I just can't stand a cluttered house. Roger made some coffee if you want some."

"Thanks," I said again.

It was all too weird.

I felt like a guest.

I felt like an interloper.

I felt like a stranger in my own home.

"Girls, help your mother with her coat," Roger said. "And her purse."

"No," I said a little too quickly. "I mean, I can handle it. I wasn't expecting you guys until later."

"Sorry," Chloe said. "It was my fault. I love my parents, but I can only take them in small doses."

"Her real name is Chlotilde," Lily said. "And she hates it."

Roger stood to get me a cup of coffee and invited me to join him in the kitchen. He wanted to talk to me about something, he said casually.

"I know we already have an arrangement," Roger said when we were alone. "But I felt bad about taking the girls away from you on Christmas, so I was thinking that it would only be fair to let you have them on New Year's Eve."

"Do *they* know about this?" I said.

The coffee pot was three-quarters full, and I still hadn't taken off my coat.

"I may have mentioned it," Roger said.

- 149 -

"So I really don't have much of a choice, do I?"

"A choice?" Roger said. "I'm doing this for you."

"Please, Roger. What came up? Whose big party are you going to?"

"I only thought you'd like to spend a little more time with the girls. If you don't want them, I'll take them."

"Don't put words in my mouth."

"Either you want them or you don't," Roger said.

"Of course I want them," I said, because what else was I supposed to say? That I was planning to get high on New Year's Eve? That I wanted to do a few lines of coke with my new partner in crime and probably smoke some dope with her, too? In the end, however, I knew that taking the girls was for the best. Owen would be home from Vegas by then, and we could all spend a quiet evening together. No big parties, just the four of us ringing in the New Year with champagne and sparkling cider. "I just wish you wouldn't spring these things on me at the last minute. What if I had plans?"

"Bring the girls along," Roger said with a shrug. "You'd be surprised at how adult they can be."

"That isn't my point, Roger."

I laid my purse on the kitchen table and folded my coat over the back of a chair. Roger poured a cup of coffee and handed it to me. My table, my chair, my coffee, my cup, yet Roger seemed more comfortable in my kitchen than I did.

"By the way," he said. "We've settled on a date."

I told myself it didn't matter.

I told myself I didn't care.

Roger and Chloe had been engaged for months now, so the fact that they'd finally settled on a date came as no surprise at all. They deserved all the happiness in the world, I said as Roger started, once again, to tell me that he wanted the girls to be a part of the ceremony and that he'd be honored if I would attend as well. After all, he said before I could protest, we were still the best of friends, and nothing would make him happier than having me on hand to bear witness to what promised to be the happiest day of his life.

I held my coffee mug in both hands and didn't say anything for a long time. The coffee was hot, and I could feel the smooth ceramic surface of the mug burning the tips of my fingers. Even so, I didn't put the drink down, didn't alter my grip, didn't take the mug by its handle and blow across the steaming black surface of the beverage as every instinct in my body told me to do. Instead, I squeezed the mug and allowed the pain to pierce right through me and penetrate deep into my heart.

"What the hell," I eventually said. "I'll be there."

If he was expecting a more enthusiastic response, Roger didn't let on. Instead, he smiled and said that we'd have to go on another double-date sometime because he really enjoyed the last one, and so did Chloe.

"That Owen of yours seems like a decent guy," Roger said. "Really good for you, I mean. I'm glad you found him."

"You're right," I said. "He *is* good for me."

"And I hope he appreciates how wonderful you are."

"*Someone* has to," I said.

"Believe me," Roger said. "I do."

"Obviously."

"Come on, Audrey. You're not being fair. We fell out of love. It happens."

"In the best of marriages," I said. "I know."

"We'll always be friends," Roger said.

"The best," I added, in case he forgot. "Which is why I'm so happy for you, Roger."

I raised my mug to toast my ex's impending nuptials, and Roger did the same.

Sipping my coffee slowly, I savored the burn as it traveled down my throat.

CHAPTER NINETEEN

Iᴛ ᴡᴀs a minor miracle that I didn't get high as soon as Roger and Chloe left my house. I *did* have fifty-five packets of cocaine in my purse, after all, and the girls were still distracted by all of the Christmas gifts Roger and I had showered upon them in our quietly escalating war for their affections. Nobody would have thought twice if I picked up my purse and locked myself in the bathroom for a private little party of one, but getting coked up didn't even occur to me. Instead, I just thought about Owen and how badly I wanted him to be the perfect boyfriend Roger seemed to think he was.

Or not the perfect boyfriend so much as the perfect husband.

And the perfect father figure for the girls.

What I wanted was the total package: the house, the car, the career, the children, *and* the adoring husband. I wanted to be married again. I wanted to have a family—or at least the illusion of one—but I was haunted by the sneaking suspicion that if I wanted Owen to pop the question any time soon, he'd need more incentive than the Stack-O-Matic record player and scratched LPs I planned to give him as a belated Christmas gift. What I needed was to show him everything he stood to gain by making our arrangement a little more permanent, and a quiet New Year's Eve with the girls might just give me the perfect opportunity to showcase everything I had to offer—in theory, anyway.

When Melinda found out that I was effectively grounded for New Year's Eve, she asked me to take the boys off her hands for the evening. They'd bring their video games, she said, and I could feel free to lock them in the basement until the following morning.

"And seriously, don't think twice about throwing away the key," she added, her voice hollow and tinny on my new speakerphone. "In fact, if you can arrange to have them run away and join the circus, then so much the better."

I was working up a sweat on my Ultimax 3000, but I had yet to experience anything even close to a runner's high. Sure, I was a little lightheaded from the exertion, but to call it a high would have been extremely misleading. It was more like the early onset of senile dementia—a suspicion confirmed when I heard myself agree to take in Melinda's monsters.

"Of course, I *will* need a little something in return," I added.

"Goes without saying," Melinda said.

"Speaking of which, any bites on our business venture?"

"A nibble or two," Melinda said. "But I'll definitely do some schmoozing at the party."

Schmoozing. Next, I figured, we'd be printing up flyers and stuffing them into mailboxes up and down the Golden Mile: *Attention drug-starved moms, dads, and other denizens of suburbia! Sick of trekking downtown to score dope from unsavory characters in seedy neighborhoods? Come to the connection you can trust! Always pure, always safe—all the buzz with none of the worry! Keep a gram on hand for birthdays, anniversaries, and all of life's special occasions! Makes a great gift!*

My breathing was heavy, and the Ultimax 3000 whined and creaked under my weight.

"You sound like you're screwing," Melinda said. "Is Owen over?"

"No," I said. "It's Captain Panther. I have him bound and gagged."

"Sweet," Melinda said.

Though Owen and I hadn't seen each other in two weeks, we'd been leaving plenty of messages on each other's answering machines, each promising the other that no matter what else happened, we'd be together to ring in the new year. He wished he could see me before then, he said in one message, but he had a lot of work to catch up on at Nick's American Grill. I understood completely, I told his machine, and I hoped he didn't mind spending the evening with me and the girls. Of course not, Owen responded, though he'd probably need to make a perfunctory appearance at a party or two before joining us. No problem, I said. I'd be happy as long as he was standing next to me when the ball dropped on Times Square.

"Wouldn't miss it for the world," Owen said; but when I left a message about our special guests, he stopped calling altogether.

"What did you expect?" Lily said when she found out. "*Nobody* likes those boys."

"Yeah," Catherine said. "They're dirty."

"How would *you* know?" I asked. "You're not even in the same grade."

"Girls talk, Mom," Lily said. "Portia Finster's cousin is in Richie's class, and she said he got sent home five times with head lice."

"That's only a rumor."

"No it isn't," Catherine said. "I know their mother's a friend of yours, but everyone knows these kids are bad. You know the one in kindergarten? He takes his clothes off and runs around the classroom in his underwear."

"The oldest one has a mustache," Lily added. "And he's always talking about how his mom grows pot in her basement."

"Don't believe everything you hear," I said.

"I don't," Lily said. "But I told some of my friends that Dad used to be on pot, and they said it wasn't a big deal."

"You *told*?" Catherine asked.

"Portia Finster told me that her grandmother smokes pot because she has cancer, and her parents smoke it sometimes, too. She said she can always tell when they've been smoking because they just sit on the couch and smile and let her stay up late to watch TV. Eileen Donohue said her dad gets high because he's a lawyer and works so hard during the week, and Chelsea Rhenquist said that her aunt makes special cookies with marijuana in them and gives them to her mom and dad for Christmas."

"That doesn't make it okay," Catherine said. "And stop telling people that Dad was on pot. I don't want the whole world thinking we're like that."

"Like what?" I said.

"Druggies."

As if to confirm the rumors, a big, dopey grin spread across Melinda's face as her little monsters rolled into my house like a thicket of angry tumbleweeds on New Year's Eve. They were a little wound up, Melinda admitted as fists and elbows flew in every direction and little hands wrapped tenaciously around little necks. But with any luck at all, they'd strangle each other before midnight.

"If not, here's a little something to help you relax."

Melinda pulled a small box from her purse and handed it over just as the girls emerged from the kitchen to greet their guests.

"What is it?" Lily asked.

"A surprise," Melinda said.

The box was wrapped in gold paper and tied with a black, velvety ribbon. The heavy crease running down the center of Catherine's face made it clear that she was thinking about Chelsea Rhenquist's aunt and the special cookies she baked for the family every Christmas. If this was marijuana, my daughter's expression said, she was calling the cops and sending all of us straight to jail.

"Can we open it?" Lily asked, and Melinda's husband leaned on his car horn.

"Sure," Melinda said. "And make sure your mom shares."

I gave the ribbon a tentative tug and hoped that Melinda had the sense not to coerce me into opening a gift-wrapped box of weed in front of my daughters. As the metallic paper fell away, the boys stopped fighting long enough to see the box of chocolates their mother had given me, then resumed their battle with renewed vigor when it dawned on them that there would be more chocolate for everyone if there were fewer children around to eat it.

"Don't worry," Melinda said as her husband leaned on the horn a second time. "They'll crash in an hour or two."

Tossed momentarily from the tangle of boys, the youngest lifted his shirt to reveal a pudgy, round belly. The grin on his face said that his pants wouldn't be staying on for very long, either, so I gave the box of chocolates to Catherine and told her to take the boys down to the basement while I said goodbye to Melinda.

"No Owen tonight?" Melinda said as we stood out in the cold.

"He's coming later," I said. "He wanted to drop in on a few parties and say hi."

"I'm sorry, darling, was that *say* hi or *get* high?" Melinda asked, slipping me three joints. "You *did* warn him about my boys, didn't you?"

"It's not like that," I said. "We're both staying clean tonight, and I'm totally cutting back for my New Year's resolution."

"Smart move," Melinda said. "By the way, tonight's BYO, so a few people might stop by for a bit of our product before the party. Just remember this is a cash-only operation. The last thing we need is a paper trail of checks with dumb-ass memos like *cocaine, two grams* scrawled across the bottom."

A cry rang out from inside the house, and Alan leaned on his horn a third time. Taking this as her cue to leave me alone with her boys, Melinda shouted across my lawn for her husband to calm the fuck down as she sauntered back to him. Two minutes later, the first of my customers knocked on my door—a bald man with a neatly trimmed beard. He drove a car like mine, and his wife was waiting for him in the passenger seat.

"My wife knows Melinda?" the man said uncertainly as the woman in the car glanced nervously over her shoulder.

"Right," I said. "How much do you need?"

"Two—ounces?"

"Grams," I told him, feigning an air of expertise. "Wait here."

I made two more transactions before a weatherbeaten clunker pulled up to my curb and a woman with a raspy voice asked me for something called an eight-ball. Her hair was dirty and her cheeks were sunken, and when I asked her what an eight-ball was, she rolled her eyes and told me it was an eighth of an ounce.

"Sorry," I said. "This operation's strictly metric. What's that in grams?"

"I don't know," the woman said. "Three? Four?"

I told her the going price, and she said I'd have to front her until she got some money together.

"Sorry," I said. "Cash only."

"But I'm a friend of Melinda's."

"I don't doubt it."

"She said you'd be cool."

"She was wrong," I said.

The woman stared at me for a full minute before I told her to get off my front step.

"Or what?" she demanded.

"Or I'll call the police."

"Yeah, right," the woman said. "You're a fucking drug dealer."

"Look at me and look at you," I whispered. "Who looks like the fucking drug dealer?"

It was a bluff, but the woman wasn't willing to gamble. Muttering under her breath, she called me a bitch and shuffled back to her car.

"Who was that, Mom?" Lily asked as I locked the front door.

"No one," I said. "She had the wrong house."

"You were talking to her for a while."

"She wanted directions."

"She's still out there," Lily said, peering out the window. "She got in her car, but she's not leaving."

"She'll leave," I said, and I thought of the words Melinda used to describe our client base: *People like us.*

Suddenly remembering why she came upstairs in the first place, Lily said that when she last saw Richie, he was shaking a can of soda and threatening to open it.

"Damn," I said as the youngest of Melinda's children traipsed out of the kitchen in his underwear. "Which one's Richie?"

"The middle one," Lily said as the little boy informed me that he was almost naked.

Before I could tell the boy to put his clothes on, there was a knock at the door, and I reminded myself that I was making easy money—over a hundred bucks in the space of ten minutes.

People like us, I reminded myself. Doctors, lawyers, teachers. People who liked to catch the occasional buzz. No one sketchy. No one to worry about.

There was a second knock, a louder knock, and I thought for a second about buying a gun. Wishing, at the very least, for a door chain, I opened the door an inch only to find Owen looking back at me with a bottle of champagne in his hand.

"For a second, I thought you'd gone to the party," he said as I let him into the house.

"I wish."

"I'm in my underwear," Scottie shouted, bouncing on the sofa as if it were a trampoline. "Richie made his soda explode, and Donnie punched him in the arm. Catherine yelled at Donnie, and Donnie called her a stupid bitch. Catherine said gentlemen shouldn't talk like that, and Donnie said if he was any bigger, he'd beat the crap out of her, but Catherine said that if he went any longer without taking a bath, they'd have to sell him to the zoo and make him live with the monkeys."

"Leave while you can," I said to Owen.

"Don't tempt me."

Handing over the champagne, Owen scooped Scottie into his arms and told Lily to follow him down to the basement where I heard a playful adult growl and a chorus of giddy screams. Turning to close the door, I realized that another customer was standing on my doorstep—a man in a black cap, who, I realized when I saw the elongated pink PT Cruiser parked out front, had to be somebody's driver. Somebody, that is, who could only get a limousine on trade.

"Six," he said, handing over three crisp hundred-dollar bills.

It was more than my asking price, but I took the guy's money and told him to say hi to Jerry and Svetlana for me. If things kept up the way they were going, I'd sell out before midnight and have enough cash in the house to put a decent-sized dent in my Christmas bill.

"Your gentlemen callers are a real handful," Owen said, already disheveled as he emerged from the basement. "But I think I have the solution."

He pulled out his car keys, and I asked if he was leaving.

"I told you not to tempt me," Owen said. "But no. I just need to grab a few CDs from my car, and we'll all sit down for a nice, long evening of jazz with the masters. A bit of Miles. A bit of Coltrane. A bit of Dizzy Gillespie. Trust me, they'll love it."

"Melinda's kids? Good luck."

Before he could leave, I grabbed Owen's wrist and led him to the dining room where the Stack-O-Matic turntable and a collection of vinyl LPs awaited his approval. The LPs weren't exactly vintage, I warned him as he tore away the green and red wrapping paper. They were just old. But I had a chance to listen to one or two tracks, and they sounded great—a few scratches here and there, some pops and clicks, but the imperfections just added to the experience.

"Oh," he said in a way that only men can, and only when confronted with gifts from the heart. "It's great."

"You don't like it," I said.

"No, I love it."

"But?"

"It's just that I already have such an extensive collection," Owen said as my heart sank. "And the sound quality on these old reissues is always a bit muddy."

Before we could discuss the issue any further, there was another knock at the door: Vic and Ellie.

"I heard you were holding," Vic said loud enough for the whole neighborhood to hear.

Owen looked at me quizzically.

"A hundred bucks a gram," I said, bluffing again.

"Our mutual friend said fifty."

Christ, even Melinda was trying to hose the guy.

"That's for our regular blend," I said. "But you don't want that."

"Yeah," Owen said, catching on. "You want the good stuff."

Vic looked me in the eye, then turned to Owen.

"How good?" he asked.

"Primo. Practically pharm grade."

"Pharm grade?" Ellie asked.

"Pharmacy," Vic said dismissively. "I'll give you seventy-five."

"Don't ask *me*," Owen said. "Audrey's the boss."

"Please," I said. "If I let you get away with seventy-five, then everyone's going to want seventy-five. It isn't good for business."

"Like I'll tell anyone," Vic said, jiggling his keys in frustration.

"Are you kidding?" Owen said. "You find a dime in the sofa cushions and it's on the evening news."

"Eighty," Vic said. "That's my final offer."

"Ninety," I said. "Or you buy the cheap stuff."

"Mom?" Catherine said, sneaking up behind me.

Spinning around, I explained that Vic and Ellie were only friends before Catherine could even ask the question.

Dropping by to wish us a happy New Year, Owen added.

Vic and Ellie smiled and waved at Catherine, who said hello and informed me that Donnie was holding one of his brothers in a headlock and wouldn't let go unless she gave him some chocolate.

"Then give it to him," I said.

"But that would be giving in."

"Good point," Vic said. "Never negotiate with terrorists."

"Just give Richie some candy," I told her.

"Donnie."

"Whatever. Just keep them busy for a few more minutes. Owen has something special planned for everyone."

"Can I have a hint?"

"It's musical."

"Oh," Catherine said. "Jazz."

My daughter turned to leave, and Vic resumed his negotiations:

"We were saying eighty."

"I thought it was ninety," his wife said, and he gave her the evil eye.

"That's right," I said. "Ninety. Take it or leave it."

"Okay," Vic said. "Ninety. But I'm only buying a single gram." He counted out nine tens and folded them into my hand.

"I'll take one, too," Ellie said, reaching into her purse.

"See what I'm talking about?" I said as I took her money. "That's twenty dollars I'm out. If anyone else comes around saying they heard it was ninety, I'll know exactly who to blame."

Disgruntled, Vic put his arm around his wife and ushered her into the cold. When I closed the door behind them, Owen shook his head in disbelief and pulled me close so I could feel his heart thumping in his chest.

"My girlfriend the drug dealer," he said. "This is pretty hot."

"Connection," I said. "And I'm only in it for the money."

"Even better. Feel like sampling the goods?"

"Not around the girls," I said. "Besides, I'm playing it clean and sober tonight."

"Just a taste," Owen said. "A tiny, tiny taste."

I was tempted, but I could already hear the kids barreling up the basement steps for their tutorial on the finer points of jazz. As everyone settled in around the ersatz vintage turntable, Owen asked if anyone knew anything about the subject, and one of Melinda's boys volunteered that *jazz* was just another word for *crap* while another whined that he was already bored. Undaunted, Owen plowed ahead. Even if there was no hope of getting through to the boys, he knew which buttons to push for the girls and had them hooked in minutes.

"Nobody even listens to jazz," Lily said. "So what's the point?"

"I know exactly what you mean," Owen admitted. "These days, it's mainly just people with money. *And* intellectuals, I suppose. No one who really matters, though."

"How much money?" Lily wanted to know.

"Intellectuals?" Catherine asked. "You mean like college professors?"

If Owen could have worked pro-wrestlers and ninjas into his pitch, he might have reeled the boys in as well, but all they seemed interested in was punching each other and drowning themselves in high-octane cola. Barely three minutes had passed when all three boys spun away from the dining room table in search of a less constricting field of battle.

A vase or a lamp or a picture frame would fall to the floor with a crash, and Owen would note that certain pressings of vintage recordings brought in hundreds and sometimes thousands of dollars at auction or that, as he'd told me once before, people had been listening to Miles Davis' *Birth of the Cool* at the wrong speed for years without even knowing it. Soaking up the trivia, Catherine and Lily barely noticed when I'd disappear out the front door for minutes at a time to deal with my clients.

Three tracks into a John Coltrane recording, the doorbell rang and I spotted Scottie running through my front yard without any clothes on. He was naked, he shouted as a man in sunglasses tried to shake me down, demanding that I give him a gram of my hundred-dollar blend for the paltry sum of ninety dollars. When I asked where he heard that ninety was the going rate, the man said that a mutual friend of ours couldn't keep his mouth shut. Meanwhile, Scottie was running circles around us, screaming into the night air that Donnie and Richie had stolen his clothes and that, as a result, he was now naked, naked, NAKED! So I did the deal, grabbed the boy by the arm and, ninety dollars richer, dragged the child back into the house where he wouldn't draw so much attention.

Inside, Donnie was trying to press an imprint of Richie's face into my living room carpet, and my coffee table was lying on its side. Both of them shrugged in unison when I demanded to know where their brother's clothes were, so I let go of Scottie and threw all of my weight into pulling the other two apart. When a stray elbow caught me in the stomach, I fell backwards and cursed at the boys. What the hell was wrong with them, I demanded? Why couldn't they behave like normal human beings? And how did their mother put up with them when they were always acting like animals?

Both boys shrugged again as Scottie, still naked, jumped up and down on the sofa.

The springs popped and creaked.

The cushions were turning brown with dirty little footprints.

Donnie resumed his efforts at killing his brother, and somebody rang the doorbell.

"I'll be right back," I said to Owen and the girls after clandestinely selling another gram of cocaine to a complete stranger. "I just need a minute to myself."

"Uh-oh," Owen said. "You boys are in trouble."

I marched upstairs to the bathroom and locked the door behind me. I left the lights off, but turned on the exhaust fan. Owen could deal with any customers who turned up, I figured as I used a long candle lighter to fire up one of the joints Melinda had given me.

Climbing up onto the toilet seat, I steadied myself with a hand against the medicine cabinet and blew smoke directly into the exhaust fan, hoping no one would get the sudden urge to pee while I was busy getting high. Holding the smoke in my lungs, I thought about Scottie running around naked in my front yard and started to giggle. It was all pretty funny, I had to admit. The broken lamps, the wrecked sofa, the spilled soda that was probably congealing into battery acid on my basement floor as the boys continued to pursue their campaign of mass destruction throughout my house. Not funny, exactly, but, okay, amusing when I looked at the big picture. Though I tried to do the math, the numbers wouldn't stay in my head. All I knew was that I'd sold a bunch of coke and was now a little more flush with cash because of it. More important, the absolute mayhem of living with boys—even on a temporary basis—reminded me of how lucky I was to have daughters. I'd have to tell them that, I thought, flushing the end of my joint down the toilet. I'd have to tell them how much I loved them and how glad I was that they were girls.

After hiding the remaining two joints in my jewelry box, I went downstairs to join Owen and the kids in their roundtable discussion of jazz. The coffee table had been righted by then, and the boys were sitting around the record player with sullen looks on their faces.

"Don't you boys have something to say?" Owen asked.

"Yeah," Lily said. "Don't you have something to say to my mother?"

"Sorry," Donnie mumbled.

"Yeah," Richie said. "Sorry we stole Scottie's clothes."

"I was naked," Scottie said.

It was okay, I told them. They couldn't help it. They were boys. They were animals. They were raised in a barn. *That* was why they couldn't control themselves, I explained, and when the girls laughed, I told them not to. The boys were our guests, I said. Even if they didn't know how to behave like civilized human beings, we had an obligation to treat them with dignity and respect.

Satisfied that he had restored the status quo, Owen laid the needle back on the John Coltrane record they were discussing, and I felt the music glide over my skin, soft as silk. The notes, I thought. I could reach out and touch them if I wanted to. I could almost smell them, almost taste them. Closing my eyes, I grinned and started to drift away, but Catherine's voice pulled me back down to Earth.

"The ball," she said. "It's about to drop."

"In five minutes," Lily added.

"Come on," Owen said. "We don't want to miss it."

I opened my eyes, and they were all staring at me.

"Sorry," I said. "I must have drifted off."

My face felt like rubber, like I was wearing a mask, and no matter how hard I tried, I couldn't shake my stupid grin.

"You smell like my mom," one of the boys said.

I wanted to respond, but I was afraid to open my mouth.

What if I said the wrong thing?

What if I admitted that I was high?

What if I started to giggle again?

I could feel my thoughts coming and going like solid objects. Like they were made of lead. Like trains on a track. One rolled in, and another rolled out, and for the life of me I couldn't hold on to any of them until one rumbled in louder than the rest:

A quick line, and I'd be fine. The coke would burn through the haze, and I wouldn't even be breaking my resolution because, technically, the new year hadn't started yet.

All eyes were glued to the television, so I grabbed my purse and headed for the bathroom where I tapped some coke onto the countertop, took a twenty from the wad of bills I'd accumulated over the course of the evening, rolled it into a straw, and snorted as hard as I could.

"You're missing it, Mom," Lily called from downstairs. "The ball's dropping. It's a whole new year."

Rubbing my nose, I went down to the living room where Owen handed me a glass of champagne and touched a finger to my nostril.

"I thought you were laying off," he whispered, licking the residue he came away with.

Smiling coyly, I sipped my champagne while the glittering ball fell on Times Square and strobe lights flashed across the midnight sky.

A whole new year.

A whole new life.

My world was wonderful, and I could do anything.

CHAPTER TWENTY

Iᴛ's ᴇᴀʀʟʏ March, and the only thing separating the gray sky from the endless line of dull, concrete shopping centers below is a partial ceiling of brightly colored signage that stretches from somewhere deep inside my rearview mirror to an ever receding point on the road ahead. Buckled into the backseat of my Toyota, Catherine sits with an open book in her lap while Lily, eyes wide behind her Chrissy Qualtieri sunglasses, gazes past the parking lots and into the windows of the shops where she dreams of spending money one day. On the stereo, a jungle beat is percolating over a breathy flute as I hit the turn signal and make the detour that twists my older daughter's face into a mask of defeat and unapologetic disapproval.

"Don't worry," I tell her, failing to make eye contact in the rearview. "I'll only be a minute."

"Are you buying our lunch at Fatso Ratso's?" Lily asks as I pull into one of a dozen empty parking spaces in front of the restaurant. "Because if you are, we need a note so we can use the microwave in the teachers' lounge. Brandi Albertini always brings spaghetti in a Ziploc bag, and Mrs. Woodring lets her heat it up in the teachers' lounge because Brandi's grandmother is Italian and she's the one who makes Brandi's lunch. She keeps a plastic fork in her desk and puts her spaghetti in a little bowl, and every day she has to give Mrs. Woodring a note that says she needs to use the microwave. Some other kids use the microwave, too, but not as much as Brandi, and they always have notes, so if you're buying us a pizza, you'll need to write us a note."

"She's not buying us a pizza," Catherine says.

"How do you know?"

"Think about it. What are we supposed to do with a pizza? Carry it around all day? Put it in the closet with the coats and lunchboxes? We'll look like idiots."

"They make small ones," Lily says.

"Trust me. We're not getting a pizza."

The flute trills up and down over the frenetic clatter of a woodblock and high hat as Nina Simone begins to hum and my heart pounds to the beat of the heavy drums. The song is called See-Line Woman, and it scares me just a little bit because it's dark and threatening like a thunderstorm and I don't really know what the words mean.

It's also the song I was listening to the first time I tried cocaine.

"Mommy just needs to pick up some trade dollars for work, baby doll," I say, killing the song as I cut the engine. "I'll be back before you know it."

"I've heard that before," Catherine mutters, but I pretend not to hear.

The line about the trade dollars isn't a lie, exactly. It's a small detail that fits neatly into the bigger picture of why it's so important for me to stop at Fatso Ratso's Pizza Depot so early in the morning.

Despite the early hour and complete lack of patrons, the depot is buzzing with the sound of coin-operated video games trying desperately to be noticed. Lost in the cacophony, I jump when a woman in a red apron asks if she can help me with anything. Her round, pockmarked face is framed with brittle, gray hair, and the first thing that occurs to me when I look at her is that someone must have assembled her out of leftover pizza dough. Nearly shouting over the noise of the game room, I tell the woman that my name is Audrey Corcoran, and I'm with *Eating Out*.

"The magazine," I add when she fails to comprehend my meaning. "Vic Charles sent me to collect on your bill."

"You'll have to talk to the manager about that."

"Fine," I say. "Where's the manager?"

"He's not in right now. He usually takes Mondays off."

"Must be nice."

"Trevor works very hard," the woman says. "Six days out of seven. If he wants to take Mondays off, I won't be the one to stop him."

"Let me guess. You're Trevor's mom."

The woman opens her mouth, but I hold up a hand before she can speak.

"Listen," I tell her. "Let's forget about the bill. Pay it, don't pay it. I honestly don't care. I'm really just here to see Michael. Is *he* in?"

"That depends," the woman says, inching away from me. "Black Michael or white Michael?"

Rubbing my temples, I close my eyes and try to tune out the maddening rumble of the video games. Usually I'm not the one who procures the package, but Melinda has a meeting with the school counselor this morning to discuss her youngest son's propensity for disrobing in the classroom. The only time I've seen the Michael in question, he was dressed like a giant rat and strumming an inflatable banjo. How to read that detail as a sign of his race eludes me at the moment, so I sigh and tell the doughy woman that I don't know how to answer her question. All I know is that he's Giant-Fucking-Rat-Suit Michael, and he has something for me.

"That sounds like white Michael," the woman says. "We haven't seen him in days."

"What do you mean?" I ask. "Is he on vacation or something?"

"No," the woman says. "He's on the schedule, but he hasn't been in."

"You must have a number," I say. "Someplace I can reach him?"

"You'd have to talk to Trevor about that."

"Wonderful," I say. "Have you always been this useless?"

This is a bad sign. If Michael is missing, then the only coke I have left is what's in my purse and the emergency stash I keep in my jewelry box. Personally, I can take it or leave it, but I have more than a few friends who count on me for the stuff lately. If they find out that I can't get my hands on good product any-more, they'll either check into rehab or find another connection. In either case, there's no way in hell I'll ever be able to pay down my credit card bills, and I seriously doubt the bank will let me use gift certificates from Fatso Ratso's Pizza Depot to make my monthly mortgage payment.

"Did you get us a pizza?" Lily asks when I slide behind the wheel of my car.

"Do you see a pizza, baby doll?"

I turn the key. Nina Simone picks up where she left off. I look in the mirror and realize that I'm a daughter short.

"Where's your sister?" I ask.

"She couldn't wait anymore. She said she was going to walk."

"And you let her?"

"She's older than I am."

We're less than a mile from Good Shepherd, but all I can think about are the four lanes of rush-hour traffic barreling down the boulevard that Catherine needs to cross in order to get to school. Throwing the car into gear, I peel out of the parking lot, and car horns scream in all directions. The trick in this instance, I inform Lily, is to avoid eye contact with my fellow motorists so they get the impression that I didn't see them. Which, as it turns out, is the exact strategy Catherine uses when I catch up with her two Exxon stations, a Best Buy, and a Honda dealership later.

"Catherine," I call across the passenger seat as I slow down and lower the window. "Catherine, get in the car."

"I'm not getting in the car, Mom."

She marches at a steady pace, eyes fixed on some invisible point in the distance.

My car crawls along the curb, snarling traffic for miles behind me.

"You're not walking to school, Catherine," I shout over the surge of angry horns and obscenities erupting all around us. "It isn't safe."

"It's three blocks away," Catherine says. "I think I'll survive."

"Catherine," I say again, hoping that the repeated utterance of her name will trigger enough guilt to make her do as I say. "You're not setting a very good example for your sister."

Much to the chagrin of the bearded little goat-boy riding up my ass in a tricked-out Chevy Nova, this last observation makes my older daughter stop in her tracks, thus forcing me to brake in kind.

"A good example?" Catherine demands. "You can't be serious."

The goat-boy leans on his horn and lets out a string of expletives.

Lily unbuckles her seat belt and turns around to wave at him.

Hanging her head in sheer mortification, Catherine grumbles her way into the passenger seat and slams the door behind her.

"Just drive," she says. "I'm late enough as it is. Lily, buckle your seat belt."

CHAPTER TWENTY-ONE

"I DON'T know what you said to that bastard's mother this morning, but he is *pissed*," Vic says before I've so much as hung up my coat. "I had to promise him a full-page write-up on Fatso Ratso's Cheezy Bread to keep him from yanking the back page on us. I'm thinking fun and sexy, and I need it to go in the next issue."

"Sexy breadsticks," I say. "Classy. You do remember it's a family restaurant, right? Little kids. Video games. Wading pools filled with plastic balls and the overflow of dirty diapers."

"I understand that," Vic says. "But where do you think families come from?"

"The suburbs?" I ask.

"Sex," Vic says, punctuating his pronouncement with a slow and steady series of karate chops to his cluttered desk. "Families come from sex. No sex, no families. It's as simple as that."

I'm tempted to ask Vic if he's holding, but I know he'll only lecture me if I do—on self-control, on moderation, on separating work from play. He's seen me go from being the poster-mom for headshaking disapproval of all things fun to his once-in-a-blue-moon coke connection, and nothing gives him greater satisfaction than reminding me that I used to be good. Even so, the prospect of laying out the magazine without a little help of the chemical variety is too much to bear, so I slip into the grimy, brown bathroom and dip once more into my dwindling supply of cocaine before settling in to get the job done.

As far as I know, *Eating Out* is the last publication on the planet that hasn't made the leap from light tables and Exacto blades to Photoshop and Quark. What this means in practical terms is that twice a month, it's my responsibility to paste long strips of text onto thick sheets of cardstock and make sure they all line up so flawlessly that the average reader can only assume that a computer did the job. Before I got into coke, this process took up the better part of the morning, but now I can knock out an issue in under an hour—headlines, illustrations, advertisements, and all. God only knows what I'll do if my friend in the rat suit never returns.

To keep my buzz going, I tune the radio to a jazz station and crank the volume. Hard bop—Art Blakey and the Jazz Messengers performing A Night in Tunisia. Lee Morgan and Wayne Shorter trade soaring licks on the trumpet and sax respectively as Bobby Timmons plunks away on a skittering, nervous piano. And, of course, there's Blakey himself bashing at his drums like there's no tomorrow for nearly twelve minutes straight—perfect for pissing Vic off.

"Will you turn that the fuck down?" Vic says, barging into my office. "I can barely think out there."

"So what else is new?"

"Funny," Vic says. "By the way, your boyfriend just pulled up."

"Owen?" I say.

"No," Vic says, making a pair of devil horns with his fingers. "The Captain. That guy hangs on like a bad case of the clap."

"He's not my boyfriend," I say.

"And you think Owen is?"

"We've been dating since September," I insist.

"And you were married to Roger for ten years. What's the difference?"

There's a knock, and Vic curses under his breath before I can tell him to go fuck himself. Taking a peek at the front door, I see our visitor pressing his nose to the window to get a better view of the sales office. Lingering in his line of vision for a split-second too long, I retreat into the shadows of my cubbyhole, then inch forward again, smiling as if I couldn't be happier to see the man.

"Audrey!" he says, tapping on the window with an elegantly manicured fingernail. "Audrey! It's Chris! Chris Parker!"

"What should I do?" I hiss at Vic through gritted teeth.

"What *can* you do?" Vic asks. "Tell him you're on your way out. Tell him your house is on fire. Lay down and play dead for all I care. But whatever you do, don't tell him I'm here. That guy's a wacko, and I want nothing to do with him."

The good news is that my gentleman caller is in his civvies today and not the pointy-eared half-mask he was once known to wear in his capacity as America's favorite just-say-no superhero. The bad news is that he can't take a hint.

"I've been thinking a lot about my comeback special," he says, clutching a three-ring binder under his arm as I reach for my coat. "I know we have a few weeks before the Good Shepherd gig, but I'm really getting pumped."

Maybe it's his tousled mop of sandy, blonde hair. Maybe it's the clear gaze of his big, blue eyes. Or maybe it's the chiseled pecs, abs, and buns that don't need the help of a vulcanized rubber costume to complete the illusion, however preposterous, that he may, in fact, be a superhero, but being in the same room with the man makes me ashamed of who I've become in the space of just a few months.

"Glad to hear it," I say. "I'm actually on my way out."

"I only need a minute. Did you know that Elvis had a comeback special?"

"Of course," I say. "Where do you think I got the idea?"

I still haven't seen him in costume yet, but the eight-by-ten full-color promotional shots of the man in his purple tights, flowing yellow cape, and golden epaulettes have ruined me forever. If I live to be a hundred, I'll never think of him as Chris Parker, mild-mannered purveyor of overpriced exercise equipment. To me, he'll always be the Captain.

"So I'm thinking that if it worked for him, it'll work for me, right?"

"It only stands to reason."

"Not on the same scale, of course."

"No, of course not."

"But it never hurts to dream."

The Captain opens his binder, and I pull on my coat to let him know that I really do have somewhere to go.

"You've contacted the media, right?"

"Wheels are in motion," I say, angling for the door.

"Do they want to see my bio? My set list? Lyric sheets?"

"I'll let you know if it comes to that."

"What about interviews? Should I do them in character, or is that too much?"

"We'll play it by ear," I say, inching forward despite his reluctance to step back.

"And the profile you promised?"

"In the works."

The radio in my office is still playing—swing, heavy on the drums. My guess is Gene Krupa, but the grinding of my teeth is too loud for me to say for sure. Reaching into my coat pocket, I rattle my keys, but it fails to spook the Captain the way it spooks the neighborhood cats, and as we continue to rock back and forth in an awkward shuffle, I wonder if I'll ever reach the door.

"I talked to my manager at Dr. Treadwell's," he says. "And she's open to corporate sponsorship."

"Wonderful," I say.

"She'll have to run it by some people first, but she's very optimistic."

"Who wouldn't be?"

With my store of noncommittal responses running dangerously low, I sidestep the Captain and reach for the doorknob.

"One more thing," the Captain says as I step into the daylight.

"Yeah?" I say without slowing down.

"Thanks," the Captain says.

"For what?"

"Believing in me, I guess. If not for you, my tights would still be in mothballs."

"No problem," I say, unlocking my car and refusing to look at the man. "It was nothing."

"No, Audrey, you really made a difference in my life."

"Don't say that," I tell him.

"You did."

"I have to go."

I shut the door and start the car. Glancing at my mirror as I pull onto the road, I see America's favorite just-say-no superhero theatrically flexing his muscles and gritting his teeth by way of goodbye as he grows smaller and smaller in the distance behind me.

CHAPTER TWENTY-TWO

I ANSWER my cell phone, and Melinda asks if I've picked up the dry cleaning. It's her clever way of inquiring as to whether or not our friend in the rat suit came through with the package this morning—in case of a wiretap, in case she's on speakerphone, in case she hits the wrong button on her speed dial and asks the school secretary if she's holding. The only problem with this system is that we haven't ironed out all the wrinkles yet, so when I tell Melinda that the dry cleaning isn't ready, there's nowhere for the conversation to go but into the realm of the literal.

"What do you mean it's not ready?"

"Our friend wasn't there."

"So you're saying what? The dry cleaner was closed?"

"No, the dry cleaner was open, but our friend wasn't working."

"That's impossible," Melinda says. "Our friend *is* the dry cleaner."

"I'm confused," I say. "Is the dry cleaner a person or an establishment?"

"He's the person who works in the establishment."

"Michael."

"Yes, Michael. The guy in the rat suit."

"He wasn't working this morning."

"So who did you talk to?"

"I'm pretty sure it was Trevor's mother."

"Trevor?"

"The dry cleaner."

"Wait, I thought Michael was the dry cleaner."

"No, Michael only works for the dry cleaner, and Trevor's mother hasn't seen him in days."

"That's not good," Melinda says.

"No," I say. "I don't imagine it is, but we'll figure something out, right?"

It's lunchtime, and the boulevard is flooded with vehicles. Ahead of me, a line of cars is waiting to make a left turn into a Taco Bell parking lot. Behind me, the bearded little goat-boy from earlier this morning is still stringing expletives together behind the wheel of his tricked-out Chevy Nova. If the area weren't so insular, I'd worry that this was more than a mere coincidence, but there's no need that isn't met by the myriad of supermarkets, drugstores, and shopping malls that populate the Golden Mile, and therefore no real reason for anyone to travel beyond its limits. Following this line of thinking to its inevitable conclusion, it's not unreasonable for me to assume that I'll be seeing the same ten or twenty faces in my rearview mirror for the rest of my life, and if the bearded little goat-boy is one of them, then it's a cross I have to bear—which isn't to say I have to do it gladly.

"Fuck you, asshole!" I scream, making eye contact with the goat-boy as he leans on his horn and his face turns red. "You think you're special? You think you're the only one with some-where to go?"

"Who are you talking to?" Melinda asks.

"Some asshole," I say. "Don't worry about it. How was your meeting?"

"Meeting?"

"With the school counselor. Don't tell me you forgot about it."

"Scottie takes his clothes off. It's no big deal."

"You didn't go, did you?"

"He's a kid. He'll grow out of it."

"Or he'll grow up to be a pervert."

"Whatever. What do we do about the dry cleaning?"

"You don't know anyone else? Someone who can hook us up?"

"What am I? Some kind of kingpin? Rat Boy was an accident. I ran into him at a party. He knew some people who knew some people. He was young and stupid, and he took risks that no one with any sense would take."

"What risks?" I ask.

"What risks do you think? Watch the news. You'll see I'm right. Six-foot rat found dead on the banks of the Delaware."

"You think he got whacked?"

"*Whacked?* This isn't a game, Audrey. These people don't fuck around."

"Then what's our plan?" I ask, realizing perhaps a few months too late that all of Melinda's talk about being a connection and staying under the radar was nothing but a front.

"You're the Catholic school girl," Melinda says. "Get down on your knees and pray."

CHAPTER TWENTY-THREE

I CAN do this, I tell myself, standing in the center of the kitchen where Roger and I told our daughters that the only life they knew wasn't good enough for us, that we were looking to make a few changes, and that, as a result, we needed to shake their world to its foundation. Sure, every second I spend in here reminds me of the family that used to be mine, but it's not like the room is haunted or anything. It just needs a good cleaning, and all I need to do is focus on the task at hand. If I start with an easy project like replacing the liner in the trash can or taking the dishes that Catherine washed this morning and putting them back in the cabinet where they belong, I can move onto bigger projects like tearing down the miniature city of appliances sprawled across my countertop.

Anchored by the utilitarian simplicity of the Krups coffeemaker I've been toting from one life to the next since college, the loose affiliation of tiny skyscrapers and Soviet-era municipal buildings straddling both sides of my kitchen sink consists of the gleaming silver dome of the Chef's Choice International electric teakettle Roger brought to the relationship because he preferred tea to coffee, the stolid linebacker bulk of the white Cuisinart food processor we received as a gift on our wedding day, the upright servile dignity of the two-speed Waring blender that arrived shortly thereafter, the expansive Black and Decker toaster oven that's always been too big to make toast but too small to cook anything anyone might conceivably call a meal, the toaster we bought when we got fed up with the inadequacies of the toaster oven, the hunter green KitchenAid stand mixer my mother gave me when Catherine was born, the boxy bread maker whose tendency to waddle forward while in use prompted Roger to name it Bread Man Walking, the vaguely phallic Primo drink frother designed to fit into any drawer as long as the drawer is completely empty, the five-liter refrigerated Heineken beer tap that Roger purchased mere months before our divorce, and the nickel-plated espresso maker I ordered a little over a week ago, opting in a fit of impatient anticipation for overnight delivery but failing to make use of the machine beyond placing it on the countertop among its theoretically practical but rarely employed cousins. If the bathroom is the most dangerous room in the house, then the kitchen is easily the most depressing.

What I really need is more shelf space.

What I really need are wider countertops.

What I really need is a bigger house.

Since none of these is forthcoming, I slouch up the stairs to my bedroom where I change into my pajamas and climb under the covers, muscles heavy with fatigue. Closing my eyes, I feel a chill spread from my heart to the tips of my toes and fingers, and I imagine my body turning to ice. Blue lips, frosty skin. Hours pass like days until I hear the sounds of the girls coming home from school. First, the diesel-engine rattle of the school bus. Next, the *whoosh* and *thunk* of the front door opening and closing, followed by the light thunder of book bags falling to the hardwood floor. Finally, the off-rhythm patter of little feet in the dining room and kitchen, the near-harmony of Catherine and Lily calling out to let me know that they've arrived home safely, that they'll be starting their homework in a moment, that they want to know exactly where I am.

"Mom?" Catherine says, tapping gently on my bedroom door with the tips of her fingers when experience and process of elimination tell her where I have to be. "Are you okay?"

"I'm fine, baby," I tell her, though I barely have the energy to say it. "I think I'm coming down with something."

"Again?"

"I took out the trash," I say. "And put a new liner in the trash can."

"That's great, Mom."

"I wanted to do more."

"It's okay, Mom."

"I wanted to clean the kitchen."

"I'll take care of it."

"And the rest of the house, too."

"Don't worry, Mom. Just get better."

"You know I love you, right?"

"I know, Mom."

"And Lily, too. I'll always love both of you."

"Mom?" Catherine says, and the pause that follows fills me with dread. "I want you to get better, okay?"

CHAPTER TWENTY-FOUR

P<small>ER USUAL</small>, Vic calls a staff meeting and starts tearing everyone a new asshole as soon as the latest issue of *Eating Out* hits the street. We need more ads, more photos, more color, he seethes from within his acrid cloud of cigarette smoke. On top of that, *someone* placed a pair of quarter-page ads from competing seafood houses at the bottom of the same page. That the article above the ads is a profile of a chef that a third restaurant pinched from one of the other two is only icing on the cake, and Vic blames me for the fact that he now has to bump each of them up to half a page at no extra charge to make up for the error.

"My fault?" I say. "You're the one who blue-lined the damn thing."

"For Christ's sake, Audrey, you're the fucking editor. It's your job to catch these things. It's your job to look out for the best interests of the magazine."

"Asshole," Melinda mouths, rolling her eyes when Vic isn't looking.

"Prick," Jerry coughs, a fist in front of his mouth as Vic paces the floor like an angry general.

"It's okay," Raj whispers, sliding his chair incrementally closer to mine and laying what I imagine is supposed to be a comforting hand on my lap as Svetlana files her nails and a new guy with red splotchy skin and a buzz cut takes notes in a spiral-bound notepad. "I'm here for you if you need me."

"Thanks," I whisper back, brushing his hand away. "But I think I'll manage."

We know the meeting is over when Vic stops midsentence, raises his hands in frustration, and slumps into the wooden swivel chair behind his desk. As we all retreat wordlessly to our respective private corners of the office, I check the messages on my cell phone and close the flimsy door that separates me from everyone else.

Evenly split between polite inquiries from the Captain about my progress on arranging for the press to cover his just-say-no comeback special and a wide range of poorly coded requests for cocaine, my inbox plays out like a schizophrenic map of my life. The Captain wants to know if I thought to call the local network TV affiliates. Holly Park, who does Melinda's nails, wants to know if I'm expecting snow anytime soon. The Captain asks if I think *USA Today* might be interested in running a piece on his efforts at turning kids onto fitness. James McChesney, who manages a tile outlet on the Golden Mile, says he enjoyed meeting my gram and would love to see her again sometime. The Captain wonders if we should buy some time on public access cable or post a mini-movie on the internet. My *gram*, James McChesney adds in a second message in case I didn't catch the reference the first time, was a hell of a woman, white hair and all. The Captain asks whether he should open the show with his old standard, Panther Time, or shake things up by starting with his newly penned Drug Free in the School Zone. Bunny Hoffman, who played bass for Melinda's band in college, comes right out and asks if I have any cocaine.

The messages are still rolling in, one after another, each more incriminating than the last, when Melinda slips into my office and closes the door behind her.

"We're back in business."

"Rat Boy?" I ask.

"Fuck Rat Boy. He's dead to me. I just got off the phone with someone who can hook us up. Are you holding?"

"No," I say, still holding my cell phone to my ear. "Are you?"

Melinda shakes her head, and I know she's lying.

"Shit," she says. "There's no way I'm doing this without a buzz."

"Doing what?" I ask.

"You still have the cash, right?"

I nod. Two-thousand dollars earmarked for a man in a rat suit lies at the bottom of my purse next to the cocaine I just said I wasn't holding. This really isn't where I saw my life heading as recently as six months ago.

"Good," Melinda says. "We're going to need all of it."

"I thought we never paid up front," I say.

"That was with Rat Boy. This is different."

"Different how?"

"For one thing, we won't be making the purchase at Fatso Ratso's."

"And for another?"

"You don't want to know."

Before I can complain, I hear Owen's voice in my ear and press a finger to my lips. He says he's sorry we haven't seen much of each other lately. He says he's been busy. He says the restaurant's been crazy. He says he's left messages that I apparently never received. He says to call him sometime soon. He says he loves me. And before he hangs up, he says there's something more he wants to ask, but it can wait until we see each other again.

In my head, I know he's only looking to score, but in my heart, I hope it's a hint at happily ever after.

MELINDA RUBS her nose as she exits the bathroom, a puffy gold purse tucked under her arm. Our eyes meet as we squeeze past each other in the doorframe, and the look that passes between us says it all—*bitch*. Each of us knows the other is holding, but we can't let on because we have business to conduct.

"Have fun," Melinda says, stepping aside with a smirk.

"Oh, I will."

Since Melinda won't tell me what the plan encompasses, I err on the side of caution and do more than my usual midmorning hit. Which isn't, I remind myself as I tap some coke onto the gray porcelain rim of the sink, to say that there's anything especially usual about my midmorning hit. It's not like I need it. It's not like I do it every day. Most days, in fact, I hardly touch the stuff. All I'm saying, I tell the woman checking her nose in the tarnished mirror, is that if I happen to indulge in a midmorning hit on a Monday or a Tuesday (or even a Wednesday or a Thursday), it's usually much smaller than the line I've just snorted.

"Where do you think you're going?" Vic asks, looking up through a cloud of gray and yellow smoke as Melinda and I pull our coats from the nails in the pressboard wall. "We have a magazine to run."

"Emergency," Melinda says, slipping an arm into her black leather biker jacket.

"At school," I add, donning my long wool coat. "The kids."

"Head lice," Melinda adds. She throws a thin, pink scarf over her shoulders and pulls a matching hat over her hair. "It's an outbreak."

"An epidemic," I say, masking my eyes beneath my sunglasses. "We got the call a minute ago."

"Not even."

"You guys aren't?" Jerry says as we stand in front of Vic awaiting dismissal.

"Contagious?" Melinda asks, slipping a long, bony finger under her hat and scratching away violently. "I don't think so."

"But maybe we should check," I say, giving my scalp a good scrub with my fingernails. "Would you guys mind?"

Vic takes a long drag on his cigarette and squints through the smoke. Already Jerry and Raj are starting to scratch at the imaginary bugs laying eggs in their skin, hair, and clothing, but our boss remains unmoved. Technically, we don't need his permission to leave. Technically, we're free to come and go as we please. Technically, we're both on the books as independent contractors so Vic doesn't have to worry about retirement plans and health benefits, but it's more fun to let him believe that he has some degree of control over his business than to remind him at every turn that he's nothing more than a toothless old dog.

"Whatever," he sighs, smoke escaping from his nose and lips as if he's been shot in the head at close range. "Just go."

THE EASTERN end of the Golden Mile peters out into what city planners and other champions of gentrification have, in alternating years, referred to somewhat optimistically as either the Silver Mile or the Silver Lining, but which everyone who's ever passed through the region thinks of as the frayed borderland between West Philadelphia and the rest of the world. Lacking both the glowing plastic sheen of the retail giants along the Golden Mile and the artificial folksiness of the lamp stores and clothing boutiques that punctuate its western frontiers, the shops in this crumbling netherworld are nothing if not functional.

Omar's Stereo and Electronics, reads a hand-scrawled collection of dripping red letters on a white cinderblock wall behind a chain-link fence topped with razor wire. *Ooh-La Nail's* reads a sign in a beauty shop window next to a corner bar whose only identifying mark is a neon Miller Light ad glowing in the murky darkness of a glass-block window. Stray cats roam broken sidewalks. Thick vines take back abandoned brick structures. Stripped cars rust on curbsides. We're barely five miles from my safe, tree-lined suburban neighborhood, but it's a whole different world.

"What was it you said about Rat Boy?" I ask as Melinda turns off the main artery and guides us down a narrow one-way street. "Something about taking risks no one in his right mind would consider?"

"Something like that," Melinda says, taking her eyes off the road long enough to root around in the backseat of her bright yellow Nissan Xterra and come up with the latest issue of *Pretty Easy*. "Read this. It'll make you feel better."

"Owen called," I say, flipping through the magazine. Billy Joel is singing something lame and syrupy on the radio. "He said he left a few messages, but I guess I never got them."

"You believe that?"

"Maybe."

"So, what? Your voicemail crashed? Your answering machine refused to take a message?"

"Something along those lines."

"And Owen only ever happened to call when you were away from the phone."

"Sounds good to me," I say. In the pages of the magazine, skinny moms sit poolside with infants and toddlers, their broad white smiles competing with pink bottles of sunscreen for my full attention. "You're the one who said we should get together."

"I said you should do him," Melinda says, searching in vain for street signs. "And you did, so it's time to move on."

Choosy mothers choose Jif, or so *Pretty Easy* would have me believe. Life happens over coffee. It's a good day when my bank pays me for saving. Having sexy underarms is no sweat. I can find true happiness in my own backyard. My kitchen is my canvas. Me-time should always come drizzled in chocolate.

"What if I don't want to move on?" I ask.

"You think it's up to you?"

"Who else?"

"It's a matter of compatibility," Melinda says. "You need to ask yourself if you really think you and Owen are a good match."

"We both like jazz," I say.

"And you both like getting high. That doesn't make you a couple."

"So what makes a couple?"

"I don't know. Look at me and Alan. He's not too pretty, he has a gut like a roll of pizza dough, and his eye tends to wander. But there's a connection there. I can't say what it is, but at the end of the day, I know whose bed he's sleeping in."

"You don't care if he looks at other women?"

"I'm not saying I like it," Melinda says, slowing to a stop in the middle of a block of row homes. "But it's part of his nature. A small part, if he knows what's good for him. Smallish, anyway." She looks over her shoulder and guides her yellow SUV into a tight space between an abandoned shopping cart and a rusty old Datsun whose side windows have been replaced with masking tape and black trash bags. "The point is, there are things we can forgive, and things we can't."

"That's bullshit," I tell her. "Look at me and Roger. Where did I go wrong? What did I do that was so terrible that he had to leave me for Chloe?"

"You got old," Melinda says, satisfied with her parking job despite the fact that the front of her car is a foot from the curb and the rear is pushing two feet. "Simple as that."

Gripping the magazine like a security blanket, I join Melinda on the sidewalk. The house in front of us has a tiny brown lawn that's littered with rotting leaves and broken glass. Beyond the lawn is a concrete porch ensconced in an ornate lattice of wrought-iron vines and flowers. Consulting the address scrawled on the palm of her left hand, Melinda checks the house number one last time and says this is the place.

"Should we go in?" I ask.

"You first."

"You're the one who brought us here."

"It's not like you tried to stop me."

Fuck it, I figure. Taking a breath, I stride up the short concrete path that leads to the house, climb three steps to the gate, and press the white button on a battered black intercom dangling precariously from a pair of wires looped over the latticework of the porch. When a voice crackles over the intercom and demands to know who I am, I think of Dorothy entering the Emerald City in *The Wizard of Oz*, but that's not exactly what comes out of my mouth.

"It's Party Girl," I say, pressing the white button. "Who the fuck is this?"

"Shit," Melinda mutters, grabbing the intercom from my hand. "We know Gerhard."

"Gerhard?" I ask when her finger lets up on the button.

Before Melinda can say anything more, the gate buzzes, and she pushes it open. When we're both on the porch, the gate swings shut behind us, and the lock in the front door buzzes like the gate did. Pitted with small craters, the door is heavy and windowless. Upon close inspection, even the windows that look out on the porch turn out not to be windows at all but sheets of burnished gray metal covered over with the same ironwork that twists and turns like a stand of metal vines all around us. Pushing the door open, Melinda steps into what appears to be a narrow foyer, but when I follow her inside, I realize that we're facing another locked door and there's barely enough room for the both of us to stand.

"This was Michael's connection?" I whisper.

"Michael should have had it so good."

The sliver of daylight between the door and the jamb disappears as the lock catches behind us, and the darkness that falls is black and complete.

"Got the money, bitch?"

A slot in the door slides open to reveal the eyes of a child who can't be much older than Catherine. His voice is thin and high despite the rasp he attempts to employ. A shaft of red light pours through the slot. Inside, I can hear gunshots, explosions, and the crunch of a pump-action shotgun. Though I know it's only the latest version of whatever the kids are playing these days to sharpen their skills in savagery and homicide, I cringe as I feel around in my purse for the roll of bills that never made it to the grubby paws of our friend in the rat suit.

"Come on, bitch," the boy says. "I ain't got all day."

I pass the roll of bills through the slot, and the slot closes. Melinda and I stand quietly in the darkness for what feels like hours, but is probably closer to a few minutes. Long enough, anyway, for the boy to count the money I gave him and return with a small package that he shoves through the slot without warning. All in the same heartbeat, the slot snaps shut, the package falls to the floor, Melinda drops to her knees to retrieve it, and the buzzer sounds in the door lock. Snatching up our coke in the blinding daylight, Melinda shoves it into her purse, and we stumble back onto the porch where the gate buzzes just long enough for us to scramble down the steps, over the sidewalk, and into her overgrown banana of a sport utility vehicle where she turns the key and the saccharine chorus of Neil Diamond's Sweet Caroline makes us jump.

Killing the radio, Melinda pulls into the street without checking her mirror, and a blue cargo van screeches to a halt behind us.

Melinda hits the brakes.

We lurch forward in our seats.

The driver of the van raises two hands to the sky, his scarred face a bolt of aggravation beneath his red wool cap.

Twisted into a scroll in my left hand, Melinda's copy of *Pretty Easy* is my only reminder of the world I've left behind, so I cling to it like a lifeline as Melinda stomps on the accelerator and we drive back to the Golden Mile in tense and jittery silence.

CHAPTER TWENTY-FIVE

A WEEK after my trip past the outer reaches of the Golden Mile, I've caught up with the majority of my clients except for Bunny Hoffman. The first time I met the woman was on New Year's Eve, and my guess when she cursed me for refusing to front her for what she called an eight-ball was that she was either homeless or a cop. Not long after that, Melinda admitted that Bunny used to play bass in her band and that she owed the woman a favor or two. Since then, I've come to discover that it's not a good idea to sell cocaine directly from the home, that an eight-ball is far too much of the stuff to front anyone of Bunny's disposition, income, and odor, and that no matter how many times I tell her to call my cell phone and arrange to meet somewhere with cash in hand if she wants to make a purchase, Bunny will, without fail, show up on my doorstep unannounced and insist that she's good for whatever astronomical amount of coke she happens to be in the mood for. When she rings my doorbell one afternoon just minutes before I'm slated to host a GESTAPO meeting, Catherine informs me that, as she so judiciously puts it, my friend is here.

Bunny's skin is gaunt and ashy in the fading daylight, and her eyelids droop as if she woke up somewhere between getting out of her car and ringing my doorbell. This is so not me, I think, rigid and a little jumpy because I know that my fellow concerned parents will start showing up at any minute, and the last thing I need them to see is scummy Bunny Hoffman trying to shake me down for a free eight-ball.

"I told you not to come here."

"No, you told me to call first."

"So we can arrange to meet somewhere else."

"Should I say I forgot or that I don't give a fuck? I tried it your way, and you never called back."

"Maybe that's because you're an embarrassment to society," I say, glancing up and down the block to make sure nobody from the GESTAPO is coming. "What do you want? I'm expecting people."

"You think I want to stick around?" Bunny says. "My guy's waiting for me in the car. Give me a gram, and I'll go away before anyone shows up."

"Too late," I say as a white Volvo station wagon squeezes into the space between my car and Bunny's. "They're already here."

"Then how's this for a deal?" Bunny says as Lyle Lesovitch gets out of his Volvo and gives me a wave. When I wave back, he pops the gate in the rear of his station wagon to retrieve the latest incarnation of the GESTAPO deli tray. "Give me whatever you have on hand, and I won't tell your friends about your little business venture."

I want to tell Bunny where to shove her new deal, but Lyle is halfway up the path to my house, the plastic tray of pink cold cuts and cubes of orange cheese resting on his shoulder. Huffing and puffing as he waddles forward, he stops at the foot of my steps and, reading a woman in ragged denim the same way he'd greet the sudden appearance of a grizzly bear in lederhosen, says that it looks like our little group has a new member.

"We sure do," I say. Because what else *can* I say? That Bunny's here to cop some coke and she'll be leaving any minute? "Lyle, this is Bunny Hoffman."

"Bunny," Lyle says as two more cars park behind mine and a third prowls the block in search of an open spot. "Just in time for Easter. More or less, anyway."

Bunny shoots me an evil look, but when she turns around to greet Lyle, she's a new woman. Still stringy. Still grungy. Still redolent of patchouli oil and cigarette smoke, but friendly enough to mask the scent.

"Easter," Bunny says as if the lameness of the joke isn't reason enough to get high. "That's a good one."

"I told you Lyle was a card," I say. "The heart and soul of the GESTAPO."

"The GESTAPO, yes," Bunny says, picking up on the cue as she follows Lyle through my front door. "I've been meaning to join for years."

"Well, we're glad to have you," Lyle says, laying the tray down on my coffee table. "And your kids are in?"

"Second grade," Bunny says. "Twins."

It's news to me, but who am I to judge?

"I hate to be a pain, Audrey, but can I use your bathroom?"

"Absolutely, Bunny," I say, matching her broad smile tooth for yellowing tooth. "Let me show you where it is."

Upstairs, Catherine is hard at work on her studies—even harder than usual, maybe, because she knows that Mrs. Woodring will be dropping by for the meeting. Lily, meanwhile, is watching television in her Chrissy Q sunglasses, fake pearls, and a faux leopard-skin pillbox hat of unknown origin. Looking away from the TV, my younger daughter gives me a quizzical look, and when I mouth the word *GESTAPO*, she nods as if it explains everything.

"Here's the deal," I say, lifting the lid on the toilet tank and fishing out a watertight Pepsi can with a false top. "I give you a gram, and you go downstairs and suddenly remember that you have somewhere to be."

"I have a better idea," Bunny says. "You give me everything in that little can of yours, and I walk out the back door without a peep."

"Are you on crack?" I ask, holding up a small packet of coke between two fingers. "A gram, and we tell everyone you just came down with food poisoning."

"An eight-ball," Bunny says, snatching at the gram. "Or I go downstairs and lay a nice, fat line on your coffee table."

"Two grams, and I don't tell Melinda about all this bullshit you're trying to pull."

"Melinda?" Bunny says. "What'll *she* do?"

"You think she hasn't planned for something like this? You think she doesn't have some muscle on retainer? The woman knows where you live, for Christ's sake. Rip us off, and she'll let the dogs loose."

"You're bluffing."

"There's only one way to find out, isn't there?"

I pluck a second gram from the phony Pepsi can, and Bunny calls me a bitch by way of acquiescing to the terms I've dictated.

DOWNSTAIRS, MY living room is filled with strangers I've known for years, faces of parents and teachers I knew in a former life. Their children used to roller-skate in my driveway and play house in my basement when the girls were younger. On Catherine's seventh birthday, all of her friends came to the house for a sleepover and constructed elaborate ice cream sundaes in disposable plastic baseball helmets on my kitchen table. When Lily turned five, we hired a woman to paint the faces of all of her friends, and when one of the girls broke out in a rash, it was understood among the parents that there was no way I could have known, that life throws minor curveballs at us all, that in time we'd all look back on the incident and laugh. I was the mom they could trust. We were the family they believed in. But then Roger left, and I became a different kind of animal altogether—a ghost, an outsider, a pariah—separate from the pack despite the fact that I still wore the same clothes as everyone else and proudly displayed all the same magnets on my car: *Live Strong. Hugs Not Drugs. Proud Parent of a Good Shepherd Elementary School Honor Student.* Now they all look away when I walk into the room. They pretend I'm not here. They squirm in their seats and try not to breathe, because what if divorce is contagious? What if family is just an illusion, light as a soft-soap bubble and not nearly as resilient. If it happened to me, it could happen to anybody.

Cocking an eyebrow, Lyle Lesovitch waddles over to me. We're about ready to begin the meeting, he says, but there's something he and I need to talk about first. In private, he adds, tugging at my elbow and leading me away from Bunny as the voice of my latent paranoia bleats like a car alarm: *HE KNOWS!*

"This Captain Panther character," Lyle says quietly. "What can you tell me about him?"

My mouth opens. My mouth closes. I don't say a word.

"I hear he's a fruit," Lyle says. "I hear he isn't even in the business anymore."

"He is," I say. "I mean, he's coming back. That's what the show at Good Shepherd is for."

"The show?"

"The assembly, I mean. He's billing it as his comeback special."

"What, like Elvis? That's exactly what we don't want. I'm not talking for everyone in the GESTAPO, Audrey, but I *am* talking from experience. These acts are a dime a dozen, and they don't do any good. If you want to keep kids off drugs, you bring in a cop, and he gives it to them straight. You do drugs, you die. Simple as that."

"Is it?" I say.

"I know this whole assembly is your baby, but I have a buddy on the force who can come in for free. Say the word, and I'll give him a call."

"Sounds good," I say as the doorbell rings. "I'll let you know."

The man at the door is wearing a red bandana on his head and a black tee shirt that reads *Mustache Rides: 25 Cents!* Before the stranger can say anything, Lyle jumps once again to the only conclusion he's capable of formulating, extends a hand, and tells the man that the meeting is about to get under way.

"I'm looking for Bunny?" the man says as Lyle waddles out to my living room.

"Don't look at me," I say. "She was supposed to come down with food poisoning."

I squeeze onto the sofa between Lyle and our new guest, and soon we're all up to our necks in GESTAPO business. Bouncing my knee up and down, I interrupt Lyle three times while he's reading the minutes of the previous meeting to ask if anyone needs a glass of water. Bunny raises a hand, and Catherine's teacher asks if she can have a twist of lemon in hers.

A twist of lemon? Fuck. It's a possibility I should have prepared for, but the house was so grimy and needed such a thorough scrubbing that I didn't have time for a trip to the grocery store. If I were a better mother, the voices of the other GESTAPO members seem to say as they all turn their heads in my direction and request water with a twist of lemon, I'd be standing by with a whole refrigerator full of citrus—lemons, limes, and oranges if necessary—but clearly I'm a failure. Clearly, they say with their bodies and eyes as I tell them that, sorry, I'm fresh out of lemons, I'm not half the mom I used to be.

In the kitchen, I fill glasses of all sizes and points of origin with water from the tap and place them on a tray. The effect, I hope, will be one of rustic charm, but I know the juxtaposition of Ronald McDonald, Strawberry Shortcake, and the cartoon Brontosaurus painted on what used to be a jelly jar will come off as yet one more example of my failure as a hostess to plan for even the most obvious of contingencies.

The talk when I return from the kitchen with everyone's water (*sans* lemon) is of raising funds for the music program and obtaining a grant to purchase more computers, but beyond the basics, I can't focus on anything. Hands go up, votes are cast, and I circle the room like a vulture.

"I'm fine," I say, though no one asks. "A little warm is all. Should I open a window?"

They know, the voice in my head insists. *They know. They know. They all know.*

"No they don't," I mumble quietly.

I need sleep, I suppose. I need to eat better. I need a joint to mellow out or a little coke to get my head together, but I can't leave the room because Lyle is saying something to me in a way that implies that I should probably nod or laugh or smile as a sign that I have at least a vague understanding of the issue at hand. Opting for the nod, I'm relieved when the expression on

- 196 -

Lyle's face tells me that it's the proper response. Though I can't for the life of me begin to guess what I've agreed to, it's apparently enough to bring our meeting to a close. As everyone stands to leave, Lyle thanks the newest members of the GESTAPO for joining us, and, eyeing the newcomer's tee shirt, Catherine's teacher suggests that maybe we can try to work mustache rides—whatever they are—into our next fundraiser.

"Hell," the man in the bandana says. "If money's an issue, why don't you just sell weed at the soccer games?"

Everyone freezes when he says this, but Lyle laughs, and we all realize it must be a joke.

Selling weed at soccer games?

What's next? Dealing coke at GESTAPO meetings?

CHAPTER TWENTY-SIX

"It's the restaurant," Owen says, fumbling with the hooks of my bra like a clumsy teenager. "I have so many plans. There's so much I want to do. Nick's, you know, it can be so much more. A new chef, a new menu, daily specials, live jazz. The kind of place I always wanted. The kind of place I can be proud of."

"It's okay," I say, looking at my watch as he kisses my neck. If we make this fast, we can still hit the town and catch a set at Zanzibar Blue, so I reach back and help Owen with my bra. "Life happens. We're busy people. I understand completely."

"I left you messages."

"So you said."

"I did." He unbuckles his belt, and I hike up my skirt. "With Catherine and Lily."

"Shh," I say, pressing a finger to his lips as I lower myself onto him. "Not while we're fucking."

"I love when you talk dirty."

"And I love when you keep your mouth shut."

"But I'm serious. I left messages with both of them. Or one of them, anyway. I'm not sure. It's hard to tell on the phone, but I think it was Catherine."

"Whatever you say."

"The girl has an attitude."

"Stop," I say. "She's my daughter."

"I don't think she likes me."

"Can we talk about this later? I'm kind of in the middle of something."

"Or something's in the middle of you, anyway."

"Clever boy. Now keep quiet, or I'll never finish."

"And that's a bad thing?"

"You promised we'd go out tonight."

"When we're done."

The sex is mechanical. The sex is cold. The sex feels perfunctory, incidental to the two of us, yet necessary to the relationship. If not for the coke, it would be unbearable.

"You have to admit," Owen says. "The girl can be bitchy."

"Everyone can be bitchy, Owen."

"But especially Catherine."

"What do you want me to say?" I ask, sliding off him. "That my daughter's a bitch? I don't see it happening."

"I left a message," he says, reaching for his razor and straw as I readjust my skirt. "You have to believe me."

"Why does it matter?"

"I need to know where I stand," Owen says. "In your life, I mean. Do you take my word, or do you side with Catherine?"

"Where *you* stand?" I ask. "What about where *I* stand, Owen? What *are* we to each other?"

"I don't know," Owen says. "Fuck-buddies? This coke, by the way, is total shit."

"Nice."

"Come on, Audrey. You know I'm only kidding."

"Then answer the question. Am I your girlfriend? Your lover? Something more serious?"

"Do we have to do this now?"

"I'm not getting any younger, Owen, so I need to know where our relationship is going."

I reach for the coke, and he swats me away.

"Get your own," he growls.

"It *is* my own," I remind him.

I could dump him right now. *Should*, in fact, dump him right now—tell Owen to go to hell or go fuck himself or go fuck himself in hell—but the words don't come. Instead I just stand and watch quietly as he lifts a remote to crank the volume on his stereo and leans over the coffee table to do another line. Because who am I trying to kid? It's not like guys are beating a path to my door, and I can only imagine what my profile would look like to potential mates on internet dating services: *Divorced mother of two seeks love and conversation. Must be into jazz and cocaine. Restaurant owners and self-absorbed assholes need not apply.*

Angling to get at my coke, I ask what we're listening to, and Owen looks up from his mirror in disgust.

"Lee Morgan," he shouts over a bouncing, blaring trumpet as if any fool could have given me the same information. "Boy genius. Played with Dizzy. Played with Coltrane. Wife shot him dead when he was only thirty-three."

"Sounds like the Gong Show," I say. "Like listening to polyester."

"Fuck you," Owen says. "This is Lee-fucking-Morgan."

"Boy genius, I know."

He surrenders my coke with a grudging shake of his head. I do one line, then another, and soon we're fucking and fighting and fucking some more. When it's not cold and mechanical, it's ugly and hateful, but there's no point in stopping because what else are we supposed to do?

CHAPTER TWENTY-SEVEN

AGAIN, THE Lincoln Navigator.

I want to know what Chloe does to my babies, what she did to my husband, how she captures their hearts and rewires their brains and wins their trust while they're in her care, but there's no way to be sure, no way to ask, no way to say anything without letting on that I know what she's doing, that I'm onto her game. To let her know too soon would be to tip my hand, I think as she returns my babies a little bit older, a little bit taller, a little more poisoned against me. And I don't have all the pieces of the puzzle yet. Don't have all the cards. *Don't have my ducks in a row* is a phrase that occurs to me as I smile and ask the bitch why Roger couldn't make it this time and accept her answer, whatever it is, with a nod and a knowing shake of my head, as if to say, yes, that's our Roger, always busy, always preoccupied, always working on *something*.

I'm seeing the world through a veil of static, white snow swirling across a TV screen. The picture is fuzzy, the voices garbled. I know that Chloe is explaining something. About the wedding, maybe. Or the vacation Roger will take them on in two weeks. When she speaks, I can see the exclamation points piling up all around her like spent bullet casings streaming out of a machine gun in a bad action movie. She's the Terminator of overstated enthusiasm, the Rambo of vapid excitement. Is this what Roger sees in her, I wonder as she prattles on about her wedding dress, the photographer, the band, the reception hall?

Not that I can hear any of it, of course. We've simply run this tape a million times before, and it's getting to the point where I can play both roles—the tossed-aside yet preternaturally accommodating ex-wife and the perky, skinny, bubbly other woman whose happily-ever-after promises so much wonder and joy that she can't help but heartlessly inflict her good cheer upon everyone she meets. And make no mistake—it *is* an act. Because deep down, the woman knows what she's doing. Deep down, she's torturing me on purpose. Deep down, she's stealing my daughters just to fuck with me. Deep down, she's shoving my face in the best days she'll ever have while I struggle to hold my own life together.

This, children, is your mother's brain on drugs.

Awake, alert, and firing on all cylinders.

Paranoid? I think not.

Your father's lover just happens to be the living embodiment of all things evil.

She hands me a list, folded neatly in quarters, of items the girls will need on their coming vacation: swimsuits, sunscreen, sunglasses, flip-flops. Comfortable shoes for shopping and hiking. Sweatshirts, clean socks, underwear, and pajamas. "Something nice" in case they go out to eat.

"Catherine and Lily should already have most of these things at home," Chloe says, lingering on the word *should* as if leveling an accusation, as if to say they *should* have these things, but knowing you, Audrey, you dumpy, frumpy, raggedy-ass, gnarled old hag, they probably don't. "But if you need to buy anything, save the receipt, and Roger said he'll pick up the tab."

"Providing for his own children," I say. "How kind. How generous. How downright magnanimous."

Chloe doesn't know what to say to this, so she smiles uncertainly, and I smile back to let her know that she doesn't need to worry, that I'm only kidding about Roger, that I love her list and how she took the time to write it, and that as far as I'm concerned, she and Roger are such a great couple, so perfect, so pure, so precious that they probably shit twenty-four-karat gold bullion. The girls and I will get to work on her list right away, I say, purposely folding the page against her fussy, meticulous creases before stuffing it into my back pocket.

"Is everything okay?" she asks as I lay my hands on my daughters' shoulders and draw them closer to myself. "You seem a little—stressed."

"Maybe a little," I tell her. "Work, you know."

"Tell me about it," Chloe says. "But at least we'll be taking these two off your hands for a while, right? A little vacation from being a mom?"

"I suppose so," I say.

Bitch.

Despite the lingering frost of March, the pale mannequins at Target are decked out in their floral, summery best. The little girl mannequins clutch beach bags. The little boy mannequins wear baseball gloves. The mom and dad mannequins set picnic tables, operate barbecue equipment, and take long, romantic walks, arm in arm, beneath exquisitely photographed sunsets. Lurking among them a half-hour before the store closes on a Sunday night, their gloomy keepers eye my daughters and me with suspicion. The worry isn't shoplifting so much as our potential for gumming up the works as they try to bring their shifts to an early end. All they want is to go home to their kids, their dogs, their microwave dinners, and their big screen TVs, but the girls and I have every right to be here. In fact, we *need* to be here because their father is taking them to Hawaii in two weeks and it's easier to buy new flip-flops and swimsuits and whatever else they need than it is to climb up to the attic and rummage through trash bags full of clothing in search of last year's summer fashions.

"Mom," Catherine says as I hold a two-piece up to Lily's small body. It's not exactly the label my younger daughter would choose if it were entirely up to her, but it's a free swimsuit on a Sunday night when she should probably be in bed, so she's not complaining. "Couldn't this have waited? I have homework to do."

"Loosen up, baby doll. You're going on vacation."

"Yeah," Lily says, swiveling her hips and snapping her fingers. "We're going on vacation. Loosen up."

"Don't call me baby doll," Catherine says.

The nearest stock girl clears her throat loud enough for me to hear it. The store manager locks a series of doors, leaving only one exit. A recording announces that the store will be closing in twenty-five minutes and that all purchases should be brought to the checkout counter. Slowly and stubbornly, our fellow shoppers emerge like sheep from the outer aisles of the store. Some push shopping carts. Others carry baskets. Still others juggle armloads of rugs, light bulbs, picture frames, and toilet paper as they're herded steadily toward the cashiers.

"Ma'am?" the stock girl says.

"I believe I have twenty-five minutes."

"I think we should go, Mom," Catherine says.

"We have twenty-five minutes, Catherine, and we're taking it."

"Yeah," Lily says. "I haven't even started looking for flip-flops yet."

Catherine hangs her head and sighs. The lights around the perimeter of the store go dim. A call goes out for a price-check on ping-pong balls, and the stock girl gives up on the three of us to seek out more docile, less recalcitrant hangers-on.

"And don't give me any of your holier-than-thou attitude," I say to Catherine. "I know all about what you did."

"What I did?"

"I saw Owen this weekend, and he told me everything."

"What do you mean?"

"Come on," I say. "Don't act like you don't know what I'm talking about."

"I don't," Catherine says. "Really."

"He called," I say. "He called and left a message, and you didn't bother to tell me."

"He didn't," Catherine says, shaking her head. "I would have told you."

"No," I say. "You wouldn't have. Because you don't like him. Because you've never liked him. Because you don't want me to be happy."

Catherine bites the inside of her lip. She looks at Lily, who shrugs as if to say she doesn't want to get involved—not if it puts her free swimsuit in jeopardy, anyway.

Good Lily, I think.

Faithful Lily.

The recording gives us twenty minutes to finish our shopping.

"Mom, I never talked to Owen."

"Why would he make something like that up, Catherine?"

"I don't know. Maybe he's confused. Maybe he talked to Lily."

Eyes wide, Lily shakes her head.

"Look, it's neither here nor there," I say. Because it's not like I'm a monster, not like I'm vindictive, not like the coke has addled my judgment. "It's over now, and everything's fine between me and Owen. I just want you to know that he's an important part of my life now, and I don't appreciate you trying to get between us."

"Mom, I didn't. I swear."

"He loves me, Catherine. And he loves you, too. Both of you."

"Ma'am?" the stock girl says, apparently unable to find anyone else to harass.

"Christ," I say. "I have twenty minutes coming to me, and I'm in the middle of a moment with my daughters. If you don't leave me alone, I'll call the manager and have you fired."

"Mom?" Catherine says. "Can we please go home?"

"In a minute, baby doll. All I'm trying to say is that we're going to be a family again. You and me and Lily and Owen. All of us together. We'll be happy. We'll—we'll have fun. It'll be just like old times. Before—you know. Before."

"I know, Mom," Catherine says. "I'm sorry."

"It's okay, baby doll. I'll always love you. You know that, right?"

"I know," Catherine says.

I give her a squeeze, and I give Lily a squeeze, and, standing among the mannequins as the lights go out at Target, I know for sure that it isn't just a dream, that if I stay the course and tough it out with Owen, we really will be a family again.

I know it in my heart.

And that's all that matters.

CHAPTER TWENTY-EIGHT

THE GOOD news is that my job is so easy, a monkey could do it. The bad news is that Vic refuses to spring for the monkey, so it's up to me to crank out the reviews and profiles that make *Eating Out* such an engaging and delightful read. As with all feats of magic, the trick to writing what I write lies in the art of cunning misdirection. If the cooking is terrible—which it almost invariably is—the focus is on size. If the portions are paltry, then price is what matters. And if every item on the menu is egregiously expensive, then I go on at length about ambiance and charm, both of which leave plenty of room for further exercises in chicanery, prevarication, and other forms of verbal prestidigitation.

Burnt becomes blackened.

Cramped becomes cozy.

Dirty becomes rustic.

Slow service becomes an unhurried, leisurely atmosphere, and a line of ants crawling from the dining area to the kitchen becomes a steady stream of faithful gourmands beating a path to the head chef's door. Our advertisers pay good money for these euphemisms, and, as the tagline beneath the masthead clearly states, *Eating Out* always delivers.

Jerry and Vic are nowhere to be found as a typo transforms an expensive Caesar salad into an expansive one, but Melinda is on the phone, and Raj is pacing back and forth outside my office. Once or twice, he stops in my doorway, rests a hand on the flimsy frame, and draws a breath as if to speak, but whenever I look up, he lowers his head and resumes his pacing.

"I am betrothed," he eventually says after opening Vic's desk and pouring himself a shot of Old Crow. "She is sixteen years old, enjoys painting and water sports, and comes from a well-to-do family of wheat farmers in Punjab. Her mother has a good child-bearing body, and so do both of her grandmothers. My bride-to-be dreams of being a doctor but will settle for marrying an American. We will be wedded in five years' time."

"Congratulations," Melinda says. "Sounds like a catch."

"Does she have a name?" I ask.

"Her name doesn't matter," Raj says. "I have only one love, and her name is Audrey."

"That's funny," Melinda says. "Audrey's name is Audrey, too."

"And I love her."

"I'm flattered, Raj," I say. "But I'm kind of seeing someone."

"Please," Raj says. "Say no more. I want to remember you just as you are."

Raj swallows the shot and places the glass upside-down on the cluttered surface of Vic's desk. Replacing the cap, he puts the bottle away. It would be greatly appreciated, he says, if I would refrain from mentioning any of this when next we meet.

He walks to the door.

He lays a hand on the doorknob.

He glances over his shoulder, heaves a sigh, and leaves in silence.

CHAPTER TWENTY-NINE

When a black van pulls into the parking lot at Good Shepherd, I check my nose and give the Captain a wave. Decked out in full superhero regalia, he wears a rubber half-mask with pointy ears and a broad feline snout. Purple satin lines his heavy black cape, golden epaulettes perch upon his shoulders, and the vanity plate on his van reads NO2DRGS. Hopping out of the driver's seat, he takes a few swift punches at the air in front of him and does some fancy footwork in his black tights.

"You're a monster," he growls to himself as he unloads equipment from the back of his van. "You're an animal. You're a god."

"How about all of the above?" I say, creeping up behind him. "Where were you on the night of my Halloween party?"

A tacky computerized drumbeat percolates in a boom box, and the Captain asks if I can give him a hand with his smoke machine, his sound system, and his portable light show. We'll have to make a second trip for the main attraction, he says as a synthesized trumpet arrangement stabs through the monotonous thumping and I help America's favorite just-say-no superhero pile the contents of his van onto a metal hand truck. Falling right into his trap, I ask what the main attraction might be, and, with a theatrical flourish, he pulls at a black tarpaulin to reveal an Ultimax 3000 cross-country skiing simulator with a massive rubber panther head bolted to its frontispiece.

"Custom made," the Captain says. "What do you think?"

"Dr. Treadwell sprang for that?"

"Actually, I did," the Captain admits. "The Ultimax is mine, and I bought the panther head on eBay. But Dr. Treadwell gave me a pretty nice banner to hang at the foot of the stage, so I'm not complaining."

"A banner?"

"It doesn't mention me by name, but it does imply a certain degree of corporate sponsorship. With any luck, the people at Gatorade or Nike might see it and throw some serious money in our direction. From there, the Captain Panther brand can only snowball. Once we get a few big names on board, we'll have to beat the offers away with a stick."

"*We*, Kimosabe?"

"Absolutely," the Captain says. "You're part of my team. You did alert the media, didn't you?"

"They'll be here," I say.

"Good," the Captain says. "Because this will be my best show ever."

"Assembly," I say.

"What?"

"Nothing."

The Captain locks his van, and we push the equipment-laden cart toward the school. Inside, the halls smell of paste, magic markers, and gym socks, and a sign near the entrance instructs all visitors to check in at the principal's office before conducting any business. When he stops in her doorway, the school secretary looks up at the Captain with a start and reaches instinctively for the telephone—apparently superheroes, even those who are invited, don't normally show up in costume on a regular basis here at Good Shepherd. Before the secretary can call the police, however, I say that we're here for the assembly, and she gives us a pair of laminated guest passes.

"Okay, kids!" the Captain shouts at the empty auditorium as a custodian in a blue flannel shirt shows us to the stage. "It's Panther Time!"

For the next half-hour, the Captain sets up his light show, his smoke machine, and his sound system while asking me at regular intervals in his deepest, throatiest, growliest voice if I'm ready for some panther action. Each time I tell him that, yes, I am ready for some panther action, he adopts the attitude of a drill sergeant, raises a hand to one of his pointy rubber ears, and complains that he can't hear me.

Apparently, someone with the local CBS affiliate has fallen for my promise to deliver "the most addictive anti-drug experience the world has ever seen" hook, line, and proverbial sinker, because a TV crew is setting up in the rear of the auditorium. In addition to the TV crew, a pair of newspaper reporters sit at opposite sides of the front row, notepads open, cameras at the ready in the event that the press release I sent out earlier in the week wasn't complete bullshit.

"Put your hands together for the P-Man!" the Captain growls into his microphone for his miniature audience. "Put your hands together for the P-Man! Put your hands together, put your hands together, put your hands together for the P-Man!"

Unfortunately, this is about as interesting as his lyrics get, but when I turn away from the stage to say a few words to the press, I find myself face-to-face with a police officer in full uniform. His name, he informs me, mustache twitching with a mix of concern and curiosity as he glances at the stage where the Captain has set up his customized Ultimax 3000, is Stan Panakowski, and he's here to talk about drugs.

"I'm a friend of Lyle Lesovitch," he adds, shaking a black briefcase. "Don't tell me I'm sharing a stage with this guy."

"I'm afraid so," I say. "Lyle mentioned your name, but I didn't realize he'd already made the arrangements."

And what you have to understand, officer, is that I may have been just a tiny bit high on cocaine when we talked about it, so I missed one or two of the key details in our conversation. In fact, you should probably bear in mind that I'm probably a little coked up right now, so you might not want to hold me accountable for anything that goes down today, either, okay?

Laying down his microphone, Captain Panther hops off the stage to join me and Officer Panakowski.

"Who's this guy?" the Captain growls quietly, dripping with sweat.

I explain the situation, and the men eye each other up and down.

"Good of you to come out today," the Captain says with a smile for the benefit of the media. "But Captain Panther works alone."

"Cute," Officer Panakowski says. "But you might want to consider the fact that keeping kids away from drugs is serious business, and the last thing these kids need is some clown in a monkey suit telling them not to get high."

"And *you* might want to consider the fact that these kids grew up in the age of television. You need to rope them in. You need to grab their attention. You need music and smoke machines and flashing lights."

"What's wrong with grabbing their attention with the facts?" Officer Panakowski demands, his voice taking on the flinty edge of a middle-aged man who's seen too many Clint Eastwood movies. "Like the fact that if they mess with drugs, they'll go straight to jail—unless, of course, they die first."

By now, the kids are filing into the auditorium, so I step between the men and suggest that they each give a presentation.

"And let the kids decide who's best," the officer says. "I like the sound of that—on one condition. The Captain goes first."

"I don't think so," the Captain says. "Captain Panther is no opening act."

"And *I* am?" Officer Panakowski asks.

"Flip a goddamn coin," I say as the reporter from the local paper fiddles with her camera and tells us all to smile.

Backstage, Captain Panther loses the coin toss and spends the next five minutes complaining in my general direction. He's a professional, he mutters, and he shouldn't have to put up with this kind of bush-league bullshit. He's been on *Mr. Belvedere*, for the love of God. On top of that, he's shot pilots in Hollywood and done countless commercials for products ranging from Irish Spring and Kentucky Fried Chicken to Old Spice and Kellogg's

Frosted Mini-Wheats. And now he's being upstaged by Officer Friendly and his traveling deadly medicine show?

"This is bullshit," the Captain mutters. "Complete and utter bullshit."

By the time the students have taken their seats, the Captain is practically frothing at the mouth. He's a winner, he reminds himself as the stage fills with wispy clouds of smoke and the computerized drumbeat kicks into action.

He's a monster.

He's an animal.

He's a god.

Lights flash, trumpets blare, and a prerecorded voice commands the children to put their hands together for the hardest-working superhero in showbiz as the Captain bounds onto the stage in a single leap.

"Hey, kids!" he shouts into his microphone. "Does anyone know what time it is?"

The younger children fidget nervously. The older children roll their eyes. From my vantage point backstage, I can see Catherine trying her best to turn invisible while Lily sneaks glances at a partially concealed fashion magazine amidst a sea of blue jumpers and plaid clip-on neckties.

"It's always the same with these guys," Officer Panakowski gloats. "All flash and no substance."

"You got it, kids!" the Captain shouts, though no one has volunteered an answer. "It's Panther Time!"

The lights flash. The drums thump. The children in the front row place their hands over their ears as the Captain starts to rap:

I'm Captain Panther, and I'm here to say
That drugs are never, ever the way!
Acid, weed, cocaine, and smack?
Everyone knows that stuff is whack!

"This is pathetic," Officer Panakowski shouts over the din. "I better go out there and help him."

There's a very brief window of opportunity for me to stop the officer from picking up his briefcase, grabbing one of the Captain's spare microphones, and moonwalking onto the stage, but by the time I realize that the man is serious, he's already part of the show.

"Hold on there, buddy," Panakowski says, interrupting the Captain mid-rap. "Before we get into all the razzle-dazzle, let's start with some fundamentals. Do any of you kids know what happens if you mess with drugs?"

A few students raise their hands, but Officer Panakowski answers the question for them.

"That's right, kids. You *die*."

"Thanks for the insight, Officer Friendly," Captain Panther says. "But I'm in the middle of a show right now."

"They put you in a little box, they dig a hole, and they lower you into it. *And no one ever sees you again.*"

Sensing that something is amiss, the kids perk up and start to show some interest in the proceedings as Officer Panakowski grooves to the Captain's lame electronic beat.

"Have you kids ever heard of marijuana?" the officer asks, opening his briefcase and holding up a bag of lawn clippings. "Some people call it grass, some people call it weed, and other people call it pot, but it's what we in law enforcement call a gateway drug. Your local drug dealer might tell you it isn't bad for you, but what he won't tell you is that almost everyone who smokes marijuana ends up trying other drugs, too."

"Which is why you need to get hooked on exercise!" Captain Panther adds. "Do any of you kids like to exercise?"

Again, a show of hands as Catherine sinks deep into her seat.

"You want exercise?" Officer Panakowski asks. "Try this on for size. Next time someone offers you drugs, run to the nearest police officer."

"But if you're already into physical fitness, it won't even come to that."

"Unless you're in the gym and someone offers you steroids," Officer Panakowski counters, opening his briefcase once again and pulling out a syringe. *"You're* not on steroids, are you Panther Man?"

"It's Captain Panther," the Captain growls. "And you know it."

"You're dodging the question, Captain."

"These muscles are pure Panther," the Captain says, flexing. "And if you kids want to get in shape like me, you might want to try out my special exercise machine. Has anyone here ever heard of the Ultimax 3000?"

"I have a better question," Officer Panakowski says. "Has anyone here ever heard of LSD? It's what we call a hallucinogen. That means it makes you see things. It messes with your mind. So, for example, you might go around thinking you can fly. Then you jump off a roof and break all your bones. Or maybe you start seeing monsters, so you pull your eyes out. Alternately, you might start dressing like a lion because you think you're some kind of superhero."

"Let's get one thing straight," Captain Panther roars. "I'm America's favorite just-say-no superhero, and that doesn't happen unless you *just say no!"*

"Whatever you say, Captain. But what I'm here to tell you kids is that you don't even get a shot at *being alive* unless you just say no, got it? You mess with drugs, you die. End of story. Just you in a little box under six feet of dirt."

The music stops.

Officer Panakowski and Captain Panther stand toe to toe, glaring at each other.

The janitor pulls on a heavy rope, and the curtains come together.

Grabbing the microphone from the police officer, the principal fights with the curtain for a second before appearing on the other side and calling on the kids to give their guests a warm round of applause.

"That was a huge waste of time," the officer says, brushing past me as Captain Panther starts breaking down his sound system and loading his amplifiers onto the hand truck.

"You're telling me," the Captain says, but Officer Panakowski has already left the building.

"I'm sorry," I tell the Captain. "I had no idea he was coming."

"So much for my comeback. I looked like a jackass out there."

What can I say? The man's dressed like a panther.

"Maybe I can arrange for another assembly."

"A do-over? I don't think so. In this line of work, you only get one shot."

"How about lunch, then?" I say. "I know a great little place where you're sure to fit in."

CHAPTER THIRTY

N<small>OBODY LOOKS</small> twice when Polly the octopus greets me and the Captain at the door to Fatso Ratso's and seats us in a booth beneath a painting of the giant rat piloting a gondola through the canals of Venice. Peering across the table, all I can see are the Captain's pointy black ears sticking up from behind a menu. In the next booth over, a woman in a fuzzy turtleneck is cutting a slice of pizza into impossibly tiny squares and feeding them to an octogenarian in a wheelchair. Across from them, a couple of teens playing hooky from high school hold hands and stare at each other, blissfully stoned. Hovering over us, our eight-armed hostess lingers a little too long, and I begin to wonder if she's one of my customers.

"It's Audrey, right?" she eventually asks.

I nod cautiously.

"Listen, you're not, um?"

"Having lunch with America's favorite just-say-no superhero?"

"Oh," the pink octopus says, the word *holding* on the tip of her tongue as she notices, perhaps for the first time, that my companion is wearing a mask, cape, and tights. "Wow. That's so weird. My roommate was just talking about you."

"Really?" the Captain says, his mood brightening for the first time since the coin toss.

"Yeah. You were on TV a few days ago."

"That wasn't me," the Captain says, storm clouds returning. "It was somebody else."

"Oh," the octopus says by way of apology before telling us that a server will be along shortly to take our order.

When she leaves, the Captain curses under his breath.

"Christ," he says. "It's the Shield, I know it."

"The Shield?"

"This guy from Texas. Ever since I dropped from the scene, he's been getting all the attention."

The Captain looks away from me, and I wonder if he's about to cry.

"If you want to know the truth, I was never really America's number-one just-say-no superhero. The Shield is, was, and always will be—but only because he jumps on every bandwagon that comes down the pike. Bullying, domestic violence, recycling, plagiarism—he has a song for everything, and everybody loves him. He even wrote a song about the evils of illegal file swapping, and it got him a big-time recording contract. Meanwhile, the only thing I ever did was tell kids to stay away from drugs. What chance did I have? What chance *do* I have? What am I even doing in this business?"

The octopus returns, stands a few feet away from us as if waiting for a confessional to open up or an ATM to become available, and I'm sure she's putting a lot of thought into whether or not this is a good time to score a gram of coke.

"You had *one* bad day," I say when the octopus finally gives up and wanders back to her post. "A minor setback. We'll get you up on your feet and back in the game in no time."

"You don't understand, Audrey. This was my one shot. My comeback special. Do you know how much money I sank into that smoke machine? Into the light show? Into tricking out my Ultimax 3000?"

"So it's all about the money?"

"No," the Captain says. "It's not about the money."

"Then what is it about? Seriously. Why do you do this? Why did you *ever* do this? The cape, the mask, the tights. Was it fame? Was it power? Was it glory? Were you trying to meet women? Did you have something to prove? What?"

"I thought I could make a difference," the Captain says.

"And now you can't? Just because some dingbat in Texas is getting press for telling kids not to download Miley Cyrus songs?

If that's all it takes to beat Captain Panther, then why the hell am I wasting my time with you?"

It occurs to me that a line of coke might lift the Captain's spirits, but I can't bring myself to say it. Instead, I sit quietly while he takes a deep breath and counts to ten.

"You're right," the Captain says. "I can beat this."

"Sure you can," I say. "You know why?"

"Because I'm Captain Panther," he says.

"There you go."

"And Captain Panther doesn't give up."

"Of course not."

"Because Captain Panther's a winner."

"Absolutely."

"And you know something? I don't give a damn about the Shield."

"Fuck the Shield," I say. "What does he know?"

"And fuck his record deal, too."

"That's the spirit," I say. "Fuck his whole operation."

"I'll write some new songs, put together another comeback special, and before you know it, I really *will* be America's favorite just-say-no superhero."

The Captain pounds his fist on the table, and the octopoid hostess hurries over to ask if everything's okay. Except for the fact that we haven't seen a waiter yet, I say, everything's coming up roses. Apologizing for the delay, Polly shuffles her feet and is about to speak again when the Captain interrupts her.

"I think I know what you want," he says. "And today's your lucky day because I happen to have a fresh stack of glossies in my van."

"Glossies?" the pink octopus asks.

"Headshots," the Captain says, sliding out of the booth. "I'll be right back."

While he's gone, the octopus gets around to asking the question she's been dying to ask ever since she spotted me.

"You're not, uh?"

"Holding?" I say.

I look around the restaurant at the glassy-eyed teenagers, the woman in the fuzzy turtleneck, and the old man in the wheelchair. I doubt any of them are undercover cops, but one can never be too sure.

"Let's go for a walk," I say. "I need to use the restroom."

CHAPTER THIRTY-ONE

A LINE of coke with a pink octopus in a toilet stall at Fatso Ratso's, a quick hit at work in lieu of a coffee break, a few lines with Owen on a Friday night. Even when the girls are home, I rarely think twice about getting high anymore. I lock myself in the bathroom, tap out some coke and run the sink. Not every night, but often enough. And I wouldn't say I'm getting high, exactly. Just trying not to sink too low. Because Roger never listens to a word I say. Because every date with Owen turns into a fight. Because all the girls can talk about is leaving for Hawaii. Because Melinda keeps talking about taking our business to the next level. Because strange people keep calling me and asking me to meet them in unfamiliar places with increasing amounts of cocaine. Because I can't look at a police car without flinching. Because I have a purse full of cash and a house full of illegal contraband, and I can't eat, and I can't sleep, and I'm edgy and nervous and paranoid and jumpy, and the only thing that makes it all go away is doing a little more coke.

Less than a week before the girls are supposed to leave on their trip to Hawaii, I come home from work to find Lily doing her tightrope act on the back of the sofa again. Her arms are outstretched, and she's reciting the names of states and their capitals as Catherine informs me that there's a message on the answering machine. It's from Lyle Lesovitch, she adds, looking away, and when I check the machine, Lyle's message informs me that I'm being removed from my post as the GESTAPO's drug czar. The vote was unanimous, he adds as Lily continues to recite her state capitals in the next room, but maybe I can volunteer for a less taxing office when I host the organization's next meeting. The message goes on and on as Lyle enumerates all the benefits of my continued membership in the GESTAPO, but I stop listening when I hear a thump in the living room and Lily falls silent.

Adopting my most self-righteous mother voice, I call out to Lily and tell her she should be more careful. If I told her once, I told her a thousand times—the sofa isn't a playground.

"Lily?" I say when she doesn't respond. "Stop fooling around. This isn't funny."

"Mom?" Catherine calls from the living room. "I think she's hurt."

In a flash, I'm in the living room and picking my baby up off the floor, cursing myself because the first thing that comes to mind as I spot a drop of blood on the carpet and the cut on Lily's scalp is that I'll need a line of coke to get through this. But I know there's no time to sneak off to the bathroom, no way I can lay my daughter down now that I've picked her up, no excuse for doing anything other than rushing out to the car with Lily in my arms, calling for Catherine to hurry up as she locks the front door behind her, and promising both girls that everything will be okay, that Mommy has everything under control.

All the way to the hospital, Catherine holds Lily close and whispers state capitals in her ear. *Montgomery, Alabama. Juneau, Alaska. Phoenix, Arizona. Little Rock, Arkansas.* There's a cut on the back of Lily's head, and I don't know how deep it is. *Sacramento, California. Denver, Colorado. Hartford, Connecticut.* Catherine presses a towel to the cut, and Lily cries softly. *Dover, Delaware. Tallahassee, Florida. Atlanta, Georgia.* I take the tears as a good sign. *Honolulu, Hawaii. Boise, Idaho.* At least she's conscious, and maybe the cut isn't so bad.

"I forget what's next," Catherine cries after Springfield, Illinois. "Mom?"

"I don't know, sweetheart."

"Why not?" Catherine demands.

"I just don't, okay?"

"It's Indianapolis," Lily whispers through her tears. "Indianapolis, Indiana."

"Indianapolis, Indiana," Catherine says, and continues her litany until we arrive at the hospital.

In the emergency room, the attendants try to take my daughter away from me, but I refuse to let go. I'm holding Lily the way I used to hold her when she still sucked her thumb and would fall asleep with her head on my shoulder, arms wrapped gently around my neck, legs dangling limply against my body. It's standard procedure, the attendants say. I need to trust them. My daughter will be in good hands.

"It's okay, Mom," Catherine says, her calm voice cutting through my panicky haze. "They know what they're doing. You can let her go."

I clutch Lily for a few seconds longer, then surrender her to a woman in pink scrubs who assures me once again that everything will be okay. Then my baby disappears behind a swinging door, and I find a seat in the waiting room where I sit for what seems like an eternity with Catherine and all the other negligent parents whose children have managed to maim themselves in the scant few hours between school and bedtime. We're all holding clipboards and filling out insurance forms, and a large television is tuned to the early edition of the evening news. Fires and beatings and tales of corruption interspersed with ads for Pillsbury Crescent Rolls and Glade PlugIn room fresheners. When the news resumes, every parent in the room casts nervous glances at the TV screen to make sure her child's injury isn't the next item on the agenda, her own lack of vigilance the next big scandal.

"I'm a good mother," I say to Catherine as we wait for the prognosis.

"I know," Catherine says. "It was an accident, Mom."

I hold my breath as the news anchor mentions a major drug bust, but it's in the city, and I don't recognize any of the names. Maybe the authorities got Rat Boy to crack, I think as an attendant calls my name. I've seen the movies. I know how it works. A week or so in holding, a few dozen rounds of good-cop-bad-cop, a deal with the D.A., and Rat Boy spills his guts. He'd be out on the street within twenty-four hours. Ten minutes after his release, however, someone in a black car would pull up next to him and ask him to go for a ride. Sensing that he had no choice, Rat Boy would climb into the car and disappear forever. The only question left as the hospital attendant calls my name a second time is whether my erstwhile connection ratted me and Melinda out to the cops or to the kingpins. Either way, we're screwed.

"Mom?" Catherine says, tugging at my sleeve as the attendant calls my name a third time. "I think they want to talk to you."

I stand. I step forward. I let Catherine guide me.

My bones feel like lead. My muscles feel like sandbags.

I wonder if I have time for a quick hit of coke.

Behind a thin, white curtain, a stringy doctor is holding fingers in front of Lily's eyes and asking her to count them. His face is long, and a tangle of curls falls down to the stethoscope draped across his shoulders. My guess is that he can't be more than sixteen years old.

"Your daughter has a small cut on her scalp," the doctor says. "And an extremely mild concussion, but otherwise she's in good shape."

"We're leaving for Hawaii on Friday," Catherine says. "So we need to know if she's fit for travel."

"I don't see why not," the doctor says.

"And the cut?"

"Negligible. A bald spot until the hair grows back. Any scarring will be completely hidden."

The doctor prescribes a topical antibiotic for the cut and tells me to keep an eye on Lily. Because the concussion is so mild, he sees no reason to keep her overnight. What she needs more than anything is to get out of the antiseptic glare of the hospital and back into her own home where she'll feel safe and secure. I nod at all of this information and, thanking the doctor repeatedly, hug Lily to my breast. My daughters mean the world to me, I say, forcing a smile and hoping it will convince the entire medical community that I am, in fact, a good mother and that our house is absolutely the safest, most secure place in the world for a little girl to recover from a concussion.

So what if I do a little coke every now and then? I want to say as the doctor acknowledges my thanks and goes about his duties. *It makes me feel good. It keeps my weight down. It gives me energy and helps me focus. It makes me more outgoing, more friendly, more confident. It helps me keep my act together. And dealing? Please. It's barely a hobby. Believe me, doc, I know what I'm doing, and you can rest assured that I'd never even dream of putting my daughters in danger.*

CHAPTER THIRTY-TWO

SOMETHING ISN'T right.

When I turn the last corner on my way home from the hospital, I spot a gray Chevy Nova parked in front of my house. It's the same car I've seen the bearded little goat-boy driving up and down the Golden Mile for weeks now. Perpetually enraged, he always shakes his fist at me, pounds on his steering wheel, and gestures in ways that are meant, I've supposed up until now, to convey his nagging sense of existential angst, voice his lingering suspicion that life holds no meaning beyond the roar of his souped-up engine, and exorcise the festering spirit of malaise that haunts his work in the retail sector. In other words, I assumed that he was just another asshole; but when I see him sitting on my front step wearing nothing but a tank top despite the chilly weather, it hits me that his ongoing outbursts have not simply been part of some larger, general complaint to an uncaring, unfair universe, but a series of aggravated entreaties aimed directly at me. The man, it would seem, has genuinely wanted to chat, and I've blown him off every time. Now he's on my doorstep, and my daughters want to know who he is and why he's talking to himself.

"He's probably a salesman," I say, gliding past my driveway and rounding the next corner. "And he's psyching himself up for his pitch."

"He has a lot of tattoos for a salesman," Catherine says. "Why did you drive past our house?"

"Just in case," I say, looking over my shoulder as I park the car.

"What's he selling?" Lily asks.

"I don't know yet, baby doll."

"Just in case what?" Catherine asks.

"I'm locking the doors," I say, all too aware that I haven't answered her question. "I want you to stay here until I come back."

"Just in case what?" Catherine asks again. "Mom?"

She's still demanding to know exactly what she should be worried about as I get out of the car and close the door, but the glass muffles her voice. Peeking around the corner, I can see the bearded little goat-boy frothing at the mouth on my front step.

I should turn back, the sensible mother in me argues as I stride down the block. I should get in my car and call the police and drive my daughters to safety. But what then, I'm forced to ask as the goat-boy catches a glimpse of me and puffs out his chest? Do I tell the dispatcher that I hate to be a bother, but an angry young man who looks like a goat is waiting for me on my doorstep? That it probably has something to do with the fact that I've been running a teeny-tiny drug operation out of my home for the past three months? That I'd appreciate it greatly if they could please ignore anything the goat-boy says, especially if it might incriminate me?

Given these questions and the fact that the goat-boy and I are currently staring each other down as we both tread forward, fists balled at our sides and steam pouring out of our ears like we've both stepped out from a caricature of people itching for a fight, the sensible mother in me backs down and hands the reins over to the coked-up, angry, self-preserving, hyper-protective, and admittedly terrified she-beast I've become.

"What the fuck?" I say, handling the situation the way I imagine Melinda might.

"'What the fuck?'" the goat-boy says as we square off on the concrete path in front of my house. "What the fuck, 'What the fuck?'"

So it's come to this. Four years as an English major, another five as the editor of an admittedly crummy magazine, approximately six or seven months as an occasional cocaine user, nearly three as a small-time connection, and I've boiled the entirety of the language I once loved down to three ugly syllables.

"'What the fuck, "What the fuck?"' What the fuck are you doing on my front step?" I ask, raising our level of discourse a notch, though I know that doing so runs the risk of alienating my audience. "Do I even know you?"

"Know me?" the goat-boy says. "You fucking owe me two-thousand dollars."

"Michael?" I say.

The goat-boy's lips are chapped and gray. His hair is wild. His cheeks are hollow. He's skinny and unshaven, and his blue tattoos appear to be self-administered. I'd give any amount of money to make him disappear right now, do anything to make him go away.

"Michael's out of the picture. I'm the one you're dealing with now."

"What happened to Michael?" I ask.

"You'll find out soon enough. Were those your little girls I saw in the car?"

"Fuck you," I say.

"Two grand, bitch."

"I don't have it."

"Then we'll have to figure something else out, won't we?"

He takes a step closer and licks his lips.

"I'll call the police," I say.

"And tell them what?"

He touches my hair and opens his mouth, and my stomach clenches with fear.

"You know you want it," he breathes.

"I can get you the money."

"I know you can," the goat-boy says. "But first I want to have some fun."

He brushes my cheek with the back of his hand. He puckers his lips and asks me how I want it. We can do it all night, he promises. Get coked up and fuck until dawn.

His breathing is heavy, his breath like bad meat.

"And if your little girls get tired of waiting," he starts to say, but I knee him in the testicles before he can go any further.

He falls to his knees. He calls me a bitch. He rolls on the ground as I run for my front door. Fumbling for my keys, I can almost feel him breathing down my neck, and I'm trembling so violently that I need both hands to work the lock.

"Fucking bitch," he moans, struggling to his feet. "You just fucked with the wrong guy."

Slipping inside, I slam the door behind me as the goat-boy lurches forward and begins to howl obscenities at the top of his lungs.

"You're dead, you fucking whore," he shouts, pounding on my door. "Do you understand me? *You're fucking dead when I get my hands on you!*"

I sink to the floor and hug my knees and beg God to keep my little girls safe.

"Go away," I cry. "I'm calling the cops."

"You're bluffing," the man growls, but before he can remind me that I'm nothing more than a two-bit drug dealer, the entire neighborhood is flooded with flashing lights.

"Shit," I mutter to myself, but mostly I'm relieved.

Cutting his losses, the goat-boy tears off into the night. An eternity later, there's a knock at the door, and a police officer identifies himself before asking if I'm okay. The voice sounds familiar, and when I open the door, Officer Panakowski is standing in front of me. The suspect has been apprehended in the backyard behind my neighbor's house, a radio clipped to the officer's shoulder informs us—and he's claiming that I'm a drug dealer.

"Not likely," Panakowski says into his radio. "She's on the drug squad at Good Shepherd."

Apparently he hasn't gotten the memo.

"That's junkie logic for you," Panakowski explains as he walks me to the neighbor's house where he says my girls have taken refuge. "Some guy gets it in his head that you're a drug dealer, and he won't let it go."

"It's crazy," I say. "Completely insane."

"What's crazy is the guy probably had your house confused with someone else's."

"A crackhouse in *this* neighborhood?"

"Not a crackhouse, exactly, but yeah. All the streets look alike around here. The guy probably took a wrong turn and ended up at your place by mistake. Then he became agitated when you didn't have what he wanted, and we all know what came next. Unfortunately, that means the real drug dealer must live within a few blocks of here."

"Hard to believe," I say. "What's the world coming to?"

"You'd be surprised," the officer says.

Or maybe I wouldn't.

"The gray car," I say. "I think it's his."

"We'll take care of it," the officer says.

"And if he comes back?"

"Don't worry. He won't."

"But if he does?"

"He has no reason to come back," the officer says. "No real reason, anyway. Besides, he'll probably be locked up for the foreseeable future."

"How foreseeable?" I ask.

"You're shaken. I can see that. But you don't need to worry. We'll keep an eye on things."

At my neighbor's house, the girls are drinking hot chocolate from a pair of massive blue mugs that could easily double as soup bowls. They called the police, Lily says, but Catherine, ever interested in keeping the record straight, corrects her. The neighbors called the police when Catherine and Lily told them what was happening.

"I know you told us to wait in the car, Mom, but we were scared."

"It's okay, Catherine. I'm just glad you're safe."

"Who *was* that man?" Lily asks.

"I don't know," I tell her, but Officer Panakowski corrects me.

"The worst kind of scum there is, kids. That man was a dope fiend."

Ah, yes. The worst kind of scum.

Now why didn't I think of that?

CHAPTER THIRTY-THREE

I SPEND a whole day making deals with myself.

A taste in the morning, and I'll never touch the stuff again. A trip to the restroom when nobody's looking, and I swear it's my last hit ever. One tiny blast to keep me going while I make dinner for the girls, and—hand on the Bible, no fooling around—cocaine will be out of my life for good.

No more using.

No more dealing.

No more putting my daughters in harm's way.

But then comes the next day, and the day after that, and it's always the same story. All week long, I help the girls get ready for their trip to Hawaii, so all week long, I have the perfect excuse. Under normal circumstances, I could stop getting high without giving it a second thought, but with Catherine and Lily leaving, I need a little something to lift my spirits.

"Don't worry about me," I say as my daughters pack their shorts, tee shirts, bathing suits, sunscreen, sandals, and sunglasses. "I want you guys to have fun."

"Are you kidding?" Catherine says. "Of course we'll have fun."

"It's our first real vacation," Lily adds. "The first time we're taking a plane, anyway."

"No it isn't," I say. "Your father and I took you to Disney World two years ago."

"More like *five*," Catherine says. "And it hardly counts for Lily because she was just a baby."

"She was four years old," I say. "She *must* remember."

"Three at most," Catherine insists. "And everybody knows that you don't take a three-year-old to Disney World. It's a total waste of money."

"Actually, I *do* remember," Lily says, trying to keep the peace. "I think I was four. We took a plane to Disney World and stayed at a hotel. What I meant to say was that this is the first time we're flying first class."

The flight is scheduled for six in the evening, and Roger wants to pick the girls up at four on the dot. Given my hours, I have plenty of time to clock out of work and see my girls off, but at the last minute, Roger changes his mind and decides that safe is always better than sorry.

"You know how it is," he says when he calls my office on Friday afternoon. "Rush-hour traffic, long lines, security checkpoints. Better to leave room for a healthy margin of error than to miss our flight completely, right?"

"But I haven't said goodbye yet."

"You'll see them in a week," Roger says. He's calling from my house. From my own telephone. "It's no big deal."

"I can be home in five minutes."

"Don't worry about it. The girls are fine. They're in the car and ready to go."

"Roger," I say, but there's no point in arguing with him. "Tell the girls I love them, okay?"

CHAPTER THIRTY-FOUR

A STAND-UP bass is percolating on the radio. A dirty trumpet sings the blues while a saxophone belches like a foghorn over a nervous, rattling drumbeat. Charles Mingus. No one could swing harder, Owen says, revving his engine while the music sweats with the scent of trashy gun molls in cheap perfume and zoot-suited gangsters barreling through dark alleys in cars shaped like zeppelins, cars straight out of Dick Tracy cartoons.

"*Mingus Mingus Mingus Mingus Mingus,*" Owen says, pleased with himself and the way the name sounds as he shouts it over the music and pounds on the steering wheel. "*Mingus Mingus Mingus Mingus Mingus!*"

"I like it," I say. "It's dirty."

"He's the only musician Duke Ellington ever fired," Owen informs me. "They were playing at the Apollo, and this trombone player named Juan Tizol told Mingus that he was totally off key. Then Mingus told Tizol that he didn't know shit, and just as the curtain was rising, Tizol ran at Mingus with a bolo knife."

"What's a bolo knife?" I ask.

"It's a big fucking knife," Owen says with an air of exasperation. "So Tizol's charging at Mingus with this bolo knife, and Mingus scrambles off the stage with his stand-up bass only to come back five seconds later swinging a fucking axe at Tizol."

"Where'd he get the axe?"

"That isn't the point," Owen says. "The point is, you don't mess with Mingus."

Owen orders a beer at the Chinese restaurant, and I order a glass of wine. The fountain gurgles. Couples murmur in the close quarters of dimly lit booths as Asian-sounding strings plink on the speakers overhead. It's our first date all over again, except that neither of us makes a move to share our food. Instead, we pass a packet of cocaine back and forth under the table and take turns running to the bathroom.

"She's hot," Owen says at one point, eyeing the hostess. "I'd totally do her."

"You could at least pretend I'm in the room," I say.

"I said I *would* do her," Owen says. "Not that I *will* do her."

"Like there's a difference," I say.

"There is a difference," Owen says. "I *would* do her tonight if I had the chance, but I *will* be doing you."

"When did you become such an asshole?" I ask.

"I don't know," Owen says. "When did you become such a bitch?"

When our food goes untouched for nearly an hour, the waiter asks if anything's wrong, and Owen tells him that the music in the place is absolute shit.

"It sounds like a fucking karate movie in here," Owen complains. "Or a Chinese funeral home. Put on some jazz, for Christ's sake."

The waiter apologizes and explains that the music we're listening to is traditional Chinese dinner music. Feigning expertise on the subject, Owen calls the waiter a liar and says there's no such thing. When I tell Owen to relax, he glares at me and tells the waiter to take our food away and bring another beer.

"But you're driving," I say.

"And I'm coked up," Owen says as the waiter clears our plates. "They balance each other out."

The waiter keeps his eyes down and pretends not to hear what we're saying. Glancing nervously around the room, I struggle to make eye contact with anyone who's willing to look my way, but nobody is. My date is only kidding, my embarrassed smile does its best to explain. *Cocaine?* How ridiculous! Neither of us ever touches the stuff.

Owen's beer comes with the check and two fortune cookies. I crack mine open and read it aloud: "You see the world in a different way."

"That's bullshit," Owen says. "Different from what?"

Different from before I met him, I imagine.

Different from before I started using cocaine.

"I don't know," I say. "Do you want me to read yours?"

"Not particularly," Owen says, but I crack his cookie anyway.

"Nothing in the world is accomplished without passion."

"Genius," Owen mutters. "Pure fucking genius."

Back at home, I light some candles while Owen fiddles with the Stack-O-Matic turntable I tried and failed to give him for Christmas. It's such an archaic machine, he complains, stacking a series of LPs on the spindle. Sure, the so-called experts bitch and moan over the alleged coldness of digital music, but they're all full of shit.

"Scratches, pops, clicks, background noises? The whole point of the digital revolution was to eradicate these imperfections, not to fetishize them."

"I get it, Owen. It was a horrible gift."

"You want to make it up to me?"

"Not especially," I say.

He pulls a lever, and after a few seconds of mechanical effort, the record player starts playing a composition by Miles Davis, one of two tracks on an album called *In a Silent Way*. Owen calls it space jazz for all the echo and reverb the producer used to sweeten the instruments. It's minor Davis, Owen explains dismissively as the record turns on the spindle and the low hum of an organ gives way to the nervous tick of a hi-hat cymbal. Nothing compared to, say, *Kind of Blue* or *Birth of the Cool*, but not terrible either. Great music for getting stoned, in any case, but when I ask if Owen wants to share a joint with me, he sneers and tells me that pot is such a low-rent drug.

"Do a line and talk dirty to me," Owen says. "Tell me about this guy who showed up on your doorstep. Was he dangerous? Did he threaten you? Did you like it?"

"No, Owen. It was terrible."

"Come on, Audrey. Play along. Tell me you liked it. Tell me it turned you on."

"That's sick," I say.

"Did he threaten the girls?"

"Stop it, Owen."

"Tell me what it was like." He grabs me from behind and wraps his hands around my breasts. "Tell me you had a little party. Tell me you made the girls watch. Tell me you threatened to have their father killed if they breathed a word to anyone."

"I don't play this game," I say, my hands touching his.

"You do now," Owen whispers. "If you want me to stick around."

"No," I say, grabbing his little finger and bending it back to his wrist. "I don't."

Owen lets out a scream and calls me a bitch as I pull away from him.

No wonder Roger left me, he seethes. I'm no fun at all.

"Get out," I say quietly. "And don't come back."

CHAPTER THIRTY-FIVE

T HE LAST thing Owen deserves is an apology, but someone needs to make the first move if either of us expects our relationship to go anywhere, so I give him a call and say that I'm sorry for nearly breaking his finger. I was edgy and bitchy and a little coked up, I say as if the last reason weren't a given lately. On top of that, the girls were gone and, quite frankly, I missed them. I knew his little game was nothing more than a game, but he picked the wrong night to play it. Other nights, I would have simply told him to stop—or so I've convinced myself, anyway—but last night? Let's just call it a case of bad timing and let bygones be bygones.

"You're right about one thing," Owen says when I finish. "You were definitely coked up."

"I know. I've been using way too much lately. I really need to cut back."

"You're not the only one," Owen admits. "I was actually thinking about getting into a program."

"Seriously?"

"There's a place I know in Colorado."

"Sounds great," I say. "Assuming I can get some time off."

"It wasn't an invitation," Owen says. "This is for me."

"What?"

"I'll have to ask you to keep your distance, Audrey. It's no secret that you're a bad influence on me, and a relationship would only hamper my recovery."

"You're kidding, right?"

"No," Owen says. "I'm perfectly serious. It's like I'm someone else when I'm around you. Someone I don't like. The moodiness, the aggression. You bring out the worst in me, and it's not healthy. I wish you all the best, Audrey, and I hope you get some help, too, but I don't think we should see each other anymore."

"So, what? I'm on my own? What about our relationship?"

"Sorry," Owen says. "But I think it's for the best. You'll only bring me down."

Part of me wants to take a trip up the Golden Mile and hurl a brick through the window of Nick's American Grill, but somehow I feel that solution lacks elegance. If I really want to get back at the man, I need to call Melinda. Sure, they're supposedly good friends, but Melinda and I are in business together, so she'll have to take my side over his if only to keep the money coming in. Besides, if anyone has a moral obligation to help me take the man down, it's the woman who introduced me to him.

"I warned you," Melinda says when I apprise her of the situation. "The worst part is that when he comes back, he'll be unbearable—saying he feels better now than he has in years, telling us that nothing beats the high of being clean, looking down on us with contempt and asking how we can keep on poisoning ourselves like we do. It usually lasts a month or so, maybe longer if he gets religion. Fortunately, he tends to keep his distance, the bastard. The best thing you can do is forget about him."

"How?"

"Don't worry. I have a few ideas."

Melinda tells me to dress for a night on the town and to be at her place in an hour. She'll make a few calls, get a few friends together, and we'll have a regular girls' night out. When I arrive at her house, however, Alan answers the door with a can of Natural Light in his hand and says he wasn't expecting me.

"That's because no one told you she was coming," Melinda explains, sneaking up behind her husband in a tight tee shirt that at first glance looks as if it's imprinted with the Coca-Cola

logo, but upon closer inspection turns out to be an advertise-
ment for our own product line. "He gets weird when he knows
you're coming over. Don't take it personally, though. He has a
fetish for redheads."

Alan's face turns red as his sons begin to swing wooden baseball bats at each other in the living room. Looking me up and
down, Melinda asks how I expect to get laid if I insist on dressing
like someone's mom. If I want to turn any heads, she says, I need
to at least *try* to pass for seventeen.

"In the Hollywood sense, of course," she adds quickly. "The
way Mel Gibson passes for twenty-seven."

"You're going out?" Alan asks as one of the boys lets out a
scream.

"Catches on quick, doesn't he?" Melinda says before leading
me to her bedroom where I change into a pair of tight jeans
and a bright yellow tee shirt emblazoned with a giant marijuana leaf.

"But it's cold out," I complain. "I'll freeze to death."

"Your health doesn't matter in this situation," Melinda says.
"Our goal is to get you a man. Nothing permanent, of course.
Just a one-night stand to help you forget about our mutual
friend. What's your type, by the way?"

"Owen," I say. "Only nicer."

"Not an option, and we don't say that name tonight."

"Smart, funny, big on jazz."

"And coke," Melinda adds.

"I don't know," I say.

"Don't tell me you're jumping on *that* bandwagon."

I gesture helplessly and realize not only that Alan is
standing in the doorway, but also that he probably saw me get
undressed—and didn't say anything to stop me. Before he can
make a last-minute plea to get out of watching the kids, Melinda
ushers me downstairs and out the door. The boys are his problem
tonight, she says as we get into my car, but she'll make it up to
him on his birthday.

"What do you have planned?" I ask.

"Just drive," Melinda says as I put the car in gear. "We'll talk about it later."

J OHN C OLTRANE and Miles Davis trade licks to a frenetic drumbeat on my stereo as Svetlana barrels out of her apartment building and charges at my Toyota like a football player. The woman's cheeks are caked in rouge, her lips cherry red, her eyebrows more than likely drawn on with a black Crayola marker. Shrugging as if to say who else did I expect on such short notice, Melinda braces herself for the inevitable seismic shift that occurs when our zaftig Romanian friend bounds into my backseat.

"We go to club, yeah?" Svetlana says, popping a pacifier into her mouth so that it muffles her next sentence. "Score some E?"

"No way," Melinda says. "We're looking to get ripped, not all touchy-feely. You want to get high, you do a line like the rest of us."

"But your coke is shit," Svetlana complains. "Everyone knows this. Even Jerry."

"Shit coke beats ecstasy any day."

"Then you do shit coke," Svetlana says. "I'm scoring some E."

"Cute pacifier," I say.

"Cute is not the point," Svetlana says. "It keeps me from grinding my teeth when I fly."

A left, a right, a handful of identical streets named after dead presidents, a few for ivy-league universities, a brief flourish of avenues named for Greek gods, and finally we hit the cul-de-sacs named for bushes and shrubs. Holly. Rose. Azalea. Bladdernut. It's this last name that sends a shiver up my spine because I know where we are, and I know who lives here.

"No," I say. "I'm sorry, I can't."

"It's too late," Melinda says. "She's already expecting us."

"We can call her right now. Say we got lost. Tell her there's been a change of plan."

"Be nice, Audrey. She's our designated driver."

"Does she know that?" I ask.

"No," Melinda says. "But she'll find out soon enough."

At the tip of the cul-de-sac, Ellie is standing on her front lawn next to a knee-high statue of the Virgin Mary. Clad in her thick librarian glasses and a long, puffy parka, she clutches her purse with both hands and smiles into the glare of my headlights. If it weren't a dead-end street, I'd lay a heavy foot on the gas pedal and peel away in a cloud of burnt rubber and exhaust fumes, but since the quickest way out of the neighborhood leads straight through Vic's living room, escape is hardly an option.

When she climbs into the backseat with Svetlana, the first thing Ellie wants to know is whether anybody's holding. There's some coke in my purse, I tell her, and Melinda adds that it's fifty bucks a gram. Biting her lip, Ellie mulls the proposition over and asks if she can owe it to me.

"*Owe* it to her?" Melinda asks. "Fucking *owe* it to her? Could you be any more insensitive?"

"Insensitive?" Ellie asks. "What do you mean?"

"Like you don't know," Svetlana says, picking up on the joke.

"I don't," Ellie says. "Honestly."

"Owen," I say in a soft, sad, faraway voice. "Owen, Owen, Owen."

"He dumped her this afternoon," Melinda says.

"I had no idea," Ellie says. "I swear."

"Sure you didn't," Melinda says. "Bitch."

"Yeah," Svetlana agrees. "Fucking bitch."

"Bitch," I add to let Ellie know that it's unanimous.

Reaching into my purse, Melinda finds my little packet of coke and shovels some into her nose before spooning out a small quantity for me. We're on a major artery now and heading for the Golden Mile. I'm going about forty miles per hour as I press a finger to one side of my nose and snort. It's a good thing I'm not feeling *too* suicidal, Melinda says as we turn onto the main drag, or Ellie's question might have driven me over the edge. Taking this as a cue, I press down on the gas pedal and gun the engine.

"Maybe we should slow down a little," Ellie says as a strip mall zips by in a blur.

"Maybe *you* should be a little more sensitive," Melinda says.

I swerve into the next lane. The driver behind us blares his horn. Svetlana raises her middle finger, and Melinda tells the driver to fuck off.

"I said I was sorry," Ellie cries.

"Sorry doesn't cut it, kid. This is a broken heart we're talking about."

"Where's the nearest bridge?" I ask as we reach the end of the Golden Mile and pull onto the highway. "I've always imagined myself dying in icy waters."

We're going faster and faster, swerving across multiple lanes, zipping past increasingly angry motorists. The coke makes me feel indestructible, like I can slam the car into a brick wall and walk away completely unscathed. I feel like a character in a movie, or like I'm back on my plastic motorcycle, dodging missiles and attacking giant spiders at Fatso Ratso's Pizza Depot— like the world is a vast coin-operated video game and I have plenty of quarters to spare.

"Dying in icy waters," Svetlana says. "I like that."

"Very poetic," Melinda agrees. "*She died in icy waters.*"

"*They* died in icy waters," I say. "I'm taking all of you with me."

"The car went out of control," Melinda says. "And plunged into the icy waters below."

"Officials speculate that mechanical failure was to blame."

"The manufacturer of the automobile was unavailable for comment."

"Family members said that no group of friends had ever been closer."

"For Christ's sake," Ellie gasps. "Think of your daughters."

"Ooh," Melinda says as I zigzag through a convoy of tractor trailers. "Sore subject."

By the time we reach the city, Ellie's face is as white as a sheet.

"Are we almost there?" she asks as I guide my car through a neighborhood with no working streetlamps. "I could really use a drink."

"Not a good idea," Melinda says. Up ahead, strobe lights flash in the windows of a giant warehouse. The surrounding streets consist mainly of abandoned cars and crumbling row homes, so it's unlikely that anyone ever complains about the heavy, thundering music that originates deep inside the mammoth cinderblock structure and radiates outward like an angry, ugly heartbeat. "You're the designated driver."

"Sucks to be you," Svetlana says.

"No kidding," Ellie says.

Outside the warehouse, the parking lot is packed, and Melinda decides that serving as our valet falls well within Ellie's job description as our designated driver. Resigned to her fate, Ellie takes the wheel, and as the rest of us pay a large bald man twenty dollars to gain entry into the loudest circle of hell, I wonder if I'll ever see my car again. Inside, the club is lit with blue and red laser lights, and heated, as far as I can tell, entirely by the seething throng of young, sweaty bodies that shake and jiggle and bounce on the dance floor. If I can't find a one-night stand here, Melinda shouts in my ear, then I'm a lost cause.

"I'm not looking for a one-night stand," I shout back.

"Have a few drinks before you make up your mind," Melinda says, flagging down a waitress who's shilling drinks from a rack of glowing test tubes. "This isn't the kind of decision you want to make with a clear head."

Though they look like something out of Dr. Frankenstein's laboratory, our drinks taste like candy when we toss them back. Melinda pays the waitress and slips her a joint by way of a tip. When Svetlana leans in to ask a question, the woman shakes her head and gives us all a look of apology.

"You really think she'll tell you where to score?" Melinda shouts. "She has her own line to push."

"Was worth a shot," Svetlana says.

"Keep sucking on that pacifier. They'll find you."

Like teenage girls at a high school mixer, we stick to the outer perimeter of the dance floor. The Sandbag Dykes played here once, Melinda shouts, craning her neck as if she's looking for someone she knows. There's seating upstairs, but before we go anywhere, she wants me to put some serious effort into scoping out the talent.

"The talent?" I say.

"Find yourself a man," Melinda says. "Or a woman, if you feel like experimenting."

"Are you kidding? I'm the oldest person here. The place is filled with babies."

"Age ain't nothing but a number, darling. We need to get you another drink."

The waitresses wear heavy eye makeup and walk the floor in platform shoes. Their glowing drinks are easy to spot in the relative darkness, and after word gets out that the older woman in the *Cocaine* tee shirt is handing out joints in lieu of tips, Melinda barely has to look sideways to get the service she wants. Holding out for psychedelics, Svetlana declines to partake of what Melinda calls the sipping of the green because the alcohol might dull the effects of the ecstasy.

"You're trying too hard," Melinda says as Svetlana holds her pacifier in the air like a beacon. "Everyone here thinks you're a narc."

Svetlana pops the pacifier back into her mouth, and a hairless, shirtless man with glitter sprinkled across his chiseled chest takes a look at my shirt and puts a finger and thumb to his lips to pantomime smoking a joint.

"How would you like to take *that* home?" Melinda asks.

"I don't think I'm his type," I tell her. "He's dancing with another guy."

"Big deal," Melinda says. "That's what three-ways are for."

"Gross."

"You never know," Melinda says, giving a coy one-finger wave to the hairless man and his dance partner. "You might like it."

"I seriously doubt it."

"A little coke? The right setting?"

"I'm not going home with two guys, Melinda."

"Fine," Melinda says. "Would you settle for one?"

She nods in the general direction of the bar at the center of the dance floor. Dressed in what would, in any other setting, be his sharpest, coolest three-button suit, Raj is sitting by himself and sipping beer from a brown bottle while the rest of the world thrashes and squirms all around him.

"No," I say.

"Why not?"

"He's nineteen."

"And?"

"He's a kid, Melinda."

"A kid who wants you," Melinda says, bouncing on her toes and waving at the boy to get his attention. "Every woman should be so lucky."

"You planned this, didn't you?"

"Of course I planned it. You think he'd come here on his own?"

Raj spots Melinda, and his face brightens with a look I know all too well. It isn't that he's glad to see her, specifically, or even that he's glad to see me standing next to her. Instead, it's a look of relief, as if he's simply glad that someone—anyone—would admit to being his friend in this room full of absolute strangers.

"Shit," Svetlana says, spitting out her pacifier as Raj wades across the dance floor. "It's Ellie."

"Fuck," Melinda says. "Let's bolt."

"What about Raj?"

"Collateral damage," Melinda says, grabbing my hand and pulling me into the sweating throng of bodies. "Besides, it's not like you want to do him."

It's not like I want to abandon him either, but apparently I don't have a choice in the matter. As Svetlana loses herself in the crowd to continue her quest for ecstasy, Melinda drags me to a metal stairway at the edge of the dance floor. Halfway up the steps, I pause on a landing and see Ellie swirling helplessly amidst the sea of bodies in her puffy, gray parka, but Melinda urges me onward and upward.

"So you don't want a three-way, and Raj is too young," Melinda says when we find a private nook on level two where the club is less crowded and a few decibels quieter. Though we can still feel the heavy thump of an electronic bass drum shaking the floor, walls, and ceiling, we can talk without having to shout too much. "This leaves us with very few options as far as getting you laid is concerned."

"Who says I'm looking to get laid?" I ask, rolling a twenty-dollar bill into a tight little straw as Melinda uses a credit card to tap out two lines of coke on the small wooden table in front of us. "All I want is to forget about Owen."

"One and the same," Melinda says. "So let's make a deal. Either you score tonight, or you absolutely swear to God that you'll do everything in your power to seduce Captain Panther."

"I thought you wanted the Captain for yourself," I say.

"I'm willing to live vicariously," Melinda says. "Now repeat after me. *I, Audrey Corcoran, swear to God and all of creation that I will do everything I can to make Captain Panther so horny that he'll have a few drinks, do some coke, and make love to me until neither of us can move.*"

"I'm sure God's taking a real interest in this one."

"Say it," Melinda insists.

"It won't work," I say. "The guy's totally clean."

"I don't care," Melinda says. "Swear to God that you'll do this, or I'll never talk to you again."

"Fine," I say. "I swear."

"To God?"

"To God," I say. "Are you happy?"

"Very," Melinda says.

We each do a line to make the deal official, and Melinda leans into me as if moving in for a kiss. There's something we need to talk about she says, but before she can say anything, Svetlana appears at the top of the steps with Ellie following close behind.

"Good news, guys," Ellie shouts. "I found Svetlana, and we scored some E!"

"Not E," Svetlana says, placing four yellowish pills on the table in front of us. "But close enough."

"Close enough?" Melinda says. "What's that supposed to mean?"

"The man in the floppy hat said it was even better," Ellie says.

"The man in the floppy hat," Melinda says, nodding thoughtfully. "I've heard good things about him."

"Really?" Ellie asks.

"No."

"Don't be a bitch," Svetlana says. "Just tell us if it's safe."

"Hmm, let's see. You bought an unmarked pill from a man in a hat. Does this strike me as safe? Stick with a product you can trust, darlings. Have a little coke."

"He called it GHB," Ellie says.

"Hillbilly acid," I say, and all three women look at me as if to say, *Who are you, and what have you done with Audrey?* "I read about it in a pamphlet. Supposedly it stands for Great Bodily Harm."

"Wouldn't that be GBH?" Ellie asks.

"Not if you're a hillbilly," Melinda points out.

"Fuck hillbillies," Svetlana says. "Is it safe or not?"

We stare at the pills. Melinda says she's a cocaine girl, but I'm up for anything as long as someone else tries it first. Suddenly remembering that she's the designated driver, Ellie bows out as well, and we all look to Svetlana, who reaches for one of the pills and is about to pull the pacifier from her mouth when Raj shows up in his gradually rumpling three-button suit.

"*There* you are!" Melinda says before anyone else can speak. "We've been looking all over for you. Svetlana just scored some ecstasy, and we're all flying."

"Quality stuff," Svetlana adds, rolling her eyes for effect. "You want a hit?"

"I don't know," Raj says. "I don't usually take pills."

"Come on, Raj," Melinda says like a pusher from a bad public service announcement. "Everyone's doing it. Even Audrey."

What the hell, I figure. It's probably fine.

"You'll love it, Raj," I say. "It's a whole new buzz."

Svetlana holds the pill in her open hand. Raj knits his brow. All he needs is a little push in the right direction, so I take the pill from Svetlana and tell Raj to open his mouth like a good boy.

"Only for you, Audrey," he says. "And only in the name of love."

"How sweet," Melinda says, and I place the pill on Raj's tongue.

Swallowing hard, he asks what to expect, but the color is already draining from his face as Melinda tells him to sit back and enjoy the ride. A split-second later, he starts to sway. Still conscious yet barely coherent, Raj nods when we ask if he wants to sit down, but his skinny legs go out from under him before we can help him to the tattered couch.

"This isn't good," Ellie says. "This isn't good at all."

"Come on, kid," Melinda says, tapping Raj's cheek. "We have the whole night ahead of us."

Raj stirs, but barely. His eyelids flutter. His body makes a weak groan.

"We better get him to a hospital," I say.

For a second, I worry that Melinda might put up a fight and tell me that it isn't a big deal, but when she agrees with me, I know the situation is serious. Pulling a limp arm over each of our shoulders, Svetlana and I walk Raj down the stairs and through the loud, crowded dance hall. Parting the crowd ahead of us, Melinda smiles nervously and rolls her eyes at curious onlookers to suggest that our dapper Indian friend has simply had a few too many beers. When we step out into the cold night air, Ellie looks to the right and to the left and tells us that she can't remember where she parked.

"Christ," Melinda groans. "Please tell me you're kidding."

"It was dark," Ellie says, holding my car keys at arm's length as if they might point her in the right direction. "I was nervous."

"Idiot," Svetlana says.

Snatching my keys away from Ellie, I hit the panic button on my keychain. When nothing happens, I take a few steps and hit the button again. A few more tries, and I break into a run, pressing the button for all I'm worth and praying that I haven't killed Raj.

Ten feet from the darkest end of the parking lot, my car screams to life, and we all pile in. My hands are trembling as I turn the key, but when Ellie balks at being stuffed in the backseat with Svetlana and Raj on the grounds that she's the designated driver, I growl that she can either shut the hell up or get out of the car.

"Bitch," Melinda says when Ellie apologizes.

"Bitch," Svetlana adds.

"Bitch," I say to make it unanimous, but the word only makes me feel worse.

MAYBE IT'S the hour or maybe it's the neighborhood, but the hospital is a far cry from the one where I took Lily earlier in the week. The waiting room, for one thing, smells like urine, and an old woman with a shopping cart filled to the brim with old newspapers is curled up like a cat in the hard plastic seat next to mine. Standing in front of the admitting desk, Melinda taps her foot nervously as she explains to the woman in charge that our friend Raj has swallowed a pill of unknown origin.

"We tried to stop him," Melinda insists as Ellie wanders among the vending machines and mutters that it could have been her. "Because we're totally not into that scene at all. But the guy refused to listen to reason."

A security mirror is bolted to the ceiling, eyeing us all from above, distorting the world in its fisheye gaze. When I look up, I see a cartoonish figure staring back at me—round head, wide eyes, stick-thin body.

Who are we trying to kid?

Me and my giant marijuana leaf.

Melinda and her bright-red *Cocaine* tee shirt.

Honestly, doctor. We were just out for a few drinks when our friend here showed up with this pill. We told him not to take it, but he insisted. That stuff's dangerous, we told him. But did he listen? No-ho-ho!

I tell Svetlana that I'm through with using, and Ellie makes the same pledge to me. Fifteen minutes later, all of us are getting high with Melinda in the women's room. Just to steady our nerves, we tell ourselves. Just to keep it together.

Since we're not next of kin, no one at the hospital can tell us anything beyond the fact that Raj's family has been notified and that his uncle has vowed revenge. Taking this as a hint, we abandon Raj to his fate and escape into the night.

"He'll be fine," Ellie says when we drop her off at the bottom of her cul-de-sac after a long, silent drive. "I'm sure of it."

"Yeah," I say. "I'm sure he will."

After we drop Svetlana off, I tell Melinda that I want to get out of the business. I have about a week's worth of inventory left, and once it's gone, I don't want to stock up again.

Absolutely, Melinda says. She understands completely. After the night we've just had, who *wouldn't* have doubts about our product line? But the thing I need to keep in mind is that we're not like the scumbag who sold Svetlana her little yellow pill. Our product is safe, and as long as we're in business, we're actually saving the fine, upstanding people of our community from being rushed to the hospital like our good friend Raj.

"All I'm saying is don't make any hasty decisions," Melinda says. "The money's good, we provide a service to the community, and people like our product. I'll totally understand if you decide to end our partnership, but at least take some time to think about it."

"I *have* thought about it," I tell her. "Ever since that slimy kid showed up on my doorstep. Since before that, even."

"Then think a little more," Melinda says. "I'd hate for one little incident to put an end to an otherwise beautiful friendship."

My car is idling in front of her house. The night is dark and quiet. There's one more thing we need to talk about, Melinda says. She's been trying to bring it up all evening, but things kept getting in the way. Per usual, I can feel free to say no, but first I need to hear her out.

"It's about Alan's birthday," Melinda says as if someone we know isn't lying in a hospital bed because of something we did. "I want to do something special."

"Forget it," I tell her. "I'm not watching your boys."

"Already taken care of."

"Then what?" I ask.

"You're keeping an open mind?"

"No, but go on."

"I'm thinking you could stop by."

"Stop by," I say. "On Alan's birthday. Sorry, but I don't follow. How exactly does having a third wheel around count as special?"

Melinda holds my gaze for a second and smiles when I realize what she's talking about.

"No," I say. "I'm not into that."

"You promised to keep an open mind."

"No," I say. "I specifically told you that I was *not* keeping an open mind, and this is why."

"Come on," Melinda whines. "The guy has a huge crush on you."

"This is your husband we're talking about."

"The father of my children, I know. After this, he'll owe me forever."

"It's not who I am, Melinda. I'm not wired for this kind of thing."

"Then *get* wired for it. It's not as if you have other plans. We'll get a little baked, we'll have some fun, and in the morning we'll act like nothing happened. Very chic. Very sophisticated."

"I'm sorry, I can't do it."

"So you're saying?"

"No," I tell her.

"Okay," Melinda says, opening the door. "I'll take that as a maybe, and you can give it some more thought."

CHAPTER THIRTY-SIX

On Monday morning, I sit at my desk and throw together yet another issue of *Eating Out* as Vic goes ballistic on Melinda and Jerry in the office next door. For reasons undisclosed, the entire Patel Cartel has pulled out of the magazine, and Vic's only clue is a barely audible message from Raj stating that he won't be in for the foreseeable future.

"Can you believe this?" Melinda asks, barging into my office and slamming the door behind her when Vic's tirade devolves into a barrage of personal insults. "The guy's been foaming at the mouth for two hours straight. Why aren't you out there with us?"

"I'm busy," I say.

"Have you called the Captain yet?"

A heavy layer of concealer hides the circles under my eyes, and the wastepaper basket next to my desk is filled with tissues. Since I got home two nights ago, I've eaten three cough drops and a saltine cracker, slept a total of five hours and twenty-seven minutes, thought seriously about taking a shower, and settled instead for applying a fresh layer of deodorant to my armpits.

"No," I say. "I haven't had time."

"Don't forget, darling, you swore to God."

"I know," I say as Vic stomps around the office next door, a spleenful of blistering curses caught in his throat. "And all of creation."

"So you'll call him today, right?"

"And say what? The guy's probably still pissed over the Good Shepherd fiasco."

"No problem," Melinda says. "Tell him you're having trouble with your Ultimax 3000. The man's under contract."

"Then what? Get him hammered and break out the coke?"

"More or less. The key is to keep it casual. Get him to relax. Make him feel comfortable, then tear down his defenses with a glass of wine. Make it seem natural. Make it seem like no big deal. Two adults having a drink—how can he resist? By the way, have you given any more thought to Alan's birthday?"

Minutes before the Captain arrives, I loosen two screws on my Ultimax 3000 and do a line to steel my nerves. It isn't that I'm interested in the man romantically, of course. Seeing him in action at Good Shepherd was enough to turn me off to men in tights for the rest of my life. What I really want is to knock the man down a few pegs. What I really want is to get him high. What I really want is to make him more like me.

Putting some Miles Davis on the stereo, I try to convince myself that my motives aren't entirely selfish. If I can only prove to the Captain that he can still have a drink and enjoy the occasional line of coke, then I'll be doing him a favor. And if America's favorite just-say-no superhero can get high from time to time, then there's no reason to think I can't do the same.

"I'm really glad you called," the Captain says, making himself comfortable in my living room after tightening the screws on my exercise machine. "I've been thinking a lot about what you said the other day. That I shouldn't give up. That money and fame don't matter. That what really counts is making a difference in people's lives."

"I said that?" I call from the kitchen.

"Yeah," the Captain says. He's in the same gray overalls he was wearing the first time he visited my house, but I can't quite bring myself to call him Chris. "Even if I only keep one kid from getting into drugs, I've done a good thing, right?"

"Sure," I say, silently pouring two glasses of wine.

"So I'm thinking we need to set some realistic goals. Yeah, we still want to change the world, but we need to do it one show at a time. Enough with the hype. Let's focus on the product. From here on out, our goal is to make every show better than the last."

"Sounds like a plan." I do my best slinky starlet impersonation as I emerge from the kitchen and gaze at the Captain over the rim of the glass I'm holding out to him. "To just saying no—most of the time, anyway."

The Captain takes the glass and sniffs cautiously. He never touches the stuff, he says, setting the glass aside. He thought I knew that.

Apologizing, I ask if a single drink would be such a big deal.

"You sound like my mother," the Captain says.

"Ah, the words every girl longs to hear. Pick up your glass, Captain. I hate drinking alone."

I sip my wine.

The Captain doesn't move.

"You know, you're not the only superhero in town," I say. "And you're definitely not the only one who has a reputation to live up to. Have you ever heard of Wonder Mom?"

"No," the Captain says. "I can't say that I have."

"She cooks and cleans and drives her girls wherever they want to go. She works forty hours a week and sometimes more to give them everything they need. She stays up with them when they're sick and holds them when they're scared and checks their homework every night and meets with their teachers to discuss their grades and even watches TV with them to make sure the content is appropriate. Then she does the laundry and shops for groceries and pays the bills and balances the checkbook. But she has her secrets, too, Captain. Because sometimes Wonder Mom needs to unwind. Sometimes Wonder Mom needs to kick back and relax. Sometimes Wonder Mom needs to have a good time. And that's when she stops being Wonder Mom and turns into Party Girl. Have a drink, Captain, and you can have a little fun with both of us."

"Sorry," the Captain says. "I can't."

"Don't be sorry." I creep a little closer, and he doesn't retreat. "Just have a drink with me. One little drink, Captain. What will it hurt?"

"There's no such thing," the Captain says. "Not for me, anyway."

"Everyone needs to unwind once in a while. Everyone needs to have a *little* fun. Don't get me wrong—the Captain Panther act is great for kids, but let's be honest." I touch the inside of his thigh and lean in close to whisper in the Captain's ear. "Grownups need to be bad once in a while or they shrivel up and die. Don't make me break out the big guns, Captain."

"It's Chris," he says. "When I'm not in character, I'm plain old Chris."

"You're lucky," I say. "Some of us are always in character."

The Captain's heart is pounding, and I know it isn't me he wants or even the drink so much as to believe that I'm right, to believe that one drink couldn't possibly hurt, to believe that he can have a glass of wine and unwind once in a while or have a few drinks and let his worries drift away or have more than a few and forget about his life altogether and still wake up the next morning without feeling the urge to pour himself another.

"Maybe you're not a big wine drinker, Chris. Maybe you're into the hard stuff. Do you like martinis? Personally, I've never been a big fan. Maybe that's why I got into coke."

"Cocaine?" the Captain says.

I smile and nod.

"Trust me, darling," I say as I root through my purse for my coke, my razorblade, and my mirror. "It's for your own good."

I sit on the sofa and tap some coke onto the mirror. It's not like Raj, I tell myself. This isn't some mystery pill I'm getting the Captain to swallow. This is a product I trust, my good friend cocaine.

"See?" I say after doing a line. "It's easy."

The Captain blinks.

"Just a taste," I say, holding out the straw. "I promise you'll like it."

"That's the problem," the Captain says. "I probably will."

"I won't tell if you won't."

"You don't understand," the Captain says. "I wasted half my life on that stuff."

"It isn't heroin, darling. You can stop whenever you want."

"Can *you?*" the Captain asks.

"Hardly touch the stuff," I say. "Once in a blue moon."

The Captain shakes his head.

"Seriously," I say. "It isn't a problem."

"For you, maybe. But I doubt it."

"One line," I say. "Do it for me."

"I'm sorry," the Captain says. "I have too much to lose."

"Like what?" I ask. "Your light show? Your smoke machine?"

"You're better than this, Audrey."

"Trust me," I tell him. "This is as good as it gets."

"Do you really believe that?" the Captain asks.

"Absolutely," I tell him.

"Then give me a call when you've changed your mind."

"I don't see it happening," I say as he stands to leave.

"I'm sorry to hear that," the Captain says. "But I understand completely."

CHAPTER THIRTY-SEVEN

I miss a day of work and then another. By the end of the week, I'm alone and shivering beneath a heavy blanket as I imagine my daughters having the time of their lives in sunny Hawaii— sailing, fishing, scuba diving, swimming with dolphins and sea turtles. I picture Chloe applying sunscreen to their shoulders, noses, and cheeks. I hear their giddy little screams as their father splashes them with cold water from the hotel swimming pool. I see them sitting on beach towels and leaning against each other in the pink and purple glow of a Polynesian sunset. Already they're starting to think of that bitch as their mother, and it's killing me.

Hands shaking, I reach for my razor blade and try desperately to scrape together a line of coke from the particles of dust on my mirror, but it's no use. The trouble, however, isn't that I've been doing lines since abandoning Raj to his fate, because I haven't. I nipped at a bottle of wine all day Tuesday to break up the monotony, and I have the vague impression that I ordered a set of kitchen knives somewhere in the vicinity of Wednesday morning when an infomercial convinced me that nothing could be more important to my continued survival than being able to cut through a tin can, a running shoe, and a phone book with a single blade. The trouble—the real trouble—is simply that I'm out of cocaine.

"Look what the cat dragged in," Melinda says when I call her. "Or should I make that the panther?"

"No," I say. "You shouldn't."

"Seriously? I thought for sure you were bonking the guy when you didn't show up for work on Tuesday. Then came Wednesday, and I could only imagine what you guys were up to."

"It didn't work out," I say.

"So what have you been doing all this time?"

"Three guesses," I say, but an ugly sniffle gives away the answer.

"No kidding," Melinda says. "How much?"

"A little," I say. "Maybe a lot. That's why I'm calling."

"This isn't good business, Audrey."

"It's only for this week," I tell her. "Can you help me out or what?"

"Sure," Melinda says. "For you, anything. Stop by my house tomorrow, and we'll work something out."

My guess is that the "something" Melinda has in mind is related to her husband's fortieth birthday, but I don't care. All I want is the galvanized, bulletproof feeling that only cocaine can deliver, so I crawl back under the covers and spend the next twelve hours alone with my misery. It isn't sleep, exactly. It's simply shutting out the world. Grinding my teeth in the darkness, I feel like my brain is tying itself in knots, and every half-hour, like clockwork, I throw off my blankets in a panic because I'm convinced that my skin is crawling with ants.

On Friday afternoon, I run a hot shower and try to do the numbers. The girls will return late the next day, which gives me approximately twenty-four hours to get my life into some semblance of order. No big deal, right? One or two lines of coke with Melinda, and I'll be fine. A little hit before Catherine and Lily walk through the door, and they'll never suspect a thing. I'll be my old self—happy and caring and completely reliable. On Monday morning I'll do a final line before heading off to work, then I'll be done with cocaine forever.

One last gram is all I need.

Or maybe two.

In either case, I remind myself as the hot water bites into my back, the only way for me to get myself clean is to score some coke, and if helping Melinda with Alan's birthday present is the price I have to pay for it, then I really don't have much choice in the matter.

The trick is to think of it as just another party.

The trick is to pretend that I'm somebody else.

The trick is to convince myself that it's all a dream or a scene in a movie.

My eyes are red when I wipe the steam from my bathroom mirror.

My nose is raw. My cheeks are hollow. My lips are thin and pale.

This isn't my face, I tell myself.

This face is the face of a stranger.

I DON'T resist when Melinda removes my big, plastic Chrissie Q sunglasses and kisses me on the lips. The transaction doesn't turn me on, but it also doesn't turn me off. Instead, it's completely neutral, like applying for a car loan or paying for groceries. Even as I return the kiss, I'm conscious of the fact that it's nothing more than a means to an end. Beyond that, I don't give it a thought.

"We have a few hours before Alan comes home," Melinda says, inspecting the dark raccoon circles around my eyes. "So we might as well make ourselves comfortable."

"What about the boys?" I ask.

"Not a problem," Melinda says. "I split them up and palmed them off on other kids' parents. As a set, they're hell, but they lose their powers when they're not in direct contact with each other. That's what I told everyone, anyway."

Melinda hangs up my coat and invites me up to her bedroom where the bed is made with black satin sheets and a razor blade rests atop a mirror on her night table. Drops can take care of the red in my eyes, Melinda muses as she caresses my cheek with the palm of her hand, but the best way to take care of the dark circles is to hide them under even darker ones.

"It's funny," she says as she blackens my eyes. "I remember when you used to be good."

"What's that supposed to mean?"

"Nothing," Melinda says.

Sharing a joint and taking turns with her coke, we spend the next hour paging through copies of *Vogue* and *Vanity Fair* in an effort to get a sense of the game we'll play when Alan comes home. In every ad on every page of every magazine, skinny waifs with knobby elbows pout against vaguely gothic backdrops and gaze longingly at each other in an effort to sell shoes, handbags, dresses, designer watches, and expensive perfume. They touch each other's breasts. They whisper secrets in each other's ears. They wear baroque jewelry and antique military uniforms and curl up with each other on gilded sofas. They scratch baby tigers behind the ears. They feed each other grapes. They touch themselves in private places and sip champagne from crystal flutes. Meanwhile, Melinda is holding skimpy outfits up to my body and laying down the rules of this evening's engagement.

I'm allowed to touch her anywhere, she says. I'm allowed to kiss her, and I'm allowed to inflict pain within certain limits. Scratching is okay, but not to the point of drawing blood. Biting is definitely out, and her face is completely off limits.

"And so is Alan," Melinda says. "But that goes without saying."

"So no touching Alan."

"God, no. He's mine."

"Can Alan touch me?"

"Not if he knows what's good for him."

"So what am I doing here?"

"Getting coked up, darling. It's what you live for, isn't it?"

"Right," I say. "I almost forgot."

It's no big deal, I tell myself as I undress and slip into the silky red nightshirt that Melinda picked out for me. We're all consenting adults, after all, and after a few more hits of coke and grass, I'll be back in the zone where I don't have to think or live or feel, the world where my life is nothing more than a scratchy movie I'm watching from the back row of a grimy second-run theater.

By the time Alan comes home from work, I'm nothing more than a body. My lips are red, my eyes black, my hair a wiry tangle of orange curls. When she hears Alan's truck pull into the driveway, Melinda dims the lights, and I snort another line of coke. Seconds later, a key turns in the lock downstairs, and Melinda's hand slips inside my silky nightshirt to caress my breast.

"Don't worry," she whispers. "You're a natural."

We're sitting on the bed. I lean into Melinda, and she wraps her arms around me. I hold the mirror in my lap, a razor blade in one hand, a straw in the other. Calling out to Alan, Melinda says that she's in the bedroom. There's a pause, and then, in the still of the night, the sound of Alan cracking open a can of beer. His knees creak and crackle as he climbs the steps, and Melinda gives me a squeeze.

"Hey, baby," she purrs when her husband finally walks in on us. "So glad you could make it. Audrey and I were getting lonely."

Alan stands in the doorway, a can of beer in one hand as the other hand tugs at the hairs on his chubby chin.

"So what'll it be, Alan?" I ask. "Do you want to join in, or would you rather watch?"

"Watch," Alan says. "For now."

Melinda loosens her grip on me and reaches for the mirror in my lap. Touching the cocaine with the tip of her finger, she holds it to my lips and tells Alan that I've been a bad girl. Which is really pretty amazing, she adds, because I used to be so good.

"Remember, Alan? She was the one who never had any fun. So pure, so responsible, so careful, so boring. But I never gave up on her, never lost hope. And do you know why, Alan? Because deep down, I knew she had it in her to be bad. Deep down, I knew she was dirty like the rest of us. And all it took, Alan, was a little push in the right direction. A few lines of coke, and she was ours for life. Isn't that right, darling?"

"Mm," I say, then kiss her fingertip.

They're only words, I tell myself. They really don't matter.

Deep down, I'm still good.

Deep down, I'm still Audrey.

Deep down, I'm still a mother.

Melinda's breath is hot as we kneel in front of each other on the bed and undo the buttons on each other's shirts. My body is aching. My muscles are tense. The coke is twisting me in knots, and from a distant point deep inside my head, I'm screaming at myself to stop, to back away from Melinda, to put some clothes on for Christ's sake, to go back home and clean myself up and wait for my girls to come back from their vacation, and, above all, to promise myself that I'll never go near another line of coke for as long as I live. But my silent, desperate cries go completely unheeded, and my body keeps moving without any concern beyond the purely carnal. My hands crawl across Melinda's back, my lips kiss her softly on the neck, and my hips start swaying in tandem with hers because Melinda has the coke and all I want is more.

Tired of watching, Alan begins to unbuckle his belt, but the telephone rings before he can join us. Cursing, Melinda tells him not to answer, but apparently the man is a creature of habit. Refastening his belt, he picks up the receiver and motions for us to cover ourselves so as not to arouse suspicion.

"It's a telephone, Alan," Melinda sighs as her husband says hello. "They can't see us."

Gesturing for Melinda to shut her mouth, Alan nods repeatedly and begins a series of increasingly profuse apologies that culminate with him saying that he'll see the caller in a few minutes.

"That was Nancy," Alan says after hanging up the telephone. "Scottie won't keep his clothes on."

"How's that our problem?" Melinda asks.

"He's our son, for one thing," Alan says. "And for another thing, it's not just the clothes. He also pushed Terrance down a flight of steps."

"Terrance?" Melinda asks. "I thought the kid's name was Lucas."

"It is," Alan says. "Terrance is Nancy's husband. He asked Scottie to put his clothes back on."

"And what? Scottie threw him down a flight of stairs? I'm not buying that for a second. Call Nancy back and tell her we had a deal."

"They think he may have cracked some ribs," Alan says. "After they drop Scottie off, Nancy's driving Terrance to the hospital."

"And Lucas?"

"That's the catch." Alan snorts a line and rubs his nose. "I kind of agreed to take him in for the night."

"No," Melinda says, grabbing the mirror from her husband. "Call her back and tell her we're not interested."

"They're already on their way."

"Then we're not home." Melinda scrapes together the last of the coke on her little mirror and snorts hard. "When she knocks on the door, we turn out the lights."

"She'll know we're here," Alan says. "I just got off the phone with the woman."

"Then we don't accept the delivery. She knocks on the door, and we say we don't want any."

"I don't think it's an option."

"I don't believe this," Melinda says. "You didn't even put up a fight."

"Our son broke a man's ribs," Alan says. "There wasn't much room for negotiation."

"It's not a question of negotiation, Alan. It's a question of balls, which you obviously don't have."

Two more packets of cocaine are sitting on the nightstand. Reaching for one of them, Melinda taps its contents onto her mirror and starts to formulate a plan. Normally, she'd just buy the woman off with a gram of coke or a few joints, but Nancy is the straightest priss on the face of the Earth—worse, even, than I used to be—so the only way to deal with her is to make it painfully clear that the three of us are up to no good.

"We invite her in, we let her know we're in the middle of an orgy, and she goes away," Melinda says. "Simple as that. If she has any sense at all, she'll take the boys with her."

"And when the kids ask what we're up to?"

"That's Nancy's problem."

The argument is still going strong when the doorbell rings. From Alan's perspective, the best course of action is to answer the door alone and assure Nancy that her son is in good hands. Still clinging to her original plan, however, Melinda chases Alan out of the bedroom and calls for me to follow. Snorting a quick line, I do as I'm told, but not before grabbing the second packet of coke from Melinda's nightstand and slipping it into the pocket of my nightshirt.

By the time I catch up with Alan and Melinda, Nancy has, at Melinda's behest, taken a seat on one of the sun-faded chairs in the living room, and the boys have plopped themselves down in front of the television. Clutching her purse in her lap, the interloper insists that she really can't stay, but before she can mention her husband's cracked ribs, she spots me in my skimpy red outfit and freezes midsentence.

"Have you met our friend Audrey?" Melinda asks nonchalantly. "Her kids go to Good Shepherd with Scottie and Lucas."

The woman stares at me, eyes wide, mouth slightly open, and I can only imagine what she sees.

"You have to understand," I say as the woman gathers her wits and leaps up from the chair. "This really isn't me."

"Of course not," the woman says, calling her son's name and saying that they have to leave.

"Really," I say. "I don't normally do this kind of thing."

"Lucas!" the woman says. "Your father's waiting for us."

Glued to the television, the boy protests, but his mother takes him by the hand and tells him again that it's time to go.

"I thought I was staying here," Lucas says as his mother drags him from the room. "You said I could stay with Scottie tonight."

"That was before," the woman says, heading for the door with her child in tow.

"I mean it," I insist, mostly to myself. "I'm not like this at all."

The woman fumbles with the doorknob, and Alan stands to help her. As he approaches, however, the woman shies away and says she can open the door on her own.

"I know what you're thinking," I say, staggering toward the woman. "And it's not true. I'm really a good person."

"I'm sure of it," the woman says, still struggling with the door.

"No," I cry as the boy asks his mother why Melinda and I are both in red underwear. "You don't understand. I'm not a bad mother. I'm really, really good. You have to believe me."

My body is shaking. I look down at my sickly belly and bony knees.

"This isn't me," I sob, wilting like a flower as the door flies open and the woman drags her son across the front lawn. "I'm not like this at all. I'm good. I'm good. I'm good."

"Don't cry, darling," Melinda says, stroking my hair. "We can have our little party some other time."

I DON'T even bother to change clothes. I pull a coat over my skimpy outfit and head for my car. The night air is cold, but I don't care. I'm just glad to be leaving Melinda's house, glad to be going home, glad to put the whole incident behind me. I have a gram of cocaine in my pocket, and my daughters should be home in less than twenty-four hours. All I have to do is snort a quick line, straighten up the house a little, and everything will be back to normal by the time the girls walk in the door.

The only problem is that a little voice keeps whispering in my head:

He's waiting for you, it says. *The angry little goat-boy. He's sitting on your step, and he has a gun. Dirty, smelly, unshaven. He'll pick up his gun and pull the trigger. He'll splatter your brains across the lawn. He'll laugh and shoot you and steal your coke.*

I drive around the block three times as my brain plays the footage over and over: the dirty kid, his scruffy beard, his gravelly voice. He'll say I had it coming. He'll tell me I fucked with the wrong guy. He'll put his gun to my head and pull the trigger and steal my cocaine. I can see it more clearly than I can see the road ahead of me, and I flinch every time he pulls the trigger.

My skin is crawling. My jaw is tense. Ornette Coleman and his band are screaming in a million directions at once. After ten or twelve more trips around the block, I switch to driving up and down the Golden Mile to break up the monotony. All the lights are dead, and except for the occasional sad, forgotten desk lamp burning away in the sales office of some car dealership or linoleum outlet, all the windows are dark.

One more hit, I keep thinking.

One more hit, and I can get my head together.

One more hit, and everything will be fine.

When the sun eventually starts to creep over the horizon, my brain gives me a reprieve. The goat-boy is gone, I mutter to myself, because people like him—*dope fiends* is the term I'm looking for—are vampires at heart. No soul. No life. When the sun comes up, they turn to dust—just like I will if I don't get some coke in my system before the girls come home.

Pulling into my driveway, I scan the area for signs of danger before dashing from my car and into my house. Once inside, I lock the door behind me and reach into the pocket of Melinda's silky red nightshirt for my packet of coke. Finally alone in the safety of my home, I light some candles and put a Miles Davis record on the turntable.

The trumpet is mellow.

The piano twinkles like starlight.

I tap some coke onto an old mirror and chop lovingly at the white powder with a razor blade. Looking down on the mirror, I can't see past the cocaine, can't see the horror show my face has become, can't see the thick, black sludge congealing in ugly clumps around my eyes, can't see my raw, red nose, can't see the thin salamander lips stretched across my teeth and gums in a twisted, angry, hungry smile.

All I see is cocaine, and I know I'm in love.

This will be the one, I tell myself as I tap at the mirror with my razor blade. This will be the line that solves everything. I'll get a little high and groove to some jazz, and all the answers will come to me like magic: how to deal with Roger, how to make my daughters love me, how to get Owen back, how to stop using so much cocaine. When I'm satisfied that I've done enough chopping, I put down my razor blade and pick up my straw.

The coke makes me smart.

The coke makes me beautiful.

The coke makes me sexy and strong and funny and cool, and the more I do, the more I realize that the perfect solution to all of my problems is to do more cocaine. So I turn up the volume on my Stack-O-Matic turntable and do another line. I pile a half-dozen LPs on the spindle and do a line after that. I pull out old photo albums and look at pictures of my ex and my little girls, and I take little hits from my coke spoon. I watch old videotapes of birthdays and Christmases long past, and wonder—vaguely, because the party isn't over yet—where I might score when my current stash runs out; then I tap a little more coke onto my mirror and snort a line and watch my little girls grow up in fits and starts on the TV in front of me.

Birthday cakes.

Paper hats.

A woman with my face who looks genuinely happy.

I used to be her, I think, touching the screen as if by some miracle I might reach in and save my younger self—might, for the briefest of moments, be allowed to step back in time and whisper advice in the young mother's ear.

Don't get too comfortable.

Keep an eye on your husband.

Never get old.

WHEN I open my eyes, the TV screen is crawling with static and my record player has gone silent. Spilling the remainder of my coke onto the mirror, I start once again to divide my precious powder into skinny white lines but stop suddenly when I hear the unmistakable sound of a car door slamming shut—then another and another.

I don't even bother to look out the window. Pausing long enough for the quickest of sniffs, I pile my paraphernalia onto the mirror and carry it all upstairs to the bathroom where I resume the work of chopping up lines while the girls let themselves into the house and start calling for me. They're home, they shout, excited footsteps heading for the family room and then for the kitchen as they sing of the previous week's adventures.

They went snorkeling and petted a stingray, Lily exclaims.

They took a boat out to sea and swam with dolphins, Catherine shouts.

They ate pizza topped with pineapples and played miniature golf every night. The course was right on the grounds of their hotel, and Lily scored a hole-in-one. Roger let Catherine drive her own go-cart, and Chloe won a hula contest on the last night of the vacation.

Sitting on the edge of my bathtub, I put the straw to my nose and snort hard.

Fuck snorkeling, I mutter, the mirror teetering precariously on my knee.

Fuck stingrays and dolphins and miniature golf.

I'm their mother, for Christ's sake. If they can't appreciate that, then my daughters can go to hell.

Vaguely aware of the footsteps on the stairway, I put the straw to my nose again.

Not quite cognizant of the fact that I never closed the door, I lean over my mirror.

Completely oblivious to the little girls standing in the doorway, I snort another line.

"Mom?" Catherine says tentatively.

I freeze and, for the first time, look down past the coke to see the dark, runny rings around my eyes.

"Shut the door, baby doll," I say. "Mommy's busy."

Turning away from my own reflection, I look up at the girls and force a smile.

"It's okay," I say. "I'll be done in a minute. Close the door, and go downstairs."

But the girls don't move.

They can't.

All they can do is stand and stare, paralyzed with fear.

I'm not their mother, their faces say.

I'm a stranger, a wolf, a monster.

"Really," I say. "You don't need to worry. I have everything under control."

Another line is all I need. One quick line, and I'll wash my face and put on some clothes and go downstairs to make my girls lunch, and they can tell me all about their exciting adventures, and I'll smile and listen and tell them how much I missed them and how happy I am that they're home. Because that's what good mothers do, and I'm a good mother, and all I need is a little more coke to pull myself together and get back to business as usual. But the girls are just standing in the doorway and staring at me with their sunburned faces and their mouths hanging open, and all I can think as the mirror crashes to the floor is that I hope my cocaine is okay.

"Could you girls leave Mommy alone for a minute?"

More footsteps on the stairs, Chloe's voice hinting at mild concern.

"I thought I heard something break," she says. "Is everything okay?"

There's blood on the floor. The girls are shaking.

When Chloe appears in the doorway, she looks at me and catches her breath.

"What are you looking at?" I croak.

Quickly and quietly, she places protective hands over my daughters' eyes and guides them, one inch at a time, out of the room. Everything will be okay, she says softly. Mommy just isn't feeling well right now.

One more line, and everything will be fine.

But there isn't enough.

There's never enough.

I hate her so much.

I'M SITTING on the floor and hugging my knees, back against the bathtub, when the paramedics arrive. There's been an accident, Roger tells me time and again as he rides with me to the hospital, but everything will be okay. When the admitting nurse asks how he's related to me, Roger pauses for a moment before saying that he's my ex.

The nurse nods at this fact and makes a note.

Before any doctors see me, Roger places a clipboard in my hand and tells me to sign the form that's attached to it. He's speaking slowly, as if I'm a child, and he's telling me that I need to sign the form so he can talk to the doctors about my condition.

And, he fails to add, so the doctors can talk to *him*.

Roger presses a pen into my hand, but I refuse to sign the document. Even if my addiction is all I have left, it's mine, and I don't want Roger taking it away from me.

I need to be reasonable, Roger says when I push the clipboard away. Then he turns to the admitting nurse, who simply holds out a hand to take back the unsigned form.

"We were married for ten years," Roger says. "That has to count for something."

The nurse apologizes. She didn't make the rules, she says.

"What if I told you we were still married?"

The nurse shakes her head and apologizes again, addressing Roger as *sir*.

As in, *Please understand, sir, it's not me—it's the system.*

As in, *Please have a seat, sir, while we see to your ex-wife.*

As in, *Please calm down, sir, or I'll have to call security.*

I know he's only trying to look out for me, but when the admitting nurse makes it clear to Roger that he won't get his way, the tiniest spark of satisfaction flashes in my heart. Despite my best efforts, I've never been able to say no to Roger, never been able to deny him anything. But now, backed by this system that's bigger than either of us, the admitting nurse has stopped the man in his tracks, and there's nothing he can do about it.

Not that my spark lasts very long. Soon, I'm lying on a stiff hospital bed behind a heavy curtain, and a half-dozen strangers in loose-fitting pastels are shining lights in my eyes and asking me point-blank about the drugs I've been taking. Have I been using cocaine, they ask in a loud, patronizing voice?

All I can do is nod.

What about heroin, a woman's voice asks while a man with a goatee pulls my lower eyelid down with the tip of his thumb and peers into my right eyeball.

I shake my head, then shake my head again when the woman asks if I've been using any hallucinogens like LSD, angel dust, mushrooms, or ecstasy, or painkillers like OxyContin, or uppers like crystal meth.

They poke me and take blood and say they need to run some tests. I hardly flinch when a nurse shoots a local anesthetic into my foot and a doctor removes three slivers of glass. I barely nod when a different doctor asks if I understand that I'm dehydrated—that my body needs water, he explains—and undernourished. The cocaine has done a lot of damage to my system, he says with a practiced frown, but the biggest problem is that it's fooled my body into believing that I don't need to eat or drink anymore. In the short term, the solution is to replenish my body's fluids and nutrients intravenously.

"In other words, we need to put a tube in your arm," the doctor says. I know he's talking down to me, but I don't care— just like I don't care that my body is wasting away or that everyone here assumes that I have the IQ of a hairbrush. "Don't worry, though. We'll have you back on solids in no time. What you do after that is entirely up to you."

CHAPTER THIRTY-EIGHT

FOR THREE days, I feel nothing. My room is spare, the walls a soft yellow. Healthcare providers of every variety check on me regularly, poking and prodding and asking how I feel. Much better, I tell them invariably, though I never make eye contact or look at anything beyond my own lap. Even as the IV tubes replenish the fluids and nutrients my body so desperately needs, I can't shake the feeling that I'm empty inside, that the coke has eroded my heart and soul.

On the day I'm discharged, Roger drives me home in Chloe's Lincoln Navigator. It's the kind of car that boasts a commanding view of the road, the kind of car you drive if you're afraid of other drivers. Looking down on all the suckers in station wagons and compact cars, I wonder if they'll ever know how good it feels to ride so high above the rest of the world—how safe, how secure, how strong, how completely unassailable.

"I can't help blaming myself," Roger says, taking a sharp turn that makes the vehicle lurch to one side before righting itself. "At least in part, anyway. Not that the divorce was my fault, *per se*, but if we both worked a little harder to keep our marriage together, then you never would have met *him*. And it goes without saying, of course, that if you never met *him*, he never could have gotten you hooked on that garbage."

"I got myself hooked, Roger."

"Well, you're clean now, and if you want to stay that way, you'll keep away from that guy."

I almost laugh. As if Owen were my only connection—or my connection at all, for that matter. As if he somehow forced me to try my first line. As if by simply staying away from him, I might resist the urge to get high and forget how numb and dead and empty I feel without my precious cocaine. As if my addiction were nothing worse than a severe staph infection that a few days in the hospital had cured for good—assuming I never go back to the leper who infected me in the first place.

As if it were really *that* simple.

"We broke up," I say.

"Good. I never liked that guy anyway. I know I should have told you, but I didn't want to interfere. You *are* my best friend, after all, and I wanted to see you happy."

"Could you please stop saying that, Roger? I'm not your best friend."

"What?" He looks away from the road long enough to give me the look he always uses to tell me I'm crazy. "Of course you are."

"No, Roger. I'm not. I'm your ex-wife and the mother of your children, but if I'm still your best friend, then something's terribly wrong between you and Chloe."

"A guy can have more than one best friend, Audrey."

"No, Roger. He can't."

We approach my house, and I can feel every eye in the neighborhood staring at me from behind discreetly parted blinds and curtains.

"We still have to talk about the girls," Roger says, piloting the hulking vehicle into my driveway and slowing to a stop behind my little Toyota. "I think it would be best if I took custody of them for a while."

"You say that as if it's up for debate."

"I don't want the courts involved, Audrey. The girls have been through enough."

"I know," I say quietly. "And I wouldn't blame them if they never want to see me again."

"Are you kidding?" Roger says. "You're their mother."

My ex-husband walks with me to the front door. I'm scared for my daughters in so many ways, and even more scared to see them again, but they greet me with hugs and a welcome-home banner made of glitter and glue and brightly colored paper. They're glad I'm okay, they say over and over again, as if repeating the phrase will make it come true, and each time they say it, I sense a question or a query, a need for confirmation.

As in *You are better now, right?*

As in *You're not on drugs anymore, are you, Mom?*

As in *You went to the hospital, and they cured you, didn't they?*

As in *We'll pretend it never happened if you will, okay?*

All I want is to hug them and hold them forever and tell them that everything's fine, but I don't have the words. The closest any of us comes to saying *addiction* is that I've been sick. The word *cocaine* is never spoken. It's like I just got home from an appendectomy or a trip to Mars, and all anyone wants is for our lives to return to normal.

I sit on the sofa with my daughters.

Roger and Chloe sit in easy chairs, sipping tea.

A week's worth of mail is stacked in neat piles on the dining room table.

Somewhere in the house, my answering machine is blinking.

Maybe Melinda called, a voice whispers in my head. Maybe she found a new connection. Maybe we can score some coke—a little, a taste, a line or two to chase my blues away, a gram to keep on hand for emergencies or special occasions.

I'll keep it under control this time.

I'll know when to stop.

Slipping into their spring jackets, the girls say goodbye. Pulling me aside, Roger says that if there's anything he can do for me—anything at all—I shouldn't hesitate to call. Hugging me, Chloe says that she admires my courage. I'm strong, she adds. She knows I'll pull through.

"I said some things," I tell her.

"It's okay," she says. "You weren't yourself."

I thank her for understanding and hug my daughters one last time, then stand in the driveway and wave goodbye as they leave me alone with my big empty house and a heart full of demons.

Inside, I check my answering machine and the messages on my cell phone. My customers want to know if I'm holding, Bunny Hoffman wants to know if I can front her an eight-ball, and Vic is furious over the fact that I haven't been to work in over a week. I shouldn't bother coming in ever again, he seethes, adding that he's already interviewing potential replacements. In the final message, Melinda tells me to give Vic a day or so to cool off, and I can probably get my job back with a minimum of groveling. The good news, she adds, is that she has a new lead on some quality product.

Would it hurt, I wonder?

Would it be so bad?

I'll give her a call, and we'll shoot the breeze.

Maybe we'll meet for coffee.

And if she's holding, who knows?

Maybe I'll have a little taste for old time's sake.

I pick up the phone. The receiver feels heavy in my hand.

It's only a phone call I tell myself as the dial tone calls to me like a siren song.

Stabbing at the touchpad, I dial a number and take a breath.

"Hi, Captain," I say when I hear his voice. "It's Audrey."

CHAPTER THIRTY-NINE

I GO to meetings now. At least once a week, I get in my car and drive to a church to share stories of my former lives with eight or nine other recovering addicts in a damp, drafty basement. We sit on metal folding chairs and nod in agreement as a man with a harelip says with a lisp that he can't look at a razor blade anymore without hearing the telltale tap of metal on glass. We shift our collective weight, and the chairs creak nervously as a woman in leopard-skin tights and a gray college sweatshirt says the phone numbers of each and every one of her connections will still be burned into her memory long after old age, psychosis, and Alzheimer's have robbed her of the names and faces of family and friends. We drink lukewarm coffee and eat store-brand butter cookies as Captain Panther, in the guise of mild-mannered fitness enthusiast Chris Parker, tells us to join hands and reminds us that we all have the strength to conquer our demons.

The coffee pot percolates on a card table.

Fluorescent lights buzz overhead.

Sometimes I keep my mouth shut and just listen to everyone else's tales of woe. Other times I talk about the girls and how I lost them to my addiction. They're with Roger now, I tell my group, and they nod sympathetically. We decided it was for the best, at least for the time being. No lawyers beyond the bare minimum required to put our arrangement into writing. No courts. No judges. No third-party adjudicators. Just two adults working out what was best for their kids. Maybe one day when I feel confident, in Roger's words, that I'm *past it*, we'll talk about *revisiting the custody situation*, but until then, the girls are his.

My new friends murmur with sad laughter when I use Roger's terminology. We all live in a world of well-meaning people who think we'll wake up one day, and the sun will be shining, and the birds will be singing, and we'll suddenly realize that we haven't even *thought* of getting high in weeks. But that's the conundrum that no one outside of our exclusive little club seems to understand. The minute you think you're getting past it is the minute all the old pangs start flooding your mind.

One taste.

One line.

One gram.

What harm could it do?

My fellow addicts nod but remain silent.

Since giving up coke, I've gotten hooked on jazz. I joke with my fellow addicts that I was just a casual user when Owen and I were dating, but now that I'm clean, I won't think twice about spending an hour sifting through stacks of dusty vinyl at a garage sale or driving sixty miles to check out the offerings at a vintage music expo. It's not like I'll ever run into Owen at any of these things, I'm always quick to point out; he was never anything more than a dilettante.

The line always gets a laugh because I've talked *ad nauseam* about Owen, but I've never once admitted the real truth—that part of me is scared to death that I *will* see him again.

And if I do?

I have no idea.

I want to say it won't lead to anything.

I want to say we'll pretend not to see each other.

But what if he's back on cocaine and looking for some cheap thrills? And what if I'm feeling low and figure what the hell—the girls are gone and they'll hate me forever, so why not let the devil himself talk me into selling my soul?

The coffee pot percolates.

The lights buzz overhead.

I talk about how I've come clean to my parents and how they support me in their own ways—Mom calling once a week and sending me books on addiction and recovery, Dad renting *Traffic* and yelling at the television. I wish I could put their minds at ease, wish I could say for certain that I'll never touch cocaine again, but I know not to make promises like that, know that the temptation will always be with me in one form or another.

In my dreams, I can never say no.

My fellow addicts nod when I say this. They've all had the same dreams. Or, more accurately, the same dream—because no matter how it begins, the ending never changes.

In one version, I'm pushing a cart through the grocery store. Past the produce, past the meat, past the soups and canned vegetables. Catherine is with me, and Lily's running ahead, gathering boxes of cereal and bottles of dish soap then dropping them off in the cart before running off for a tube of toothpaste and a can of fruit juice concentrate. They're giving out free samples again, Catherine says, and at the end of the dairy aisle, the little old woman who usually hands out tiny slices of pizza or medicine cups half-filled with low-fat yogurt is tapping out lines of cocaine. In the dream, this last detail seems perfectly normal, and when the little old woman asks if I'd like to try some, I say thank you and pick a shortened length of plastic drinking straw from the pile she's laid out for her customers, and I think, wow, it's been so long since I've done a line of coke, and isn't it great that they sell it in stores now? Then I lean over a card table decorated with plastic flowers in a vase and a checkered tablecloth, and I do a quick line.

In another version of the dream, I'm back with Roger. We're sitting at the breakfast table on a Sunday morning. He's reading the paper. I'm pouring myself a glass of juice. The girls are young again—Lily's four, and Catherine's seven. They're eating corn-flakes and sharing the comics. Thank God the divorce was just a dream, I think, and the telephone rings. It's probably Chloe, Roger says, and I'm glad to talk to her because now she's my best friend in the world. I just had the weirdest dream, I tell her, cradling the phone between my ear and my shoulder as I open the kitchen cabinet where we keep the soup, the cereal, and my cocaine. Yeah, I say, tapping some coke onto a silver tray. Roger and I were divorced, and the absolute craziest thing of all is that he'd left me for her. Chloe agrees that it's the craziest thing she's ever heard, and I tell her to hold on a second as I sit down at the breakfast table and snort a line of coke in front of my husband and kids.

That's when my mouth goes dry and my heart starts to pound like a jackhammer.

If I'm lucky, I wake up crying, which is inevitable in any case.

If not, the dream always takes a turn for the worse.

I call Catherine over and tell her there's something I want her to try.

It's fun, I tell her.

It'll make her feel good and help her come out of her shell.

I do a line myself to show her it's okay, and I hand her my little straw.

I hate myself when I wake up from that dream. My breath is short, my heart is pounding, and my mouth is dry. Though I know it's only a dream, I feel like the worst mother in the world. I can never sleep after that dream, I tell my fellow addicts. All I can do is lie awake and pray to God that it never comes to pass.

There are other stories, of course—variations on a theme— and at our meetings, we trade our tales like currency. There's the single mother of three who graduated from popping caffeine tablets to snorting crystal meth so she could stay awake while she waited tables at two different restaurants seven days a week on two hours of sleep a night. There's the wannabe rock star who got into drugs because it was part of the lifestyle. There's the Cambodian refugee who started doing coke because someone told her it was headache powder. Our lives are the stuff of nineteenth-century temperance pamphlets, old-world morality plays, and made-for-cable movies of the week. We tell our stories over and over again not so much to figure out where we went wrong, but to reassure each other that we're not alone, that everyone makes mistakes, that everyone has a weakness.

When I mention one night that I'm entertaining thoughts of attending Roger's wedding, I can tell that everyone in the room wants to jump all over me, but that's not what we do here.

We listen. We nod. We empathize.

But we never judge.

I admit to the group that this isn't the wisest decision I could make, but I've made up my mind. The only real question is whether to go it alone or to enlist the aid of the Captain. After all, if anyone can help me stay on the straight and narrow, it's America's number-one just-say-no superhero.

As our meeting breaks up, the Captain, *sans* costume, starts folding our chairs and leaning them against a wall in a corner of the room. He isn't my sponsor, but we speak almost every day—about work, about the girls, about jazz, about the latest improvements to the Ultimax 3000, about the new songs he's writing and the tracks he's laying down for his debut CD—but for the kind of favor I'm about to ask, I need to speak to the man face-to-face.

I know it's a bad idea, I say, helping with the chairs, but I *have* to go to Roger's wedding. Any chance to see my daughters and show them that I'm okay, that I'm taking care of myself again, that I'm not a monster is worth the risk.

The Captain lays the last chair against the wall and says that he understands.

There's no chemistry between us, no spark, no magnetism when he looks me in the eye, and this is a good thing. What I need from the Captain isn't romance. What I need is support. What I need is a friend, and when I ask if he'll accompany me to Roger's wedding, the Captain thinks about it for a second before asking which cape he should wear.

"Just kidding," he adds quickly. "Unless you think it would be okay."

"Probably not," I say.

"I didn't think so."

I KNOW I've made a mistake the minute the Captain and I arrive at the wedding. All of Roger's friends are on hand to wish him the best, and I can't help remembering my own wedding day. These same people once toasted my union with Roger. These same people once wished us a lifetime of happiness. These same people once called us the perfect couple and predicted that we'd be together forever, and now they're doing it all over again as if Roger's first trip down the aisle had been nothing more than a dress rehearsal for the real thing.

Sitting in the last row, I say hello to the friends Roger and I once shared. We exchange friendly hugs, and everyone makes a point of telling me that I look great.

Do they know, I wonder?

Do they see anything but an addict when they look at me?

Would a single glass of wine be so bad?

When a string quartet starts playing the wedding march, we all turn to watch as Catherine and Lily sprinkle the bride's path with crimson and white flower petals. Methodical as always, Catherine goes about her business with measured dignity while Lily, basket in hand, casts the petals into the air with a series of grandiose theatrical flourishes.

I smile at my daughters as they pass, and I give them each a tiny wave when they smile back at me. All I want is to let them know how proud I am of both of them, and to let them know that they don't have to forgive me—not yet, anyway. Trust comes with time, and it doesn't come free. In the meantime, the best I can hope for is patience and—little by little, day by day—their growing understanding that I'm human and fragile and utterly fallible just like everyone else.

"How are you holding up?" the Captain asks about halfway through the ceremony.

"Surprisingly well," I say. "Given the circumstances."

In the end, however it isn't the ceremony that gets me, but the photo session afterward. The bride has disappeared for a few minutes to have her lips re-glossed and her eyes retouched, and Roger is taking the opportunity to say hello and meet my date. It's great of me to be here, Roger says, and I tell him that I wouldn't have missed his wedding for the world. The girls are eyeing the Captain curiously, trying to figure out where they've seen him before; and when Chloe returns, the photographer asks if he can get a picture of the bridesmaids with their mother. Happy to oblige, I approach my daughters but stop dead when the photographer reaches for my elbow.

"Excuse me, ma'am," he says politely. "Just the girls and their mother."

"But I *am* their mother," I say, looking helplessly to the girls and then to Roger for affirmation.

"I'm sorry," the photographer says, shaking his head. "I don't know what I was thinking."

Covering his ass, the photographer snaps a few perfunctory photos of me and the girls in their dark-red dresses, but the damage has already been done. I'm the outsider here—that much is clear and growing clearer by the moment as the photographer arranges Roger, Chloe, and my daughters into a portrait of the perfect family right before my eyes.

"Come on," the Captain says. "Let's get some air."

"Yeah," I say. "That's a really good idea."

The chapel and the reception hall are joined by a foyer with a marble floor and a high ceiling. Waiters and waitresses weave in and out of the crowd with silver hors d'oeuvre platters and trays laden with flutes of champagne. To toast the bride and groom, a teenage girl in a red bowtie explains as she approaches the Captain and me with a tray.

God, how I want that drink—and the one after it, and the one after that, and on and on until I kill off every last brain cell that's ever cared about anything. But I'm a good girl. I send the Captain to the bar and ask him to procure me a club soda in a champagne flute so I can at least go through the motions of wishing my ex and his wife the best of all possible futures in their new life together. When he comes back with my drink, the Captain asks if I'm okay, and I tell him I'm fine.

"It just stings a little, you know?"

"I know," the Captain says.

And that's when I feel the tears welling up.

"Is there anything I can do?" the Captain asks.

I shake my head and say I'll be right back. I just need some time alone. I just need to pull myself together.

"You're sure I can't come with you?"

"I don't think so," I say, nodding in the direction of the women's room. "There are some places even Captain Panther can't go."

I run the water and dab my eyes with the corner of a tissue.

If only I had some coke, I think. I'd do a quick line and go back out to Roger's wedding. Mingling with his friends, I'd smile and make small talk, and everyone would see how well I'm doing. The band would play, I'd dance with the Captain, and all of Chloe's friends would point at me and wonder how Roger's ex managed to land a date with a guy who had such a magnificent bottom. And when the band took a break, I'd sit for a while with Roger's parents, and they'd sympathize with me for the hell their son has put me through.

It's no big deal, I'd tell them. Because now my life is back on track, and Roger is Chloe's problem, for better or worse. They'd laugh at this, and I'd laugh, too, before finding Chloe to tell her how truly glad I am that she and Roger have fallen in love. Then I'd go to the bar and order another glass of sparkling water and raise a toast to the happy couple. When the band came back, I'd dance with the Captain for a few more songs, and at the end of the reception, I'd say goodbye to my girls and give them each a hug, and they'd say that they loved me as the Captain and I strolled off into the sunset and everyone talked about how great it was to see me and how much fun I was to have around.

And the girls would hear all of this talk and be proud of me, and they'd ask their father when they could start seeing me again on a regular basis or maybe if they could move back in with me, and I'd be wonderful and charming and lovely and beautiful—Wonder Mom and Party Girl all at once—and all because I snorted some coke.

It would be so easy, I think.

A quick phone call, and—

"Mom?" Catherine asks, poking her head into the women's room. "Are you in there?"

It's the voice that brings me back to reality.

It's the voice that saves my life.

"Yeah, honey. I'm right here."

THE BRIDE and groom are being toasted in the big hall while I sit with my daughters in the chapel where the ceremony was held. The bride's father is a short man with tiny eyes and narrow shoulders. He sounds like a rusty door hinge as he speaks into a microphone and his voice spills out of the hall and across the foyer and leaks into our private little sanctuary.

He sounds like a nice man, I say, and Catherine shrugs.

Lily reminds me that he owns a tennis court, a swimming pool, and a private gas pump.

"Wow," I say. "A private gas pump. I'll bet *that's* fun."

I give my girls the hint of a smile, and Catherine rolls her eyes the way she always used to whenever I'd tell a bad joke or make a pun or, heaven forbid, say something in public to let the outside world know that she had a mother. It's a look that used to make me cringe on occasion, make me feel like an outsider in my daughter's life, but now it speaks only of our history together and of the secret, silent glances that pass between mothers and daughters. Though I know that Catherine and Lily will never forget the monster they watched me become, the loving embarrassed playful roll of Catherine's eyes tells me that little by little, they'll both begin to trust me again and that little by little, we'll all begin the slow, cautious work of rebuilding the life that I've done everything in my power to destroy.

"I know I did some bad things," I say, unsure of the path I'm on. "And it's okay if you hate me sometimes because of it."

"We don't hate you, Mom," Lily says. "We love you."

"Yeah, Mom," Catherine says. "We could never hate you."

"I know," I say, taking their hands in mine. "But it's okay if you do."

There's more to say, of course, because there's always more to say, but the band is playing in the big hall, and the MC's voice is echoing through the foyer. There are two special ladies in attendance, the MC announces, and the groom wants to dance with both of them.

"That's us!" Lily says. "Dad wants to dance with us!"

"Mom?" Catherine says.

I give their hands a playful squeeze, and the girls run off to dance with their father. Alone in the little chapel, I take a deep breath, then head out to the foyer where the Captain is waiting for me.

"Are you okay?" he asks as I stand in the doorway to the big hall and watch my little girls take turns dancing with my ex-husband.

"Not really," I say. "But I'll survive."

WE LEAVE the reception early, and the Captain drives me home. Ever the gentleman, he walks me to my door and gives me a friendly hug before I let myself into the house. I'm strong, he says, and he really admires me for what I'm doing.

"Oh yeah? What's that?"

"Living your life," the Captain says.

"That's easy for you to say," I tell him, though I know it isn't—because we're all broken in some way, all empty, all longing for more, all doing our best to find a pattern in the bits and pieces we pick up in the mad rush of our daily lives. "You're America's favorite just-say-no superhero."

"Keep saying that," the Captain says. "It might come true someday."

We say goodbye, and when the Captain leaves, I go into my house and light some candles and lay the needle on a jazz record. There are numbers I can call if I want to get high, and numbers I can call if I'm afraid that I might, but alone in the house with my jazz and my memories, I'm content for the moment to watch the old LP turn on its spindle.

A sad, slow-moving piano.

A lonely, longing trumpet.

The tentative thump of a stand-up bass.

A soft, rolling snare and the hiss of old vinyl.

Worn and weathered and far from perfect, this is jazz the way it's meant to be heard, life the way it's meant to be lived. A slow embrace, a daily decision. A scratch, a click, a pop, a heartbeat.